The Reluctant Samaritan

As the carriage started—too slow for him, especially now that he was a reluctant Samaritan—Nez glared at the woman, who tried to make herself small in the corner of his carriage.

He looked at her face, wet but full of character, even to his critical eye. Spanish women, whatever their degree, have that look, he told himself. From habit, he compared her to Libby Cook, but decided comparison was unfair. She could never achieve the kind of English complexion that was Libby's birthright. Her skin was the off-white of southern Spain, her eyes brown. It wasn't her eyes that caught his attention as much as her heavy eyelids, which gave her a sleepy, restful look. Perhaps she is tired, too, he thought—more charitable now. She wiped the boy's face with the end of her sopping cloak.

He did not think she was much beyond her middle twenty years. He had no idea how old the boy was.

"Wiping his face with your cloak will hardly do him good," said Nez.

"Sometimes it is enough merely to make the gesture."

SIGNET

REGENCY ROMANCE

COMING IN JANUARY

A Rival Heir
by Laura Matthews

Nell Armstrong promised her dying grandfather to remain unwed and to care for her aging—and frightfully fitful—aunt for the rest of the elderly woman's life. But when Nell comes across the most loving man who has ever lived, she can't help but doubt her resolve...

0-451-20527-8/$4.99

Lord Darlington's Darling
by Gayle Buck

What with raising his siblings and managing his estate, Lord Darlington has little time for courting. And Abby couldn't care less about finding a husband. But that's all about to change...

0-451-20502-2/$4.99

The Ivory Dragon
by Emily Hendrickson

When Lady Harriet seeks shelter from a spring shower in an old barn, she finds mysterious wooden box—and a handsome stranger, Lord Stanhope. Even stranger is the fix the two soon find themselves in...

0-451-20535-9/$4.99

To order call: 1-800-788-6262

One Good Turn

Carla Kelly

A SIGNET BOOK

SIGNET
Published by New American Library, a division of
Penguin Putnam Inc., 375 Hudson Street,
New York, New York 10014, U.S.A.
Penguin Books Ltd, 80 Strand,
London WC2R 0RL, England
Penguin Books Australia Ltd, Ringwood,
Victoria, Australia
Penguin Books Canada Ltd, 10 Alcorn Avenue,
Toronto, Ontario, Canada M4V 3B2
Penguin Books (N.Z.) Ltd, 182–190 Wairau Road,
Auckland 10, New Zealand

Penguin Books Ltd, Registered Offices:
Harmondsworth, Middlesex, England

First published by Signet, an imprint of New American Library,
a division of Penguin Putnam Inc.

First Printing, December 2001
10 9 8 7 6 5 4 3 2 1

Printed in the United States of America

To Nick, whose help made
this book appear in timely fashion.
Thanks, Nick, for this and other things.

Patience, and shuffle the cards.

—Spanish proverb

Prologue

Pray, do not beat yourself with too many stripes because you are yet in love with my wife.

Benedict Nesbitt, seventh Duke of Knaresborough, sighed and looked out the carriage window at the endless rain, thinking of his last conversation with Tony Cook. "Damn you, Dr. Cook," he murmured under his breath, careful that his niece Sophie did not hear him. "If you were not such a good man and a kindly friend, I could certainly despise you. So what if I love your wife still?"

"Uncle, we cannot quite hear you," Sophie said, looking up from the page she was coloring with the French crayons he had bought her yesterday morning before they set out for Knare.

He looked down at her as she leaned so comfortably against him, using his bulk to steady her as she drew in the carriage. "I wasn't talking to you, Empress," he said. "I was talking to myself."

"Mama says you are an eccentric" was Sophie's only comment, as she directed her attention to the page again. "She would call that proof."

I suppose I am an eccentric, he thought, as he looked out the window again. I gave away my wine cellar—famous through three shires—to my stupid friend Eustace Wiltmore on the occasion of his marriage to my Libby's equally stupid cousin Lydia. (No, no, she is Tony's Libby, and not mine. You think I'd remember.) I have not drunk a drop in a year, which my friends think odd. I take my meals belowstairs at Knare instead of at that ridiculous table in the dining room, which could probably seat the whole drooling, doddering House of Lords. Of course, I only eat belowstairs so my former private Amos Yore will feel at home talking to me about the Knare armory that he is refurbishing. Nothing eccentric about that; I am merely practical. Besides that, the food is still warm when it doesn't have to be traipsed through a quarter mile of corridors.

"So, my dear Empress, what's an eccentric?" he asked with a wink to his butler Luster, who sat opposite in the carriage.

She thought a moment. "Uncle, we believe that eccentrics are people who cause Mama indigestion."

He smiled. "Don't you mean indignation, love?"

She thought a moment more as she colored in the tree she was drawing. "No, we mean indigestion, Uncle. Mama always asks for soda and water after you leave, so she can belch and feel better."

I wish I could take soda and water, belch and feel better, Nez thought, as Sophie returned her attention to the tree in her lap. Yet in love with your wife, Tony? Guilty as charged.

He had to admit that Tony had been nice enough about it during his recent visit to Kent. The visit was brought about by the combined effects of missing Libby so much that his sleep was troubled, and his eagerness to see some corner of England, where spring, after a long winter, had taken hold with a vengeance.

He shifted uncomfortably, which earned him a glare from Sophie, when he bumped her elbow and turned the grass she was drawing into a tall, rather palm-like frond. "We are not happy when you do that, Uncle," she said, sounding remarkably like her mother.

"We wish you would get over this phase, Your Royal Highness, and treat *us* with a little more respect, Sophie," he replied. He smiled when he said it, thinking as he did so that she was a wonderful child, and not a lump like her brother Clarence, who was throwing out spots, mercifully back in London.

As the carriage moved slowly along through the

rain, he remembered what a winter it had been, dreaming of Libby and desperately unhappy each morning. He even went down to his wine cellar after an especially bad night, just to stand there and stare at the empty racks. He wanted the bottles back, wanted just to sit on the floor in the cellar and drink, and not come upstairs until he was cured or dead. His butler had found him there, miserable and silent, and had done something unthinkable for a butler. Nez smiled just remembering. Luster had watched him a moment, then knelt down and touched his master's cheek. That was all. It was the smallest gesture, but it kept Nez from the wine cellar again.

His mother died after Christmas, but there was no reason to mourn her from inside a brandy bottle. She had outlived many of her contemporaries, and much of her usefulness, according to his sister Augusta, who could be even more censorious than he. *Sic transit glorious mumsy,* he had thought at the time from his own apartment on Clarges Street. He closed his apartment, and moved into the family house on Half Moon Street and assigned his footman the task of refurbishing the house. He accompanied Mama's coffin back to Knare and placed her beside his late father. The sixth duke had died while Nez recuperated in Portugal from a concussion received during the second siege of Badajoz. He remembered still the odd sensation of reading the letter from his solicitor over and over again as he lay on his cot, trying to get his eyes to focus.

And now Mama was gone, too, where all good Knares went, and where he would rest someday. Aye, he thought, first we're on the wall in the gallery, to glare down on future generations, and then we're worm's meat in the vault. He stayed at Knare then, spending time settling Mama's tangled accounts, and staring out the window that overlooked the formal gardens, his mother's last bit of extravagance, if he could believe the neighbors when they came to offer condolences.

"Damn this rain," he murmured, careful to speak more softly than before. After a glance at Sophie, he returned his thoughts to Libby, dragging out the memory of her two turndowns of him last year, her marriage to the bumbling and thoroughly kind doctor, Anthony Cook, and the guilt he felt when he still dreamed of her in his own bed. The welcome sight of her last week, opening the door to his knock, and then standing there a moment before flinging herself into his arms, was not calculated to ease his pain. And then to take a second look and see how gloriously, abundantly with child she was made the matter worse. Why did she still have to look so beautiful, even with her apron riding so high now, and her face rounder than he remembered? She positively glowed with love, and he knew it wasn't for him.

Maybe that's why no one chooses to partner me at whist, he told himself. I cannot hide my feelings. Instead of calling him out and shooting him dead, dear Tony had merely walked him to the nearly completed hospital being constructed with that vulgar wad he had laid down as a wedding present, and cheerfully admonished him not to flog himself because he still yearned for Libby Cook. Of course, it hadn't helped that he had cried then in Tony's arms, weary of his inability to forget, sick of the long Yorkshire winter that had driven him south, missing his mother, tired to his very soul of the effort of resisting another drink. It was all too much, and what did Tony do but let him cry, and then kiss his forehead, which only made him sob again?

"Oh, lad," Tony had told him, "I would cry, too, if Lib had turned me down for keeps."

That should have made him mad, but it didn't. In the oddest way, Nez knew that Tony understood, and chose to be generous rather than jealous. He took comfort from Tony's arm around his shoulder as they walked back to the house together. The pain became almost bearable when they both stood in the sitting room, sheltered now in shadows, to look at Libby, asleep in her chair, but with her hands curved so protectively around the baby she carried inside her. His heart stopped when she opened her eyes, and gave her husband such a look of love that he felt as though he watched them in the intimacy of their bedchamber. And then her smile extended to him, and she sat up and became the excellent hostess, but never his own wife.

Somehow the moment made it easier to want to be away from the Cooks the next morning, even though he had promised he would stay a week. He was the guest, and he knew it now; an honored guest, to be sure, but just someone who would come and then go—someone to be missed, but not yearned over.

He had been amazed all over again at Tony's diplomacy in going on to the stable ahead and leaving him behind to say good-bye to Libby in private. She had stood awkwardly sideways in his arms, and the bulk of her made him smile instead of sigh. It was easier now to tease her and tell her that since she danced, she'd have to pay the piper. Easier to leave her blushing and laughing, her hand on her baby again. If it was going to mean nights of no sleep, maybe some of his desperate unhappiness was gone now, in the face of Libby's joy in her husband and baby to come. She was in good hands, even if they weren't his.

Trust Tony to advise him. As he mounted the horse that he had ridden all through Spain and even at Waterloo, Nez accepted with pleasure Tony's request that he be the baby's godfather. "You're sure I'm the right person?" he had asked.

"None better, Nez." Tony tugged on his horse's cinch to make sure it was tight. "Next time you come to see us, though, bring a wife along."

He had returned some reply, and gathered the reins in his hands. Still Tony hung onto his stirrup. "One thing more, lad."

"My Lord, Tony, you ask me to find a wife this coming summer?" he teased. "Isn't that enough labor for one rather spoiled, lazy man?" The smile left his face when he saw how intense was Tony's expression. "Now, Mr. Cook, you know I'll do what you ask, if the bill isn't too high."

He owned to a real start when Tony bit off his words with precision. "You are neither spoiled nor lazy, Nez."

"Oh, but I am. You can ask anyone."

"You are not," Tony insisted, "but obviously this is something you have to discover for yourself. It is this, then, my friend," Tony had said as he released the stirrup and stepped away. "Make some peace with your sister. That would be a good turn."

I wish it would stop raining, Nez thought, as he pulled himself back to the present. I hope Yorkshire will be green when I get there. I wonder how on earth I can make peace with Augusta?

"Your Grace, are you well?"

Surprised, he looked across at his butler, who was eyeing him with an expression that could only be solicitous. "Never better, Luster, never better," he replied. What an amazing bit of fiction that is, he thought. I imagine Luster can see through it like gauze. "Never better," he repeated, thinking that if he said it often enough, perhaps it would be true.

Chapter One

What would my butler do if I suddenly banged on the roof, stopped the carriage, and ran from the carriage, tearing my hair and shouting, "Rain, rain, go away?" he thought. He glanced at Luster, who dozed opposite him. Heaven knows the man looks exhausted, but who wouldn't, managing two households?

He had returned from Kent to discover from Pomeroy, his own footman, that Luster was attempting to put together the shards of his sister Gussie's household, a brisk walk across Green Park to Park Place. "Chicken pox," Pomeroy said darkly, "and Sudden Death, Your Grace."

Had the footman been wearing a cape then, Nez was sure he would have twirled it. Rather than panic at Pomeroy's admission, delivered in round tones, he had waited for further enlightenment. Oh, I know you well, Pomeroy, he thought. Denied a career on the wicked stage, you continue to indulge your theatrical talents in my employment. Luckily for you, your efficiency overrules your dramatic flair. "Come, come, sir," he said finally.

"Clarence is Afflicted with Disease," the footman pronounced, "and Lord Wogan's father chose this inopportune time to cock up his toes, or so Lady Wogan described the matter to Luster, Your Grace." He leaned forward. "And we all know that Luster cannot Refuse a Cause."

"Oh, go on, Pomeroy," he had said. "We all know that Gussie employs a household staff that must have trained originally in New York, or perhaps Melbourne, if we must be generous."

"Precisely, Your Grace. Perhaps you had better Go 'Round."

He went 'round, and it was much as Pomeroy described, without the capital letters. Peace reigned, mainly because Augusta had wisely decided to remain in bed and leave her infected son to the nanny, and because he knew Luster lurked on the premises, turning chaos to order like water to wine at Cana. He looked around, wishing that Freddy, his gentle brother-in-law, were there. He wondered for the thousandth time what Fred had ever seen in Gussie besides a disgusting fortune, then squared his shoulders, and knocked on the bedroom door.

He reeled back from the smell of burned feathers. "Augusta, are you on the brink of death?" he asked when he could catch his breath. He waited for her little sob. Ah, yes; there it was.

And again. Then, "Benedict, sometimes I wish that you had ever been sick once in your life, so you could bring sympathy instead of vitriol."

"Correct me if I am wrong, but isn't little Clarence the sick one?"

She blew her nose vigorously, which went at cross grains against the way she delicately laid her hand on her head. "I suppose he is, but I declare even he conspires against me!"

"Surely not! He's only two, isn't he?"

"Yes, but at nights I can hear him crying all the way down to my chamber. Imagine! He woke me twice last night, and it took me so long to get back to sleep."

"Wretched child," he said, chilled to his bones. "What could he be thinking?"

"Exactly," she replied. "Benedict, you must do me a favor and take Sophie to Knare. I am forced to remain behind until Clarence is better."

It was on the tip of his tongue to ask why that mattered, but he remembered Tony's admonition in time. "I can do that, my dear. Tell me, how is Freddy bearing up?"

"Don't remind me!" Gussie snapped. "Didn't his father take ill last week. Nothing would do but Fred rushed off and left me alone with all these cares," she waved her hand, dismissing the platoon of servants that he knew crowded the place. "And you were visiting your shabby genteel mushrooms in Kent. And then what do I get but a special post from Frederick, drat him, telling me that his father had the nerve to die during *my* crisis!"

"Fancy that. How could old Lord Warburton have been so insensitive?"

Gussie dabbed at her dry eyes. "You do understand, Benedict. And to think I was afraid you did not care."

I hope I am never this bad, he thought, as he watched his sister. And yet we are cut from the same cloth. He stood a moment longer in the doorway, then came into the room, sat on her bed, and took her in his arms. She sobbed in good earnest while he patted her back, murmured such endearments as he could stomach, and felt, surprisingly, a little better. "Sophie and I will start for Knare tomorrow, my dear. Have her ready at nine of the clock."

"Nine o'clock!" his sister exclaimed, sitting bolt upright. "I am hardly even awake then!"

He dug deep within himself and patted her hand. "Force yourself, Gussie," he said, hoping for perhaps the first time in his life that his utter disgust did not show in his voice. "Think of the good of your children and be brave with this exertion."

One mustn't waste sarcasm on the slow-witted, he thought wickedly, as Augusta's lips trembled. "I will be brave for my children," she said, "even if it kills me."

"I shouldn't think it will come to that, my love. Just have Sophie and her governess ready."

Gussie sniffed back something (it couldn't have been tears). "The evil woman resigned this morning.

Just trooped in here and quit! I am certain you can manage Sophie without a maid. I cannot spare anyone. And you have plenty of excellent help at Knare, none of which you have ever chosen to share with me."

They would run away if I suggested working in Park Place, he thought. "Very well, my dear. I am certain that the Empress and I will manage." He got up and gently tugged his hand from his sister's firm grasp.

"Why are you so kind to me today?" she had asked as he paused in the doorway.

"You need me," he said simply.

She blew her nose again. "I will repay you, my dear, just see if I don't! When I get to Knare, I will find you the perfect wife, even if it is a lot of trouble and taxes all my strength."

Gad, what a thought, he told himself, as he looked out the window again. I know she will sic Audrey St. John on me. He looked down at Sophie, who was asleep now, the crayons fallen from her grasp and rolling around on the carriage floor. I suppose there are worse fates than Audrey. Heaven knows we are well-acquainted from living next to each other all these years. He remembered his last view of Libby, awkward-looking, but beautiful in her pregnancy. I want a family, too, he thought. Sophie is a charming child, and there is every indication that Clarence will become human in a year or so. Besides that, Tony would call it the right idea.

Sophie had been no trouble in the inn last night, demanding only that he read to her before she went to sleep, which caused him no exertion and a certain homely pleasure. "Papa always reads to me," she informed him as she patted the spot beside her in the bed.

Good for you, Freddy, he thought, as he took the book she handed him. Let us pray that your daughter will come to see your gentle qualities and never despise you for a weak man, which Gussie would own that you are. "Oh, *Children of the New Forest*! I remember that one."

"Did your papa read to you?" she asked as he found the page.

"My tutor did."

"Did Grandmama?"

"No, alas. She was generally too busy." He started to read, but Sophie put her hand over the page.

"Do you miss Grandmama?" she asked, her voice softer, less certain.

"I do." And he did, despite her frivolities, and the air of vacuity that seemed to grow as she aged. He remembered with a pang the empty feeling inside him only a month ago when he settled the last of her accounts, and put her ledger back on the shelf at Knare. There was no reason for him ever to open it again: no more gambling debts to pay, no more tears over modistes who would not wait another quarter, even though he had continued Papa's generous allowance. She was gone from his life, and he wished he had known her better. "I do miss her, Empress. Now, move your hand, and let us read this chapter."

When Sophie woke from her nap in the carriage, she complained of a sore throat, and only shook her head when he picked up her crayons and handed them to her. "We are not feeling good," she announced. "Crayons would only make us cross."

The rain thundered down, slowing travel to a crawl, and making him want to fidget like his niece. They stopped for nuncheon at an inn already crowded with people seeking a room for the night. I wonder if we should join them, he thought, after a glance outside the window. He decided to continue, no matter how uncomfortable it was for his coachman, as his concern for Sophie grew. She was listless now, and definitely warm to the touch. She leaned against him when he found a bench for her in the public house, and shook her head when he offered her almond pudding with currants, her favorite.

"Luster, I hate to think of it, but she might be coming down with chicken pox," he said in a low voice.

"The thought has occurred to me, too, Your Grace," his butler replied. "Like you, I am inclined to think that we should hurry on to Knare." Luster peered over his spectacles at Sophie. "Shouldn't there be spots of some sort?"

"One would suppose," Nez replied. "Dash it all, Luster, we're in a fix. Let's just hurry on."

Because of the rain, the light in the carriage was gloomy at best, and suited his mood. He had never seen the Empress listless before, and he felt an unaccustomed helplessness that irritated him as much as it frightened him. "Luster, I think that parenthood is not for the faint of heart," he commented as Sophie winced in her sleep and muttered. "I would rather have her pestering me with questions I cannot answer, and acting like Her Majesty."

He was desperate to see Knare, but knew it was still two days away. When the coachman came to a sudden stop, Nez was painfully aware that only Sophie's heavy warm weight against him kept him from leaping from the vehicle and giving the man a blistering scold. "What now?" he snapped.

Luster opened the door. "Your Grace, I believe there has been an accident!"

It had better be a good one, Nez thought. Better be people dead and mangled. "Find out, and get us around it! Don't let me be the only one thinking!"

My, that was rude, he thought, as Luster left the carriage. I hate when I do that, Tony. He sat another moment in frustration, then stood up, gently lowering Sophie's head to the seat. He left her there and went into the storm.

"I'm sorry, Luster," he said a moment later. "I don't think sometimes."

Luster smiled as the water dripped off his face. "You'll get wet, Your Grace."

"I've been wet before. Luster, assuage my heart and go back to the carriage. I have at least thirty years on you. I'll find out what's going on." They stared at each other, but Luster finally returned to the carriage.

Nez could barely make out a mail coach tipped on its side. He squinted and saw the passengers huddled together. Someone stood close to the road to direct other vehicles around the mail coach. He noticed a body, boots sticking out, covered with a coat, and regretted his earlier thoughts.

He found the mail coach driver, who was overseeing the unhitching of his horses. "May I help you?" he asked, surprised how easily the words came out.

The driver barely looked at him. "I wish you would shoot that off horse. His leg is broken, and I have a soft spot for me animals. Here." He handed Nez two pistols, wicked-looking things probably meant for road agents.

Nez took the pistols, and edged carefully down the slippery incline until he was standing at the head of the horse. He ran his hand gently down the animal's leg. "You'll never rise again, old sport," he said softly. The animal whickered at him. "Life's not fair, laddie," Nez whispered. After a moment, he stood back slightly, aimed and fired. Not the first time I've done that, he told himself, but at least I won't be eating this one. He started up the incline, and grasped the driver's outstretched hand offered in assistance.

"Thank'ee. I couldn't do it."

"I understand." Nez handed back the pistols.

"Do ye know who the bloke is that belongs to that carriage with the lozenge?" the driver asked, after a brief dab at his eyes.

"Mine. I'll move it."

The driver's eyes opened wide. "Damn me, sir! I'd never have troubled you about me horse!"

"No matter. I like my horses, too. What happened?"

"Too much rain, too slippery. And there's a dead one, my lord."

"Have you sent someone ahead for another coach?"

"Aye, sir." He looked around. "That farmer'll take these passengers to his croft. There'll be someone along soon."

"Is there anything else I can do?"

The driver shook his head. "In all my years, this never happened. Thank'ee again for what you did. Just have your coachman edge around slowly."

"Nothing else?" He noticed that the man hesitated. "I can do something, surely."

"My lord, maybe you could do this: one of the passengers—she has a young'un—started off walking. I tried to explain to her that there would be another coach along and we would be riding again soon, but I'm not sure she understood me. She's foreign."

"Should I bring her back here?"

"No need. Stokely's next, and you're likely going that way, my lord."

"I can do that," he said, then thought of Sophie and cursed his sudden philanthropy. "If I see her, I should explain that you will be in Stokely soon, and she is to wait there?"

"Aye, me lord. Speak loud and slow, and she'll understand ye, if she's like most foreigners."

Nez nearly smiled. I remember speaking English like that to villagers from the Douro to the Tagus, he thought, before I had the wit to learn Spanish. "Maybe she speaks a language I know."

"Loud and slow will carry the day, my lord," the driver said.

Nez went back to his carriage. "I am now a philanthropist, Luster, prepared to succor the downtrodden," he announced. "We are to keep our eyeballs skinned out for a woman walking with a child. The driver says she's a foreigner, and we're to take her to Stokely and leave her there."

"I am certain that you can adequately explain the situation, Your Grace, no matter the language."

"Luster, you flatter me," Nez said. "I wish I had promised him nothing. I would rather hurry along to Stokely and find a bed for Sophie." He sat next to his niece again, who sighed and closed her eyes. "We do not feel good," she said.

He kissed her. "I doubt we do. We'll stop soon, my dear."

They started forward again, moving carefully on the slick road, so deadly for the mail coach. Nez looked back at the driver. Now, there is a man who knows he will be looking for another situation quite soon, he thought. I wonder if the company will prosecute him for the passenger's death? He dismissed the thought; it was none of his concern. And yet . . . he cared for his horses. I hope the company is not too hard on him.

Odd thoughts, he told himself. When did I ever concern myself with a mail coach driver before? And yet . . . he has to feed himself. Perhaps he has a family. He rested his hand gently on his niece's head.

The rain let up slightly, but there was no question of speed. He watched the side of the road, looking for the woman and child, but saw no one. She must have taken shelter somewhere, he thought, and directed his attention to Sophie, who was stirring restlessly now. In another moment she was crying. "Oh, honey," he whispered. "We'll stop soon."

He looked out the window then, and there was the woman, picking her way cautiously along the edge of the highway. She carried the child, and across her back was slung a large knapsack, the kind carried by men of the artillery batteries in Spain.

He felt no charity. We cannot be that far from Stokely, he told himself. She does not know I am looking for her. Luster doesn't see her. I am too concerned for Sophie to stop, and truly this would be a nuisance. He leaned back and said nothing. He felt a twinge of conscience, but experience told him that it would pass soon enough.

"Your Grace, there she is!" Luster had spotted her. "Thank goodness! She is carrying such a burden." He looked at Nez. "You do wish me to stop the carriage, don't you, Your Grace?"

He didn't, but he did not wish the double combination of Luster's studied disfavor and Sophie's illness to plague his evening. One at a time was enough to manage. "Of course, Luster. Careless of me to overlook her."

The moment the shallow words were out of his mouth, he wished he had not said them. Thou shalt not attempt to bamboozle thy butler, he thought. I am surprised that Moses did not carry down that counsel from Sinai. "Do stop the carriage, Luster," he said, trying to make it sound like the plan was his, and knowing that he fooled no one.

Luster banged on the carriage roof with surprising vigor, and Nez knew that his butler was irritated with him. He leaned back out of the wind and rain when Luster opened the door and took down the step.

"I say, miss, do join us," Luster called. "Come, now, it is all right." He leaned back inside the carriage, his face wet. "Your Grace, I do not think she wishes to come, and that would be a terrible shame. Imagine how wet she is."

And imagine how wet this carriage will be if she does join us, he thought. "I wouldn't think we should argue with her, Luster," he murmured.

"I wish that you would try, Your Grace," Luster said. Something in his tone made Nez's face burn.

Flogged into action by a look, he squished toward the woman. "Let me give you a ride to Stokely, the next village," he said, coming close so she could hear him.

To his irritation, she backed away at his rapid advance, but not before setting down her child and standing in front of him. She wore no gloves, and her hands were balled into fists. "Look here, Miss, Mrs. . . . I mean you no harm," his irritation dissipating at the look of unease on her face. "The coach driver back at the accident told me to transport you to Stokely. Please, now, we're all getting wet."

Still, she hesitated. "It is not as though you have an array of choices spread before you, *dama,*" he snapped. And why in God's name did he address her as *dama*? She was poor and wet, scarcely a lady.

Maybe it was something about the set of her shoulders. "Please."

"It will be as you say," she replied finally. She knelt to speak to the boy, then shouldered the artillery kit and took his hand.

I do know that accent, he thought. He wanted to take her arm because the highway was so slick, but she did not move closer. He shrugged and headed back to the vehicle. What is a woman from Spain doing here on the road to nowhere? he asked himself. I rather hope she follows me now.

Chapter Two

"Oh, she's a rare one," he muttered to Luster when he got back into the carriage. "I think she was going to strike me if I came one step closer to her ragged little boy. Thank God Stokely is so close. I believe she is Spanish."

He sat down, and felt the rain beginning to seep through his many-caped coat. Disgruntled, he watched Luster help her into the carriage, and sit her down. She pulled the hood back from her face.

As the carriage started—too slow for him, especially now that he was a reluctant Samaritan—Nez glared at the woman who tried to make herself small in the corner of his carriage. He noticed the number 19 on the ammunition bag that rested at her feet. I remember the Nineteen, rather, he thought, interested. A pity they were shot to pieces at Quatre Bras, even before we got to Mont Saint Jean. We could have used them.

He looked at her face, wet but full of character, even to his critical eye. Spanish women, whatever their degree, have that look, he told himself. From habit, he compared her to Libby Cook, but decided comparison was unfair. She could never achieve the kind of English complexion that was Libby's birthright. Her skin was the off-white of southern Spain, her eyes brown. It wasn't her eyes that caught his attention as much as her heavy eyelids, which gave her a sleepy, restful look. Perhaps she is tired, too, he thought, more charitable now. She wiped her boy's face with the end of her sopping cloak. Her lips were well defined, and full, and he wondered how they would look when she smiled. Hers was a Spanish face, with that ineffable combination of pride and dignity that seemed the birthright of all Iberian women of whatever class. He could never mistake her for an Englishwoman. That's it, he thought. Englishwomen are not particularly exotic. He did not think she was much beyond her middle twenty years. He had no idea how old the boy was.

"Wiping his face with your cloak will hardly do him good."

"Sometimes it is enough merely to make the gesture." Her voice was low and melodious.

He admired her command of English, but didn't understand what she meant until she touched her boy's face. It was still wet, and he shivered, but as her wet fingers smoothed his cheek, he smiled. He knows she is doing the best she can for him, Nez thought, touched.

Nez took off his coat. He knew it was wet, but he also knew it was drier than anything the boy wore. "Here, put this around his shoulders."

She hesitated, and his irritation returned. Why in God's name is she so reluctant? he thought, and almost snatched the coat back. No, no. Be a man of charity, Benedict, he told himself. Try a little harder. "I remember Sarpy's Battery, señora," he said. "The Neverending Nineteen, eh?"

She looked him in the eye then for the first time. "Yes" was all she said, but she reached for the coat then, as though she could trust him now. When her child was wrapped tight she touched his face again, and Nez felt an odd sensation of envy. I wonder if my mother ever did that, he thought. I would remember, if she had. His irritation lingered, directed now more at himself than at her hesitancy.

He made himself comfortable on his side of the carriage, and only partly watched as she removed her cloak. She tried to wring the water from it, but the matter was hopeless. Instead, she folded it carefully and set it on the carriage floor. He observed her figure, but she was nothing spectacular—no handsome deep bosom like Libby, but not poorly endowed, either. She had the waist of a woman who had born a child, and probably never quite returned to her former dimensions. I wonder where her husband is, he thought. He remembered the Nineteen at Quatre Bras against Ney and knew the answer to that one. But why are you in England, madam? he thought, even though he knew he would never ask, he wondered why she had not returned to her own land. This acquaintance ends at Stokely. Augusta would say I know enough low company without increasing the census.

"I regret that we cannot make you more comfortable, Miss . . . Miss," Luster was saying. Good God, man, Nez thought. Don't further the relationship!

"It is not important," she said, her voice so low. "I am Liria Valencia."

He knew she spoke to Luster, so he said nothing. "Mrs. Valencia?" Luster said. When she shook her head, Nez rolled his eyes and glanced at his butler with a half smile. Lord God, a drab and her bastard dripping wet in a Knare family carriage, he thought, then was quelled, nailed, and nearly fractured by a cold look from Luster. The glance was so pointed, so rude from a servant, that he almost gave a sharp reply. He stifled his retort when Sophie woke and began to cry again.

He patted her shoulder. "There now, Empress," he said. "We'll be in Stokely soon, and I will find you a warm room." He knew he said it almost to spite the woman, as though he really said, "But not one for you and your bastard." He did not look at Luster.

Sophie only cried harder. "Dear me, Luster," he said finally, "do you have any suggestions, or must we all suffer?"

Before he finished speaking, the Spanish woman knelt beside his niece. He opened his mouth to protest such familiarity, then closed it as she smoothed her hand down this child's cheek, a child she did not even know. As he watched first in surprise, and then in deepening shame, she leaned forward until her cheek was against Sophie's. She began to hum a little tune he remembered from campfires long ago in Spain. In another moment, Sophie was silent. He watched the woman then, and found himself admiring her dark hair coiled at the nape of her neck. How tidy she was, despite the rain.

When Sophie slept, Liria returned to her side of the carriage, and gathered her son to her side. She closed her eyes, and he knew she had no wish to make any conversation with him. She knows just what I think of her, he told himself. Well, Benedict, isn't that what you intended?

He observed the boy. He knew the child was younger than Sophie, but he sat quietly, enveloped in the riding coat. Nez could see little resemblance to the woman. His eyes were lighter, and his complexion, as well. He did share her self-contained expression, which Nez thought unusual in a child not so far distant from babyhood. He seemed accustomed to finding himself among strangers. Nez had to grudge that his manners were excellent for one so young.

I suppose he has learned to be quiet in some corner when his mother services men, Nez thought, then dismissed the idea as unworthy of him. Truly there was nothing about her to indicate a woman of low fame. Nez closed his eyes.

They didn't remain closed long. Sophie sat up and started to whimper. Before he could react—not that he knew what to do anyway—the woman knelt before his niece again, this time her hands on both sides of the Sophie's face. "*Pobrecita,*" she said. "Are you not feeling good?"

Sophie shook her head, and leaned toward the woman. "My little brother has spots all over him."

"*Ay de mi,*" the woman murmured. "Perhaps you will have spots, too?"

Sophie's lips quivered. "My uncle has promised me that I could climb trees at Knare." She started to cry again.

Before Nez could offer any objection, Liria Valencia edged herself onto the seat next to him and put her arm around his niece. "My dear, I am certain this will pass. The trees will probably be there all summer." She hugged Sophie to her, and Nez saw the surprise on his niece's face. I doubt anyone has ever hugged her like that, he thought. I know it never happened when I was growing up.

Sophie settled against the woman. "You're wet," she murmured.

"Close your eyes," Liria whispered. She glanced at Nez, a question in her eyes.

"Sophie," he said, and then added, "she thinks of herself as the Empress, but Sophie will do now. Right, Sophie?"

Sophie nodded and closed her eyes as Liria gathered her closer. In another moment, she slept. When she was breathing evenly, the woman gently lowered her to the seat and took her own place in the opposite corner of the carriage next to her son. Again she sat so properly. Perhaps she has been a lady's maid, and fallen on hard times, Nez thought, remembering the turmoil of Spain. No, not a lady's maid, he amended. Only the lowest of the low ended up trailing after the British soldiers. Still, she seemed to have learned English and manners from some source. I rejoice that it is not my concern, Nez thought.

Sophie was crying in good earnest as Stokely came into view. The Spanish woman cuddled his niece on her lap and sang to her softly, with no hint of irritation. Her son had made himself comfortable on the seat with his head in Luster's lap, as though this kind of confusion was his lot in life. And it probably is, Nez thought, trying to keep his own calm at Sophie's tears. "How do you do it, Miss Valencia?" he asked at last, in spite of himself.

"What cannot be remedied, must be endured," she said in Spanish. "Do you know this proverb?"

He did. "It seems that I heard it over and over from Lisbon to Toulouse," he replied. "I cannot confess that I found it entirely satisfactory. Oh, heavens, Sophie, give over! She's doing the best she can!" he exclaimed in exasperation.

"Perhaps it helps to be Spanish, to understand that *dicho,*" she replied, and then put her cheek close to Sophie's again.

"You would be the judge of that," he said as he succumbed to the woman's calming influence. "Still, I apologize. Soon you will be able to wait for the next mail coach in peace and quiet. Oh, don't look daggers at me, Sophie!"

"Uncle, we are chagrined at your total indifference to our welfare," Sophie managed to say with some dignity.

". . . Must be endured," Liria said under her breath, and Nez could have sworn that her dark eyes held just the hint of humor.

He could not immediately recall ever seeing a more welcome sight than the Rose at Stokely. His carriage had hardly pulled to a stop before he took Sophie from Liria Valencia and carried her inside. In mere moments he had arranged for a sitting room and two bedrooms, one for him and one for Sophie, and a cot for Luster in his dressing room. With one more breath he ordered dinner.

Before he started for the stairs, Luster turned to Liria, who had followed him inside with her son. "My dear Miss Valencia, we thank you for your kindness," he said with a slight bow.

Oh, doing it too brown, Luster, Nez thought. "Yes, indeed, we appreciate your help," he said when Luster looked at him. "I'm sure the landlord will allow you to wait here for the mail coach."

Liria nodded. She took his coat from her son and handed it to Luster. "We are grateful for your assistance, sir. Come, *mi hijo*." With a nod to Luster, and a nod to him, they went into the public room.

He watched her go. "Don't you think it a little odd, Luster," he began, then stopped.

"Your Grace?"

"She didn't seem to expect anything from me."

"Perhaps she knew she would get nothing, Your Grace."

He sighed. "Should I have offered a gratuity?"

"Possibly, Your Grace."

"Or was the ride enough?"

"Perhaps, Your Grace."

I am in the dumps with my butler, he thought, as he carried Sophie upstairs. "Luster, you know I am not at my best in situations like that! I did give her the ride. At least allow me that." He was embarrassed to continue, knowing that he would not have stopped the carriage if Luster had not caught sight of her, too, and equally aware that his butler knew. "You know I am concerned about Sophie."

"Indeed, Your Grace, and you are to be commended for that."

Oh, ow, coals of fire now, Nez thought. "Well, she will be on her way soon."

By the time the doctor had come and gone, by the time the apothecary had delivered a large bottle of calamine lotion, and by the time Sophie had rejected everything placed before her for dinner, Nez knew some force had singled him out for punishment. He did not know where to begin. He sat on Sophie's bed as she wailed, remembering not-so-distant days when he had splinted two soldiers in his own regiment as they stood firm at Mont Saint Jean.

"Luster, I do not know what to do about Sophie," he said at last. "It's really not my place to doctor her." He glanced at his butler. "Do not go pale on me! I think we are both inept."

His butler hesitated. "Your Grace, if I may suggest . . ."

He thinks I do not want to hear this, but I am

desperate. ". . . that perhaps the mail coach has not arrived yet?"

"If we are far more lucky than we deserve, Your Grace."

"You are too charitable, Luster; than *I* deserve. Do you think that she will overlook how rude I am?"

"With any luck, Your Grace."

He hurried downstairs. He had not heard the coachman blowing his yard of tin, but Sophie was noisy enough to cover all that. Please let her be in the public room, he pleaded with the Almighty, who may or may not have been inclining his ear toward Stokely at the moment.

She was not there. "Damn," he said softly. "Damn."

The public room was full, and the landlord leaned on the high corner, listening to a customer.

"You there, sir," Nez said, raising his voice a little, but not much. He knew how to get people's attention.

"Yes, my lord."

At least you have glanced at the register, Nez thought. "Did the mail coach come?"

"No, my lord."

"Then, where is the woman who came with me? The one with the little boy?"

The landlord indicated the doorway behind him. "Washing dishes. My help quit and she wanted to buy a meal." He laughed. "Your old meal, my lord."

So you're hungry, Liria Valencia, Nez told himself, as his shame returned. Too bad I didn't have the kindness to ask. Libby would have. With a nod and bow to the landlord, he went through the door into the kitchen. He heard the landlord say something to him, but he wasn't interested.

There she was, a kitchen towel wrapped around her waist, belly up to the sink. Her small son stood close to her with a dish towel and a cup in his hand. He smiled at Nez and waggled the cup at him. Liria spoke to him over her shoulder in Spanish. "Have a care, *niño*," she said. "If you break it, I must wash more."

She wasn't aware of him, he was certain, so intent

on the mound of dishes before her. The boy dried the cup, then sat down for a moment—no denying his wistful expression—to stare at the remains of the meal he had picked over, and Sophie had ignored. The meat juices had congealed, and the potatoes were brown and wilted, but the little boy admired the food.

"How long since you have eaten?" Nez whispered.

"*Ven acá,* Juanito, we have more dishes," Liria said. Interesting, Nez thought. She speaks to him in a combination of English and Spanish.

"Sí, Mama." Juan returned to the sink and took another cup from the many that were draining on the counter.

Nez cleared his throat, hoping he would not startle her. "Excuse me, Miss Valencia?" he said when he was much closer.

She gasped, and he wished he had not surprised her. Maybe I should have tripped over a chair or something, he thought, uncomfortable with her reaction, but not surprised. He remembered her hesitation when he approached her in the rain. "Forgive me for startling you. I, uh, do you have a moment?" Now, that was stupid, he thought. Are we at a garden party?

She dried her hands then reached for her son, touching his hair and resting her hand on his shoulder. Does she think I would harm him, or her, for that matter, Nez thought.

"Say, now, I have a request of you," he told her. It came out more abruptly than he would have wished, but he plowed on. "I cannot manage Sophie. Will you help me? I will pay you, of course."

She indicated the dishes. "As you can see, I am occupied right now, my lord."

"But I need your help!" He hadn't meant to plead; he hadn't thought he would need to. "Just leave these dishes and help me!"

She released her hold on her son and whispered to him. He turned back to the sink for another cup and began to dry it. "Perhaps I can help after these dishes are done, and my son has eaten. But if the mail coach comes . . ."

"Oh, hang the mail coach!" he exclaimed. "Sophie is ill."

"I know, but did I not see a physician go upstairs, and then an apothecary? Surely they told you what to do."

He registered her words, and something else that puzzled him, even beyond his current dilemma. You aren't speaking to me as a lesser one speaks to a greater one, he thought. Either you know little about the height of my title, or you have a greater one. He dismissed the idea as stupid beyond belief as soon as it poured into his brain. *"Óigame, dama,"* he said. "The doctor told me what to do, and the apothecary brought a huge flagon of . . . of some pink lotion. I am to daub it here and there. Miss Valencia, I don't want to daub it here and there! We . . . we need a woman's touch." There. You can hardly misunderstand me, he thought. And if you still do, I can probably remember enough Spanish to say it in Spanish. He came closer to her, noticing, even in his distraction, that she took an involuntary step backward until she was up against the sink.

"How're them dishes coming?"

Annoyed, Nez turned around to see the landlord standing in the doorway. "See here, sir, I need this woman to help me with my niece, who is ill."

To his extreme exasperation, the landlord seemed unmoved. He folded his arms. "And I need them dishes done." He gestured with a toss of his head to Juan, who stood close to his mother. "And the little'un wants to eat the meal you sent back." He grinned. "You ask his mama which is more important: his meal or your niece."

He didn't have to ask, not the way Juan was looking at the food. "It's been a while, laddie, hasn't it?" he asked, softly, then looked at Liria. "You may be wondering if all Englishmen are as rude as I have been."

"You are concerned about your niece." Liria held out her hands. "My son must eat, and I gave my word to the landlord that I would do these dishes."

Your word, he asked himself. Well, I'm certainly diddled. He took another step. She couldn't move closer to the sink, but she did incline herself away from him slightly. "You have given your word." He looked at the landlord. "I will offer you five or ten pounds to release her from this task."

"You could, m'lord, but I still need them dishes done more than I need your blunt right now. And the little'un." He looked significantly at Juan. "Are you on a fallow pasture, laddie?"

The boy didn't answer. Nez knew he couldn't understand the question, and he felt his anger growing. Even I would not bully a child with food, he thought. He opened his mouth to speak, just as Liria stepped away from the sink. As he watched, she clasped her hands together and seemed to will herself taller. The effect was something magnificent and unexpected, and almost painful to watch because he could see how she shook.

"Sir, my son and I are doing the best we can," she said, looking at the landlord. She turned to Nez. "I will help your niece after the dishes are done and my son is fed. I gave my word and nothing will change this."

The landlord laughed, and she jumped a little. Nez felt an absurd urge to reach out and clasp her to him, just to stop her trembling, but he stood there, knowing better than to touch her.

"Well, then, my lord, I reckon you must wait," the landlord said.

"I reckon I must," he replied. I could buy this whole inn with the money in my luggage, you blue-bottomed baboon, he thought, but you have checkmated me. "Very well, sir. May I suggest this? You let the lad eat now—that roast of beef is not getting any younger—and I'll wash dishes, too."

"You, my lord?" the man exclaimed.

"Yes," he replied, hoping to match Liria's dignity. "One never knows what skills one might need, does one? Do find me another towel. I would hate to ruin a perfectly good shirt."

Laughing, the landlord opened a cupboard and tossed him an apron. "I'd like another one for Miss Valencia," Nez said. "You didn't think to give her one."

"Didn't think she used the same tailor you do, my lord," he said, but obliged with another apron. "Do them dishes up nice-like, now. Liria will show you. Go ahead and eat, laddie." He laughed and turned back to the public room.

"Well, here we are," he said, marveling at his inanity. "Allow me, Miss Valencia." He started to undo the knot that held the dish towel around her waist.

She moved away from him quickly, clutching the towel as it fell into her hand. "I can manage," she said. She went to the table, and called Juan to her side. He sat down, his eyes bright, and she tied the towel around his neck. In another moment she had arranged the half-eaten meal on a plate and kissed the top of her son's head. "Go ahead, my dear."

He watched them. "You could eat, too," he said. "I'll just carry on here at the sink."

"Oh, no," she said quickly. "I can wait."

"You've been hungry before, then?"

"I've been hungry before."

And will be hungry again; just a common drab, he reassured himself as he removed his coat, tied on the apron, popped off his cuff links, and rolled up his sleeves. Still, she was magnificent a moment ago. Of course, Spanish women are like that. I was forgetting.

He looked over his shoulder. Juan was steadily working his way through a plate of veal that Sophie had so tearfully rejected, and wonder of wonders, Liria Valencia was seated beside him, intent on a plate, too. I suppose we all hit low tide sooner or later, he thought. I seem to be coming about, and maybe Liria will, too, in her own way. I wonder where she is heading?

I could ask, he thought, then reconsidered. He dipped a plate in the rinse water. Where she and her boy are bound is really none of my concern. He set the plate on the drying rack. But wherever it is, Libby, I promise to pay her enough to get there without having to wash dishes in some bully's kitchen. They deserve better than that.

After arranging some almond cream on Juan's plate, Liria joined him at the sink. She watched his own awkward progress for a moment, then cleared her throat. Nez laughed and handed her the scrub brush. "I'm not too good with this, am I?" he asked.

She took it. "Let us say that I have washed more dishes in recent years than you, and the necessity here is speed, if the Empress is as uncomfortable as you say she is. You may dry."

She worked efficiently, intent on the dishes before her, with a glance now and then at her son. When he finished and was rubbing his eyes, she took him to a corner where there was a pile of sacking, kissed him, and left him there to sleep.

She was scouring the last pot when Nez heard the skinny wail of a mail coach horn. Liria paused and looked at him, uncertainty on her face. "I do not have enough money for another ticket," she told him.

He could tell that it pained her to make such an admission. You're a proud one, for a servant, he thought. "I meant what I said," he replied, taking the pot from her and dipping it in the rinse water. "I will pay you for your help, and you will have enough to buy another ticket. Where are you going?" There, he had asked. It was rude, but he wanted to know.

"Huddersfield," she told him. "I think it is only another day's travel."

"And a little more. I believe you will have to change to a smaller coach line at Drumlin."

"Oh, dear. They didn't tell me that," she said, and frowned into the dishwater.

Who didn't tell you, he wanted to ask. Why are you going to Huddersfield, he wanted to know. To his knowledge, it was a mill town with nothing to recommend it beyond sooty buildings and a sky to match. Was she going to seek work in a factory? Surely not. Would Juan have to work there, too? He looked at the little boy, curled up on the sacking and sound asleep. He can't be more than four or five, but I hear the mills like them young. A pity.

"I assure you that I will pay for your transportation, food, and lodging between here and Huddersfield," he reminded her. "Is . . . are you expected at a certain time there?"

She shook her head. "I suppose a day or two will not matter."

"And I am a desperate man," he joked. "Even more desperate than the landlord!"

The coachman's horn sounded again, and she listened to it, her hand to her hair. He could see that she was wavering. She sighed, and looked at her son.

"Please, Liria," he said. They could hear the coach stopping in the inn yard now.

"Very well," she replied, decisive now. She took off her apron, folded it neatly, and set it on the table, then went to the pile of sacking.

He was there before her, and scooped up Juan, who only stirred and resettled himself. "I can carry him upstairs for you, *dama*."

She paused, and he knew she wanted to ask him why he called her lady. It was good that she didn't; he couldn't have told her, himself. As long as she does not think I am mocking her, he thought, as he carried the sleeping child upstairs to his own room and put him on his bed.

"We can find a blanket for him in the corner," she said quickly, standing in the doorway, and not entering his room.

"No need. He doesn't take up much space." Quickly, Nez took off the child's shoes: muddy, broken affairs too large for his feet. He has so little, Nez thought, covering the boy with a blanket, and yet, I have rarely seen a more cheerful child. He looked at

Liria in the doorway, standing there so calmly with her hands clasped in front of her. He has a good mother. It may be that I must revise my estimation of the Valencias.

"This way," he said, and opened the door to the next room. Luster, the portrait of distress just barely under control, sat awkwardly with the Empress on his lap. Nez knew he hadn't been gone the better part of an hour, but Sophie's face was even more inflamed with the shiny blisters of chicken pox. When she heard them enter the room, she opened her eyes and burst into tears.

The tempest was of short duration. Speaking in a voice so low that Sophie had no choice but to stop her sobs in order to hear, Liria told his butler to summon a maid from belowstairs. In mere moments, a tin tub stood before the hearth. He watched in growing admiration as the Empress allowed Liria to help her from her dress. In another moment she was close to bliss in the tub, while the woman gently washed her body.

"Amazing," he said.

Liria rolled up her sleeves a little higher and shook her head. "It is only what her own mother would do, if she were here."

Nez chose not to disabuse her of that notion, even though he knew Augusta would have been at least as useless as he was. I am in the presence of female competence, he marveled. God bless the ladies. "Is there anything I can do?" he asked, compelled by a gentleman's manners to ask.

"No, my lord. You may retire now. I will take care of your niece."

It was music to his ears. He nodded and tried not to stampede to the door in his relief. "If you would just ask the landlord to have a cot put into this room for me," she said.

"Immediately, *dama,*" he said.

"My son will not trouble you tonight," she added

as she dripped warm water on Sophie's poor arms. "If he should wake up, sing to him."

"I can't sing!" he replied.

"Of course you can," she said. "He likes 'The British Grenadier.' Good night."

He delivered her message to the landlord, who eyed him strangely for a moment. "You're certain it's not the plague, my lord?" the man inquired, standing well away.

"I have seldom been more certain about anything," Nez replied.

Relief covered him like the contents of the calamine lotion bottle when he returned to his private parlor and collapsed on the sofa. "There are times when being an uncle is exhausting," he told Luster, who sat quite still in a chair. He glanced at his butler, then stared at him. "Luster, have you looked in the mirror lately?"

"No, Your Grace. Is there a need?"

Oh, Lord, why me? Nez thought. "Luster, think a moment. Do you ever recall having been afflicted with chicken pox as a child?" The question was almost as hard to ask as it was to imagine that his butler had ever been anything but a butler.

"I . . . I do not recall, Your Grace," he said finally. "Your Grace, are you trying to tell me . . ."

"Welcome to the pesthouse, Luster."

Chapter Three

Considering that he had never slept with a child before, Nez spent a surprisingly comfortable night. After he had assured Luster that he really could find a nightshirt all by himself, and then helped the man, who apologized with every step, to a cot in the dressing room, Nez took himself to bed. Juan did nothing more than sigh, and cuddle close, which turned out to be a blessing, because the night was cool. I should be worried about this dreadful situation, Nez thought as he relaxed. Churl that I am, I will let Liria worry about it in the morning.

Sleep came closer. It should be a sad reflection on the state of my mind that I am so willing to turn my troubles over to someone else, he considered. The only place where I couldn't do that was the Peninsula, and wasn't that an uncomfortable state of affairs for a man of indolence? The idea made him smile in the dark, because he knew how little indolence had ever entered his mind through Portugal, Spain, France, and ultimately Belgium. Libby is right, he thought; I could be redeemed.

Tentatively, Nez stretched out his arm and allowed Juan to settle into the hollow of his shoulder. He knew that women fit so well there; apparently children did, too. Little fellow, your mama must be missing you right now, was his last conscious thought of the evening.

Liria did miss her son. She woke once or twice to check on Sophie, and then returned to an empty bed.

The cot was soft in the right places, but it felt like a bed of rocks without Juan. Not that there would have been room for him on the cot, she reasoned. He was five now and tall for his age, tall despite poor food and a rackety life that she could never have imagined for a child of hers.

I wonder if he takes after his father in height, she thought, then dismissed the matter. Best not to dwell on it. That's what Sergeant Carr would have told me. She curled herself into a ball out of habit, then made a conscious effort to draw herself out to her full length and lie on her back, something she did seldom, even now when she could. She remembered those strange dreams after Juan's birth, when she woke in a panic because she could not find his small body there on the camp bed beside her. I would sit up and pat the covers until the sergeant told me to lie down, that Juan was in the ammunition box, his first crib. "My ma used to that, too," he whispered to her from his cot on the other side of the tent. "Da told me she did that for each of us, and didn't he laugh? Go to sleep, Liria. He'll wake you up soon enough."

She wished she had not thought of the sergeant, because she felt tears prickle her eyes. You would like me to remember that I am still alive and I have a son to raise. People depend upon me.

She contemplated the man in the next room and his butler. I do not even really know his name, she thought. I know he has a title of some sort; perhaps it is even exalted. He did appear startled when I addressed him as an equal. "But you are, sir," she said softly, "even if you have already judged me and found me wanting. I wonder if you have moments that you prefer not to remember? Do you judge yourself with so little information?"

She woke early, dressed, and went to the window and peeked out on a glorious day, something rare in her brief tenure in England. She had suffered through a long gray winter with one or another of Sergeant Carr's relatives, shunted from house to house as they tried to oblige his final plea, then gave it up as a bad business. His last wish had been that she be taken care of. "Liria, they have farms in Suffolk," he had told her, before the infection from his injury took over his mind, turned him inward, and then killed him. "I will write them a letter that you will take to them, and they will be kind to you and Juan."

They weren't. For two years they merely suffered her presence. The last relatives—cousins of some degree, as she was sent farther and farther down the family tree—did attempt to find her a situation in Huddersfield. They tell me the mill owner is kind, and there is a school for the young ones, she thought. Perhaps we may even stay together. Her next thought was the relentless one: and if we cannot? What then?

Sophie stirred then, and muttered in her sleep. Liria touched the child's head, grateful for the distraction, and yet not entirely able to put the other matter from her mind. She observed Sophie in her careful way and saw no hurt beyond the temporary discomfort of chicken pox. You will feel better soon, she thought, and climb those trees on your uncle's property that he promised would wait for you. I wonder, do you have a mother? And if you do, how could she allow you to leave her?

She heard footsteps outside the door, and then the knock she had been half expecting. Liria opened the door on the man whose butler rescued her from a long walk yesterday in the rain. "Good morning, sir," she said, keeping her voice low. "Do come in." She ushered him into the small sitting room, amused at his appearance. She had already decided that he was not a man who stood much on ceremony, and who was probably the despair of his tailor, if he employed one at all. He had stuffed his nightshirt into his breeches, and possibly run his hand through his hair; she could not be sure. He had pulled his shoes on without the benefit of stockings, and hadn't bothered with the detail of lacing them.

" 'I see before me a desperate man,' " she quoted in Spanish before she thought.

It was from an obscure comedy by Cervantes, and he astounded her by replying in the same language, " '. . . and he is ready to throttle old ladies,' " continuing the line of the story. She stared at him in surprise.

He held up his hand. "I spent one winter convalescing from a pesky fever in the house of a merchant near Ciudad Rodrigo who adored Cervantes, and thought I should, too. Amazing way to learn Spanish, won't you agree?"

She nodded, too surprised to speak.

"The Gypsy Priest?" he asked.

Liria nodded again. "Your butler is ill," she said. "He did not look well last night."

"How did you know he had the chicken pox?"

"I took a good look at him last night," she said, then wondered if she had angered him, because he was silent for a long while.

She must have had a wary look on her face, because he clapped his hands on his legs. "Oh, bother it, *dama*! I was going to come in here and complain and whine because my butler had the temerity to throw out spots and blight my life. Your expression tells me rather that I should be concerned about him and not me."

She had no idea that her expression told him anything of the kind. "As you say, sir. At this nasty turn of affairs, I would recommend tea."

"For him or me?" he asked quickly, then smiled at her. "There I go again!"

"Actually, sir, I think *you* should have the tea," she replied, mystified by his quickness of mind, something she did not expect from one who seemed so proud. "I have been long enough in the company of English to observe that it cures all ills, real and imaginary."

"Except chicken pox, eh?" he asked, and she knew he was joking this time. "Shall we give'um a good gargle of calamine lotion and direct that they take up their beds and walk?" He seemed to hesitate. "Miss

Valencia, I must continue to throw myself upon your mercy. Would you help me with my niece *and* my butler?"

He did mystify her. "I told you last night that I would help. Adding another patient does not require a new contract," she assured him. "I will insist that you help me."

"*Claro que si, dama.* Only command me. Huddersfield can wait, although I am puzzled why such a town is an attraction."

I need employment, she thought. Have you never . . . well, no, I suppose you have not. "It can wait," she agreed. "Please summon the landlord and request tea and toast for the sufferers, and how did you say? Plenty of calamine lotion to gargle."

I will have to write to Tony and Libby and tell them that I continue to lead a charmed life, he thought later that afternoon as he sat beside Luster's bed—he had given him his own—watching his butler. I am a man most fortunate to have fallen into the clutches of a woman born to command.

He had always thought his skills in command constituted his only virtue, but after a fruitless waste of time in trying to convince Luster to abandon the cot in the dressing room for the more comfortable bed, he had whined to Liria, who was giving his niece a sponge bath. "He won't do as I request," he complained.

"Oh, he will not?" she murmured. She worked swiftly, patting Sophie dry, applying more lotion, then whisking her back between clean sheets that the landlord's wife had furnished. Does this woman command us all?

"I will see Senor Luster now," Liria declared. When Sophie started to whimper, she turned back to the bed. "My dear, your uncle will sit with you for a few minutes and then I will return," she said, and touched her forehead to Sophie's.

"Your forehead is pink now," he said as she turned around. With a slight smile, she pulled up the corner of her apron and wiped her face. "My butler is wondrously stubborn, Miss Valencia," he warned her.

She merely looked at him, her eyes open no wider, her expression scarcely altered. Maybe it was the way she raised her chin, or that barely perceptible squaring of her shoulders, but he decided not to waste his breath. "I will sit with my niece," he said hastily, and felt a momentary pity for Luster. Serves you right, you stubborn old man. He nodded to Juan, who sat on the floor and drew in what appeared to be an artillery ledger book. "Do *you* ever argue with her, lad?"

Juan gave him a sunny smile and returned to his drawing. Nez glanced at the page. "My carriage?" he asked, and Juan nodded.

He leaned close to Sophie. "Chicken pox doesn't last forever, Empress," he said. "Soon we'll be at Knare, and they'll be on their way to Huddersfield . . . oh, now, why the tears?" He wanted to leap up and drag Liria back to his niece's bedside.

"Uncle, she is so good to us," Sophie said, and then sniffed back her tears. "We do not wish her to leave our presence."

Well, at least you have some of your humor back, he thought. "But I think Miss Valencia is rather a martinet, Your Spotted Highness," he replied.

Sophie nodded, and then smiled, which amused him, because her face was so dotted with calamine. She indicated that he lean closer. "She touches us, and we like that."

Oh, this is a sad reflection on my sister, he thought. "My dear, it is nice to be touched, isn't it? Well, er, perhaps we can find you a governess who does just that."

Sophie shook her head. "Liria," she said, and closed her eyes.

Well, well, he thought. A commander who is gentle, and disguised as a rather broken-down servant. At least I will not be bored for a few days. He gazed at Sophie, hesitated, then put his hand on her arm. She opened her eyes, smiled, then returned to sleep. He watched her, then looked at Juan, who had moved closer even as he continued to draw in the ledger. The boy has an eye for detail, he thought, admiring the way a few sure strokes turned into trees, and then a road, and then rain. Nez doubted whether he had ever drawn as well as the youngster who sat next to Sophie's bed, his tongue between his teeth as he concentrated.

The door opened and Liria stood there. She beckoned to her son, who put down the ledger and tiptoed to his mother. She handed him a bundle of sheets. "Take these downstairs, *mijo,*" she whispered. "*La dama de casa* will have more for you." Juan took the bundle and hurried away.

"Did you convince my stubborn servant to take my bed?" Nez whispered.

"Did you doubt I could?"

"Not at all, *dama,*" he replied, amused. "I think, even though our acquaintance is short, that I would have been more surprised if you had not succeeded."

"Pues claro," she said finally, and closed the door. He laughed softly, pleased with himself. He returned his attention to Sophie. Her skin was dry and warm under his hand, but not feverish. Gently he turned her hand over so it was lying palm-up on the sheet, and pressed his fingers onto the pulse at her wrist, not for any need to check it, but to feel the calm rhythm of her heart. It soothed him better than tea.

In another moment he released her wrist and leaned back in the chair. He knew he should be out of sorts and fretful about this delay to his plans, but a moment's reflection reminded him that he had no plans. What a pleasant toil is leisure, he thought. He followed it with the sure consideration that he would be busy enough this summer. I will see to the health of my land, and find me a wife, he told himself. The former will please me, the latter, my sister; and so it goes.

He was about to close his eyes, when his attention was caught by the ledger book lying on the floor where Juan had left it, to run his mother's errand. Talented child, he thought, and picked up the book. Perhaps I can find some scrap paper for you at Knare that is larger than an artilleryman's notebook. Out of curiosity, he turned to the front of the ledger, and there it was: Richard Carr, Battery Sergeant, 19th Battery, in the precise handwriting he expected. Funny thing about artillerymen, he considered. I never knew one to be slipshod in his records.

He thumbed the pages, knowing he would find a careful record of the guns Carr served and died for: where they were forged, precise dimensions (each gun was ever so slightly different, he knew), how many grains of powder per charge, trajectories, azimuths, arc, torque, and vectors. It was all there. Brighter than me, sir, he thought, as he turned another page and saw a long list of names, each followed by a date, and the word "letter," in Carr's careful script. "And what have we here, Sergeant?" he murmured.

He knew he was no genius, but only a moment's perusal of the chronology told the story. This list was Coruña, then a pause, then Torres Vedras, and Ciudad Rodrigo twice, and Badajoz, and Salamanca, and smaller engagements he did not recognize—Campofino, Frontera, El Paso. A shiver ran through him to know that he was looking at Sergeant Carr's butcher's bill through the length and breadth of Spain and Portugal. He turned the page. And Toulouse. "So you wrote a letter to each family, did you, Sergeant?" he asked. "I wonder if your battery commander knew it."

He could see another page of names through the thin paper. He didn't want to turn the leaf in the book, because he knew it would be Quatre Bras and Mont Saint Jean, what good Englishmen far away from the distinction of each battle were now calling Waterloo. He thought a moment. No, it would be Quatre Bras alone, Quatre Bras and the death of the Nineteen. He turned the page anyway, compelled, and found nothing beyond the long list of Quatre Bras, but not all in Sergeant Carr's handwriting. Never mind, the word "letter" followed each entry except the final one—Richard Carr 6-25-15. So you lived a week, sergeant? Then this is Liria Valencia's handwriting, is it not, sir? She wrote the letters you couldn't write.

The realization shook him because he knew what had happened to the Nineteen, how they had refused to pull back in the face of Ney's advance, buying seconds, minutes, an hour or two for an army caught with its leaders at Lady Richmond's ball in Brussels. You were there at Quatre Bras, weren't you, Liria? he thought. And Juan, too, I imagine. My God, and I whine because I give up a bed to a butler. He flipped through the remaining pages, which contained some closely written words that were covered with Juan's drawings now. He closed the ledger, and put it back on the floor, open to Juan's rendering of His Grace of Knare's carriage. The drawing made him smile. Sergeant Carr, you would be pleased to know how your son has used your ledger, he thought.

He lay awake a long time that night, thinking about war, but it was less painful than usual, as though Juan's barely glimpsed drawings were soothing his own wounds, even as they covered an artillerist's precise record of death.

Chapter Four

What followed were curious days for the Duke of Knare, so close to home, and yet too far to trundle anyone so spotted and miserable into a carriage. He knew that he could have insisted they go on, but he chose not to, for reasons he could not quite divine. There was something peaceful about cooling his heels where no one expected anything of him beyond sitting by one bedside or the other, looking appropriately sympathetic.

In low tones, Liria Valencia had warned him that his butler would be the sicker of the two, and she was right. Nez's presence in the sickroom did not help, because ill as he was, Luster could not reconcile himself to the fact that he was taking His Grace's bed and chamber. He could not offer his devastated butler any consolation, so he left him in the care of the Spanish woman, and devoted himself to his niece.

He did insist upon one homely office he could perform for his butler, and must have sounded firm enough, because Liria chose not to resist. Every morning, and through the day at her request, he carried the slops jar downstairs to the necessary. Luster would die if he knew, Nez thought, as he poured the contents down the hole. The absurdity of it all made him smile. Nice to know that someone even as starchy as Luster has to piss now and then.

Juan generally accompanied him into the yard, walking seriously beside him as though he needed an escort for this important duty. "You like to be outside, don't you?" he asked finally one morning as, empty jar in hand, he stopped to contemplate the activity in the inn yard. "Is it the horses?"

Juan nodded. "I like horses," he said in English.

To Nez's delight, the boy leaned against him for a moment, then took the empty jar and continued across the yard, obviously remembering a duty pressed upon him by his mother. Do we all march to her quiet tune? Nez thought.

He enjoyed the evenings. After Sophie had resigned herself to sleep, he sat with Juan at the table in the sitting room. Juan would generally prop his chin up with his hands and struggle to stay awake because he knew that his mama would come. "You know, I could wake you up when she comes," he told Juan in Spanish, but the little boy only shook his head.

He misses his mother, Nez thought. He can't be more than five, and he surely has never been far from her side, but he soldiers on, alert for the moment when she will come to us . . . to him. He only smiled when Juan did doze, his cheek resting on his drawing.

Liria Valencia came when Luster slept, letting herself quietly into his niece's chambers to sit at the table a moment in silence. He could see the exhaustion on her calm face, which generally revealed little emotion. She would sit as though regrouping herself, then rest her hand on her sleeping son's head, which would always wake him. In another moment he was in her lap, and they were speaking to each other softly in Spanish. Nez tried not to listen, because it wasn't his business. He focused his attention on the newspaper, surprised at himself because he was envying Juan his youth with a mother who obviously adored him. This is one for the books, Libby, he thought, I am envying the bastard son of a Spanish drab. I suppose life has its little lessons.

Liria would hardly do more than sit there, fingering her son's hair, assessing him in the way that he supposed good mothers did, asking him if he was being helpful to the senor and his niece. Juan would look at him then, and Nez would nod and assure Liria that he was valuable in keeping Sophie distracted. "*Dama,* he even escorts me to the necessary when I go on Luster's errands," he said. "He would be an excellent aide-de-camp."

His words always perked her up, as though a good report about her child was nourishment. "Sergeant Carr would be proud of you," she told Juan in Spanish. He could not help overhearing, maybe because he was listening so hard, wondering about these two castaways.

That was it. Liria would sew, or look through Juan's drawings, or sit with her hand gently fingering her son's hair, her eyes on some middle distance beyond the wall of the room. He knew the view himself, and wanted to tell her so. He and his brother officers had sat like that after a battle or skirmish, wondering what the next day would bring. I am sharing sickroom duties with an old campaigner, he reflected.

After a few moments, Liria would sit up straight and shepherd Juan to the little sofa where he slept. She covered him with her cloak, stood a moment, then went to look at Sophie. He usually followed her, not so much out of concern, but because he liked to watch Liria touch Sophie's hair, pat her cheek, and perform this loving assessment on a child she barely knew. It's a nice touch, Libby, he thought. Reminds me rather of Tony and his treatment of the sick. No wonder you love him more than me.

He knew he waited for Liria's approval of the way he was caring for Sophie, and she was generous in her praise. "Senor, she is doing splendidly," Liria whispered, tugging up Sophie's coverlet a fraction of an inch. "The credit is yours."

Her words were so simple, but he felt himself basking in the glow of her commendation. At least I do not wriggle like a puppy, he told himself, after she bid him a quiet good night and returned to the other room.

He appreciated Sophie's resilience. Three days of fretting discomfort constituted her bout of chicken pox. He reminded the Empress not to scratch, daubed on calamine lotion to ease the itch, provided copious amounts of lemonade, and read to her and Juan from a volume of children's stories from the village's lending library. Soon Liria's son was drawing dragons and knights on quality paper that Nez had found in one of the village's few shops. He calmed Liria's wide-eyed alarm upon seeing the expensive paper. "My good woman, you worry about Luster and I will deal with the infantry," he told her quite firmly. "And thank you for not arguing," he said to the closed door after she let herself out quietly.

He had to amend that thought. Liria Valencia did not seem to argue at all. She did not raise her voice, or make demands on anyone, but she had such a way about her of command. No, that was unfair, too. She did not command like the brigade major he had been, but she had a way of raising one eyebrow to Juan that never failed to get him to his feet promptly when she needed him. Maybe it was because she was tall, he thought at first, then dispatched that notion because she was not tall, probably not an inch or two beyond Libby's small height. She acts tall, he decided, rather like a good duchess should, even though the idea of Liria as a duchess made him chuckle to himself.

In an unspoken arrangement, he took the cot in his niece's dressing room, and Liria moved into the dressing room close to Luster. Nez knew he could have requested another chamber, and the landlord even suggested it, but he chose to remain where he was. These people are beginning to interest me, he told himself the second night, after bidding Sophie good night, seeing that Juan—long asleep on the sofa—was covered, and then lying down on his cot. That is it; for some odd reason, I am not bored.

Granted, Liria was a fine-looking woman, but nothing intrigued him more about her than her serene way of watching over them all, her hands clasped in front of her. She could stand so still, gaze at his fretful niece, and as he watched, Sophie would become calm before his eyes. It was not intimidation, but a deep compassion that he could only envy, and wonder about. I have seen women like this before, he thought. It came to him finally after she reported to him after dinner on the third day that Luster was much improved. "Excellent news, Miss Valencia," he said, offering her a seat at the table.

She shook her head. "I should return to Senor Luster," she said, and with the slightest incline of her head, glided from the room.

Then he knew. Well, damn me, he thought in sudden surprise as the notion took hold. You either were a nun yourself, or you are convent educated, Liria Valencia. He remembered evacuating an orphanage that happened to command the choicest view of Soult's army on the flank. At his sharp command, the sisters had shepherded their charges from the building. Their calmness was contagious; he had never forgotten it, or the memorable way they walked, seeming to glide over the stones in a manner that was utterly composed and fluid. They also stood as she did, hands clasped at waist level, some of the sisters fingering rosaries through that tense time, the sole evidence of their fear.

He imagined that Liria had been raised in such an orphanage because he could not fathom that she was a nun herself. He decided she probably was a lady's maid, after all. It seemed likely, but he couldn't make the leap from lady's maid to Sergeant Carr and the Nineteen. War does change things he knew, thinking of the long retreat from Burgos, and recalling—odd what one remembers!—a cat loping along purposefully beside his exhausted horse, carrying a kitten in her mouth. All of Spain was on the move, courtesy of Boney's appetite for others' real estate, so why not Liria and her boy?

The next morning, Sophie declared herself well enough to sit at the table and take some cheerfully rendered advice from Juan about drawing horses. Nez took the hint and went to see his butler. Luster tried to raise himself up onto one elbow.

"Heavens, Luster, you're ill," he murmured. "Pray don't exert yourself." He couldn't help a certain glee in looking at Luster in a nightshirt, his face unshaven and liberally spotted with calamine lotion. So this is the dragon who intimidated me and a whole generation of servants? Good to know that you're mortal, Luster.

"You shouldn't see me like this, Your Grace," Luster said, and Nez felt immediately chastened because the comment was so heartfelt.

"Oh, bother it, Luster. You've certainly seen me in worse straits," he replied, not even trying to hide the brusqueness in his voice because intuition told him that the last thing any butler wanted was sympathy from his duke. "Miss Valencia, I have never been a paragon. When I think of the scrapes that Luster glossed over with my departed father . . . Ah, well."

Liria nodded. "I had brothers," she replied in such a droll tone that he had to laugh.

"I rest my case, Luster." So you had brothers in the past tense, Miss Liria Valencia, he thought. And where are they now? "Luster, my chiefest desire is for your recovery, so I can continue to plague your life." He came closer, wondering when it was that this ageless man finally got himself so old. He decided on a light touch, even as his heart turned over to see the exhaustion in his eyes. "I suppose I must scold you for continuing to go to my dratted sister's house after I went to see the Cooks, mustn't I? I am no physic, but even I know it takes a while for chicken pox to manifest itself."

"Your Grace, you know how rackety Lady Augusta's household is," Luster said. "I only sought to help her staff."

Liria vacated the chair she sat in, and indicated that he sit there. He knew better than to argue. "I know.

What a shame that Augusta staffs her house with drooling idiots! Do get well, and do so by not worrying about me! I know you do not believe it, but years of vague unrest in Spain, Portugal, and Belgium taught me to manage myself. Well, never as successfully as you can manage me, but I got by from time to time, and I can do so now until you are better."

He hoped that was the right tone, and glanced at Liria. She nodded. "Your master is right, Senor Luster," she said. "Allow him to sit with you while I check on Sophie, please." She left the room before Luster could argue.

Luster lay so still, his eyes boring into the ceiling. Nez could almost read his thoughts, this strange reversal of position for a man accustomed to serve. "Your Grace," he murmured. "You cannot fathom my distress."

"Perhaps I can," he said gently. "Can I tell you that I am genuinely fond of you and genuinely concerned, without causing you further distress? I have many faults, Luster, and you know them all, but lying is not one of them. Now, sir, may I hand you a urinal?"

"Never, Your Grace!"

"Never is a long time to hold water, butler or duke. You'd prefer to hand the landlady wet sheets?"

There was a long pause. "Perhaps just this once, then, Your Grace. Oh, God, forgive me! It is behind you on the table."

He spent the next two days caring for his butler. Liria did not so much abdicate her sickroom duties, as share them. She did not know him, and none of the circumstances of his life, but some gift for discernment led her to do the absolute right things, or so he told himself as he tended his butler's needs.

Beyond a propensity to lie at attention as though he were still on duty, Luster was a model patient. He required no cajoling to eat his gruel and toast. Nez thought he would be mulish when he lifted him from his bed so Liria could change sheets. "Your Grace, I am too heavy to be lifted," he protested, but it was a feeble protest, as though he knew he would be overruled.

"That is fustian, Luster, and you know it," Nez said in his most rallying tone. "I outweigh you by at least two stone, and I stand a head taller. I intend to humor the landlady and this kind Spanish woman who has decided that we are not past redemption. If they say you are to have clean bedding, I would never presume to argue; nor should you."

Luster did not argue, and raised no more objections to his care. As a consequence, he was better within two days, which Liria informed Nez that night as they sat together. "I think that one more day will see your servant fit to continue travel, if we have not too far to go," she said.

"Knare is close enough, no more than a long day's drive."

"So close," she murmured. "You could have sent servants to tend Luster, and gone on your way."

"I suppose I could have," he agreed. "Sophie needed me, and I suppose I will imagine that Luster did."

For the first time, Liria seemed to lose some of her self-possession. "I did not mean to imply that your presence was not required, sir."

He looked at her, enjoying the sight of her face, so unlike that of an Englishwoman. I have missed the people of Spain, he thought with a pang. "I know you did not imply any such thing, Miss Valencia. I can only be grateful that you did not answer the summons of the coachman's horn—heavens, is it five days ago now?—and leave me to the fate I probably deserved." He hesitated, then plunged on. "But for Luster, I would have left you and Juan beside the road in the rain. I suppose you know it, but I feel a need for confession."

"I know," she said softly. "I do not suppose that you are accustomed to helping women like me."

It was honestly spoken and left him no room to

hem or haw. "True," he admitted. "Appearances are deceiving. Excuse the cliché."

It was her turn to hesitate briefly. "Would it anger you to know that I was having the same thought?"

He laughed. "No, it would not." He looked at her and she returned his gaze, not boldly, as one of her class and station might, but in a measuring yet friendly way that startled him even more, because he knew that somewhere down deep, they were equals.

He thought then about Huddersfield. I wonder if she is seeking work in the mills, he thought. Juan will not be able to be with her then. "Liria, are you planning to work in the textile mills in Huddersfield?" he asked suddenly when she kissed Juan, deposited him on the sofa, and went to the door.

She nodded. "I have heard of a mill owner who has a school."

"That may be, but you will be long hours at the loom. Must you do that?"

"If Juan and I are to live," she replied, and turned the door handle.

He was on his feet then. "Have you another choice? Could you return to Spain?"

"No," she said, and nothing more.

That is the short answer, he thought, but could not help noticing that she seemed to want to say more. "Is there more?" he asked, knowing how intrusive it was to question her.

He thought she would tell him, but the moment passed. "Very well. I only ask that you come with me to Knare until I can get Sophie and Luster situated. I intend to pay you for your services, and pay your fare to Huddersfield." He waited for her to object, but to his relief she did not.

"That is kind of you, sir," she said. She hesitated, and he hoped for one small moment that she would tell him more about herself. "I suppose I should have asked this sooner in our acquaintance, sir, but should I be addressing you differently? Luster told me you are a duke."

Bother it, he thought, disappointed. "I am. I live in relative splendor in a pile of stones called Knare. I am the despair of my tailor because I dress as you see me. My sister Augusta rails at me because I never bother to go to the House of Lords in velvet and ermine. Now, why should a man wear velvet and ermine? My housekeeper sighs and clucks her tongue because I insist on eating belowstairs."

"That *is* eccentric," Liria interrupted, and it pleased him, because it was almost a joke from such a serious woman.

He continued, pleased to be amusing her. "Augusta is nagging at me to marry and set up my own nursery, but . . ." He hesitated. Why am I telling you all this, he asked himself. "Well, I was in love with another, and she married someone else."

"You can't forget her?" Liria asked, when he did not continue.

"I should, shouldn't I? She married a wonderful man, someone I even like, damn his eyes."

"Forgetting is difficult," she said.

"Yes, it is," he agreed. And what are you having to forget, he thought. "Augusta is right, though. I will make a serious effort to find a wife this summer. Oh, the original question, I suppose you should address me as Your Grace, but I would prefer that you did not. It sounds so stuffy, and madam, I am not stuffy."

The next morning, after a consultation with the village's one physician, Liria assured him that Sophie and Luster were fit to travel. By noon, they were on the road. He wasn't sure whether it pleased him or not, and he almost didn't think Liria Valencia was happy about the matter, either. She gave no real outward sign of disappointment that the journey must continue, but there was something in her silence that stirred him to an odd kind of hope that she would miss him. Sitting there in his carriage, watching her when he hoped she wasn't aware, he realized with a pang that he had gone beyond the disdain of his class for hers. He only cared now what would happen to

Liria Valencia and her son Juan. Libby, you would be proud of me, he thought.

He waited for the mere thought of Libby to send him into the doldrums, but it did not. The day was beautiful and he knew as surely as though someone had told him that his melancholy would pass. I will get on with the business of life, he told himself, smiling at the thought.

Or so it seemed to him, until Juan nudged him, a gentle poke in his side that pleased him with its familiarity. He looked down at the drawing Juan held out for his view only, and not to his mother, who sat across from him next to Luster. What talent this child has, he thought, as he admired the profile drawing of the boy's mother.

Juan leaned toward him. "Mama," he whispered in Nez's ear, and the tickling of his breath touched him.

"I know," he whispered back, admiring the way Juan had caught the pursing of her lips that he knew by now meant deep concentration. Juan had also caught the depth of her brown eyes, and her clear gaze. Something was missing, Nez thought, which made him wonder, in their brief acquaintance, how much time he had already spent admiring her beautiful Spanish face. He touched the drawing. "See there, Juan, you have left out the little mole by her eye."

Juan frowned, and Nez could tell that he did not understand. Nez smiled and touched the side of his own eye, and the boy nodded, and added a dot to the drawing. "Excellent," Nez said. He wanted to ask him how he achieved that look of restfulness, which seemed to be Liria's hallmark. But knew that so much English complexity would be beyond the child.

In his companionable, adaptable way, Juan leaned against him and continued his picture. In another moment Nez found himself fingering the child's hair, and then gathering him closer, as he had watched Liria do on many a night. He felt a deep sorrow at the thought of sending the two of them to the mills. Perhaps Juan would have a school there, but would a tired teacher of mill brats have the time to look at a drawing, or the wit to recognize lovely talent? He doubted it, and the thought gnawed at him.

They spent the night in Wishart, no more than twenty miles from Knare, but he could tell that Luster and Sophie both were exhausted and in need of beds. The full moon beamed on a beneficent evening good enough for late travel, but even beyond the welfare of his constituents, he had no heart to continue the journey that would part him from the Valencias.

He flattered himself that Liria felt the same way. When Sophie and Luster were both asleep, and Juan slept on a pallet, she did not retire to her own cot in Sophie's room, but went down the stairs. After a length of time considering the matter, he followed her.

He didn't see her at once. A coach had come, and the ostlers were hurrying the tired horses away and hitching fresh ones while the coach's occupants stood stretching, or rushed inside for something to eat. For one irrational moment he feared that she was leaving, but knew the enormity of that idiocy in his next breath; Liria would never abandon her child.

He saw her then by the fence that bordered the highway. She seemed to be watching the inn-yard activity, perhaps even admiring the horses, and he wondered then if she liked to ride. That can hardly be, he thought. Women of her quality usually walked, or hopped onto the back of carts. But there was no mistaking her interest in the horses. He joined her at the fence.

"Nice animals, aren't they?" he said. "I mean, for an inn yard."

She nodded. "My brother told me that England's finest horses come from Ireland. Was he right?"

"Indeed he was. I've scoured a few counties across the Irish sea for bloodstock." He thought a moment. No harm in asking. Be casual, Benedict. "Does, does your family have horses?"

"Some," she replied. She seemed to hesitate, too,

and he wondered if she would continue. "Ours come . . . came from North Africa."

My God, Arabians, he thought in surprise. "Did your brother ride?"

"They both did."

"And you?" he asked, practically holding his breath.

"Oh, yes."

She smiled, and he suddenly wanted to hear her laugh. "A good memory, I gather?" he prompted.

"Yes again, until the *jefe del rancho* caught me and told me I didn't belong in his fields."

So that was it. He had seen scraggly-looking children hanging around his own paddocks, eager to ride, but knowing the penalties of being caught on his land. Might as well change the subject, he thought, for this one is only going where I thought it would. "Juan likes to draw horses, and I think he is quite good." He took a deep breath. "Do you think the school in Huddersfield will nurture that talent?"

She shrugged. "I do not even know for sure if there is a school in Huddersfield, sir. I hope, though."

There didn't seem to be any inane reply that would smooth that realistic statement, so he changed the subject again. "I do fully intend to compensate you for your time and trouble on my behalf," he said.

"I have no doubt that you will be fair and generous."

She replied quickly, obviously without thinking about it, and he was touched by her trust in him, the most unreliable of men. "I will be generous, Miss Valencia. Good night, now."

The whole business of saying good-bye to the Valencias left him low and uncommunicative for the rest of the journey, which ended at noon on the gravel drive at Knare's main entrance. Even in his worst days, he usually felt a lift of his heart when the road topped a rise and entered the small valley just beyond the village of Knare. He gazed at it with a frown this time. He was right; it was just a pile of cold stones, the gift of a Catholic house wrested from its owners during the time of Henry the Eighth and given to the first duke of Knare, probably for some dirty doings against the Church of Rome. True, the ivy was appealing, and the little panes of glass did catch the sun in an attractive way. At least it is well run, he thought, glancing at Luster, who looked so weary.

The carriage rolled to a stop, and he waited for the servants to pour out of the door to line themselves along the way to the entrance, ready to bow. Luster looked at him, faint surprise on his face, too, when nothing happened. "They may not be expecting you, Your Grace, but surely someone is at least watching out a window," he said, shaking his head in dismay.

"You know, Luster, I think I prefer it this way," he said. "Let me throw down the step and give you a hand." Before his butler could object, Nez opened the door and unfolded the steps. By the time he helped Luster, his hand still trembling from illness, from the carriage, the door opened and his servants emerged. He looked again, with a deep sigh this time. His sister Augusta came next, and with her was Miss Audrey St. John from next door. She grinned at him, and he couldn't help but smile back.

"Well, Audrey," he said as the footman ran up to help Luster. "I can only pray you haven't rearranged all my furniture and replaced the draperies. 'Lo, Gussie. Sophie is safe and sound, if a little crusty yet."

"Let us hope that she will not scar," his sister said, nodding to Sophie, who had started toward her, but hung back at her words.

Oh, Gussie, you could hug your daughter, he told himself.

"Mrs. Burlew has died," Augusta replied in that same tone. "It was two nights ago. In view of the fact that I had just come from my father-in-law's funeral, I thought it completely inconsiderate of her."

You would, he told himself. "Let us pray she is feeling some contrition beyond the veil," he murmured.

"My thought precisely, brother," Augusta replied.

"As a result, your household is leaderless. Thank goodness I am here to save you from some folly or other. I am ready to summon my own housekeeper from London to assume charge here at Knare."

He flinched in spite of himself and thought of that forbidding gorgon who nipped at poor Fred's bourbon, sharpened her tongue on 'tween stairs maids, and was even seen coming out of a broom closet once, straightening her skirts, followed a few minutes later by an underfootman. His heart sank. He glanced at Audrey St. John, who stood a little behind his sister and continued to grin at him. He winked at her, which caused Gussie to puff up. "Really, brother, I wish you could see the seriousness of this event! It is hard to imagine a more thoughtless scheme on Mrs. Burlew's part, with summer coming on. She knows how busy it will be, with your military friends dropping in to see your disgusting armory! What can she have been thinking? Thank God I am here to rescue you."

Well, toss me back into the arena with the lions, he told himself. Suddenly it was too much: no more Valencias, Augusta here, the country's worst housekeeper on her way soon, and Luster still weak.

He looked at the row of servants, who gazed back expectantly, ever hopeful, as if praying he would rescue them from Augusta and prevent her housekeeper from blighting their lives. He felt tired, and it was only noon.

"Who is *that?"* Augusta asked suddenly.

Startled, he looked around. Juan had just jumped from the top step. Liria stood at the carriage door. He offered her his hand. She descended gracefully, released his hand, and stood close to her son.

An idea took hold then, and he made no effort to shake it off. He could almost see Libby Cook staring at him, her eyes wide, her mouth open in shock. He took a deep breath. "You're too late, Gussie. I was preparing to retire Mrs. Burlew, and can only wish that she had been able to enjoy a pleasant retirement, poor dear. May I introduce Liria Valencia, my new housekeeper?"

Chapter Five

Augusta gasped. "You never hired a housekeeper!"

You are correct, he thought, amazed at himself. "I saw her walking in the rain and had a sudden impulse," he said. He stared at his sister, astounded that any human being could turn such a peculiar mottled shade of purple. "Gussie, do breathe."

She did finally, letting out such a gust of wind and choler than Juan moved closer to his mother.

Augusta's eyes narrowed into slits. "You are telling such a lie, brother," she declared.

"That's my story, and I won't waiver from it, Gussie dear," he replied with a shrug. I should remember that telling Gussie a lie or the truth is all the same, he told himself. "I might add that the matter has Luster's entire approval, eh, Luster?"

"Most indubitably, Your Grace," his butler said without a blink. "Now, Miss Valencia," Luster continued, "if you would lend me a shoulder to lean upon, I will show you to your domain belowstairs. Haverly, don't just stand there with your chin dragging on the gravel. Lively, now!" A footman leaped forward and took the butler's arm. "Juan may come, too, my dear," Luster said.

Nez barely dared to look at her. Oh, please, he thought. I don't care how ramshackle your life has been. You don't belong in a mill, no matter how enlightened it is.

"Aha!" Augusta exclaimed, planting herself in front of the Spanish woman. "This is the first time you have heard of this, is it not?"

Juan gulped and wrapped his arm around his mother's leg, burying his face in the fold of her threadbare cloak. Don't bully them, you witch, Nez thought. Pray, don't treat them that way. They are just two people with very little between them and ruin.

Liria looked at him, and he knew he did not know her well enough to interpret her expression. Please, Liria, he thought. *Por favor, dama.*

To his relief, she smiled at Gussie. "My lady, I have had time to consider this offer. I have already told your brother that I will enjoy managing a duke's estate again."

You are almost as cool a liar as I am, Liria Valencia, he thought, impressed.

"If you have ever managed even a duke's potting shed, then I am Caroline of Brunswick!" Augusta snapped.

"Your mustache is not nearly as dark, Gussie," he murmured. "Where was that estate, Miss Valencia? I can't recall."

"Near Bailen," she replied promptly, "in the middle of an orange grove. My lady, I will give most satisfactory service. Now, if you will excuse me, I think that Luster is starting to droop. *Ven conmigo, Juan. No ten miedo.* Your Grace, excuse us." She dropped as elegant a curtsy to him as he had ever seen in his life, right there in his driveway, a curtsy worthy of the Court of Saint James, and then gave her arm to Luster. To his further gratification, the other servants gaped, then followed them into the manor. Gussie stared after them.

"I think your dear little brother has matters in control, Augusta," Audrey said. "But really, Benedict, it is a little hard to believe that *you* found a housekeeper."

"Oh, I didn't, Audrey," he said, happy enough to tiptoe along the selvage of truth, now that Liria had not left him facedown in his own yard. "Luster discovered her, and I am wise enough never to disagree with my butler. You should have seen Miss Valencia managing two invalids. She can handle one household, and I, for one, aim to let her."

He could tell that his sister was not going to give up without a struggle. "*Miss* Valencia, and she has a son?" Gussie asked. "What will the vicar say? What about the neighbors? Benedict, *why* do you never think of consequences?"

"A's your closest neighbor, *I* have no objection, and you know how my papa enjoys a pretty face," Audrey said, and Nez could have kissed her. "As for the vicar, if I am not mistaken, didn't Mr. Potter say at dinner the other night that his sermon this Sunday would be on not judging others? Of course, I could have misheard him, Augusta." She took Augusta's arm. "Come on, my dear, and walk me to the edge of the property. I would invite you, too, Benedict, but I know that you do not possess a shred of propriety, else you would have thought of it first!"

He laughed and winked at her again. "Audrey, you remain a game goer! Tell your papa I will visit him tomorrow, and even drink some of your tea, if you will pour."

"Oh, well-done, Benedict!" she replied. "There is hope for you yet."

He watched them cross the yard, Augusta an unwilling partner, but Audrey pulling her along and jollying her as she went. Sophie tugged on his sleeve, and he looked down at her, surprised. "Heavens, Sophie, I forgot you were there. May I carry Your Highness into the house and let you be an invalid for a few more hours?"

His niece shook her head. "Liria says I should only consider the Bourbons of Spain and France, and the Hapsburgs of Austria and not pretend to be royalty. She claims it is an unsteady profession these days." She sighed. "But maybe just this once, Uncle."

He picked her up and held her close. Sophie wrapped her arms around his neck and he kissed her cheek. "And now I will take you upstairs and then root about in the kitchen for something to eat. I fear my household is somewhat disorganized."

He deposited Sophie in the chamber next to his own. "Do I even dare attempt the kitchen?" he asked himself as he strolled downstairs, content to be at his own ground again. He took the shortcut through the gallery, gazed up at his ancestors frozen in time on his walls, and wondered what they were thinking, if indeed, the dead had a thought to waste on the quick. He paused for a long moment before his favorite portrait, the first Duke of Knare, who by all accounts was the worst of the lot. He remembered the stories about a man who regularly indulged in roguery with his serving women, and had no qualms about taking Catholic lands, with Henry the Eighth's entire approval.

"I was never that bad, Your Grace," he said out loud, "although I suppose in our own way and time, we have fought for king and country." He stood a moment more in thought, considering how nice it would be someday to have other paintings here. I could put all these stuffy progenitors in some other hall that no one frequents. "Then I'll find an attic for this furniture and buy comfortable pieces," he announced to his ancestors. "Just you wait."

He looked around the long gallery with new eyes, imagining his wife reading to a child or rocking a baby, or even just listening to him as he lay on a well-stuffed sofa, shoes off, describing his day. "Heavenly," he murmured. "I must find a wife. Good day to you all. Mind your manners, won't you?"

Once he crossed the gallery, the kitchen was not far away, if down several flights. He allowed discretion to take over from valor, and directed his steps to the armory. Up another flight, and he opened the door.

Amos Yore looked up from his worktable, where he was polishing a gun lock. "G'day, Major," he said in his quiet way, as though Nez had only been gone an hour or two. He gestured to the musket resting in the vice. "You were right to send me to that estate auction for old Lord Withers. Look at these."

Nez gazed around in satisfaction at the gleaming weapons, and breathed deep of metal polish. "Private

Yore, as much as you writhe when I tell you, you truly do have an eye to the beauty of arrangement. Now, I'd have just stuck those swords over there in a row, but you've hung them to illustrate thrust, parry, and all those other positions I'm thankfully forgetting."

"It helps to have adequate wall space, Major," Yore replied modestly. He cleared his throat. "Betty Gilbert likes it, too."

"She does? Spend much time here?" he asked casually.

"If I don't go belowstairs right sharpish, she brings me my dinner, Major." Yore turned back to the gun lock, as though it needed his concentration. "I let her clean one of the bores, sir. Didn't think you'd mind, because she knows her business."

"I expect she does, seeing that her brother and father are my gamekeepers." He touched Yore's arm. "They're good shots, too, Private, so mind your manners."

"I do, Major," he said promptly, then blushed. "I mean, that is to say . . ."

"You are a perfect gentleman?"

"Well, no, Major," he said. "You know I am no gentleman."

"Consider yourself blessed beyond measure," Nez declared. "I am currently in trouble with everyone of my acquaintance, even if I am supposed to be a gentleman." He sat down at the bench by Yore. "Private, I have hired a housekeeper whom I scarcely know, and who is Spanish. She carries an artilleryman's satchel with the number nineteen stenciled on it. Did you know a sergeant with the Nineteen? I believe this particular one died at Quatre Bras. His name was Carr."

"Didn't nearly all the Nineteen die there?" Yore asked. He rested the stump of his leg on the bench and rubbed it thoughtfully. "They served in brigade with us now and then, didn't they?"

"They did."

Yore thought a moment more, then shook his head.

"I remember an older sergeant, a quiet man, but I don't remember a Spanish woman with him." He spoke in a wondering voice. "Major, I thought I would never forget those days, but there's so much now that I can't recall." He rubbed his leg again. "Betty's father took me hunting with him. You had asked him to thin out the deer over by Finders."

"I remember."

"He made me a kind of stand, so I could lean and shoot. That's what I think about now, and Betty. It's better, isn't it?"

"Much better," he agreed, touched by what he was hearing. "I suppose I just wish I knew a little more about my new housekeeper."

"Is she pretty?" Yore asked suddenly.

"Emphatically," he said, startled by his own answer. "You know I've been missing those Spanish looks."

Amos looked around dramatically. "Don't let an English woman hear that confession, Major," he said. "Revenge would be swift!"

They laughed together. "You know, Major, I think Allenby might remember the sergeant, and if he had a senora. Allenby of Pytch?"

He nodded, and couldn't help but flinch a little when he thought of his second meeting with Yore on the London street corner where he was begging only last year. "You told me his wife was taking in laundry to support him."

Yore brightened. "Not now, Major. The most amazing thing! I got a letter from him while you were gone. I nearly forgot. You won't believe this, but about a year ago, a relative he can't remember died and left him enough money to start a little business of his own. He has a sweetshop in Pytch and makes candy. Amazing good fortune, isn't it?"

Good for you, Allenby, Nez thought. I was trusting that you would know what to do with that little parcel from a relative you'd never heard of. How good of him to die at such an opportune moment. "Yes, amazing good fortune, Yore." He gestured to the weapons around him, and decided on a monumental change of subject. "And what does my sister tell me but there are visitors here all the time to tour your armory now."

"It's true, Major." Yore grinned. "I think it bothers her ladyship, but there you are."

"There I am. You said that Allenby might know something about the Nineteen?" he said, reminding the man.

"I'll write him tonight."

"Have him send us some sweets, too. After all, Yore, wasn't I a purveyor of candies once?"

"I believe you were, Major," Yore replied, and got up when Nez started toward the door. "How is that pretty lady you told me about? The one in Kent?"

He steeled himself for a pang, and it came, but not with enough force to make him flinch. "She is blooming and about to hatch. I think I'll be a godfather soon."

"Good for you, Major! I'll write to Private Allenby and see what he remembers."

Nez descended the stairs slowly, stopping by the mullioned window on the landing to gaze out at his park. My God, how peaceful it is, he thought. Was there really a time when I thought it boring? He saw a figure approaching, and hoped it was not Augusta returning from Ash Grove, girded for battle over his housekeeper. A longer look relieved his mind; it was one of Sir Michael's footmen. Maybe he will tell me that my sister sprained her ankle and must remain at Ash Grove for at least six weeks, he thought.

He walked down the stairs and opened the front door just as the man was starting around to the servants' entrance. "Over here, Cutting," he said.

The footman handed him a note, and bowed. "Miss St. John told me to wait for a reply, Your Grace."

He read the note quickly. "Tell your mistress I will be happy to dine with her and Sir Michael. You keep country hours, Cutting?"

"Yes, Your Grace. Dinner is at six. Good day." Nez took out his timepiece and looked at it. This will at least relieve Liria of the strain of organizing a meal for me tonight, he thought, provided she is even planning to stay.

He took the long way to the kitchen, seeing none of the servants. For one horrid moment he thought that everyone had deserted Knare, that they had all packed their bags and were fleeing his estate like virgins in a bad three-volume novel. "Absurd," he murmured as he approached the familiar green baize door and went quietly downstairs.

He heard the murmur of voices in the servants' hall and slowed his steps when he heard his name mentioned. "Oh, the duke's a care for nobody, but he's harmless," someone was saying. "It's his sister what gets my back up. She scolds and frets and counts the silver, and declares that we all ought to be turned off without a character."

So I'm a care for nobody, he thought, stung by the title at first, then fair enough to admit that the anonymous comment had some merit. He couldn't see through walls, but he imagined that Liria Valencia, whom he had nearly left standing in the rain, was probably nodding her head in agreement.

If she was even there; he had to know. Nez went back to the stairs, tiptoed half up to the first floor landing, then clattered down this time, making sure to shut the door at the bottom with a decisive click. When he strolled around the corner into the servants' hall, all was silent. His servants looked back at him in faint surprise, as though he had not taken his meals belowstairs with them all winter, and they were all caught in collective amnesia. Disagreeable wretches, he thought. Liria will imagine I feed you on bread, water, and kitchen floor sweepings. "Good afternoon," he said. "Miss Valencia, may I assist you in any way?"

She shook her head. "No, sir. I believe the matter is well in hand. The airing of opinion is a good thing, no?"

He looked around at the familiar faces, and noticed the red eyes of the women and the men's serious expressions. "I know it has been a difficult week with the unexpected passing of Mrs. Burlew, but please remember: we will continue as usual here at Knare. Miss Valencia, I have been invited to dine at Ash Grove this evening—it's the neighboring estate. You needn't worry about seeing to me."

"Yes, Your Grace," Liria said. "I will have a report for you this evening."

"That will be fine," he replied, wishing that she did not have to sound so formal, but knowing that it was probably necessary. "Miss Valencia, a word with you, please." He indicated the late Mrs. Burlew's sitting room, and she rose gracefully and followed him, shutting the door quietly behind her.

He almost felt tongue-tied as he stood there. "Miss Valencia, thank you for not betraying me in front of Augusta . . . Lady Wogan. I . . . I just couldn't face so much female management all at once."

She smiled at that. "Surely you have been managed before, sir."

"Of course I have!" he retorted, amused more than irritated. "Probably from the cradle! I just wish that Augusta would be more discreet in arranging my life."

"What sister can resist?" she murmured, and he was pleased to notice a lively light in her eyes.

"I can see I am taking my troubles to someone who has obviously meddled in her siblings' lives," he teased, then noticed with dismay that her eyes filled with tears. "Oh, I didn't mean to cause you distress, Miss Valencia, honestly I didn't." My God, what did I say? he asked himself.

She turned away for a moment in an obvious effort to collect herself. All her brothers must be dead on Spanish battlefields, he thought in horror. And what has become of her sisters? He stood there, not knowing whether to go or to stay, to keep silent or to speak. The moment was brief. He heard her take one deep breath, and then another, and she turned around to face him again.

"I have meddled," she said quietly. He could sense

her struggle more than see it, because she was magnificently in control of herself again. "I will say this, sir, even if you think me bold: it is nice to know that she is concerned about your welfare. Perhaps that is the light in which she chooses to manage you."

He thought not, but his own discomfort certainly made him willing to consider it. And why am I engaged in so serious a discussion with a shabby woman I found in the rain only a week ago? he asked himself. "I know her pretty well," he said at last, "but you are correct; this is not what I came to ask you." He paused, wondering again at his impulsive suggestion in the driveway, then forged ahead. "Miss Valencia, I do hope you will seriously consider the position of housekeeper here."

"You know nothing of me or my skill in managing a household such as yours" was her quiet reply, and he felt his heart sink.

"All you know of me is that I am a care for nobody—yes, I overheard that—and a man who leaves women to walk in the rain," he said. "The plain fact is that I need a housekeeper right now, and you need employment that will keep you from a workhouse, and Juan from a life not, I think, of your choosing."

She waited a long time to speak, and again he was struck by her ability to master a situation when all reason would suggest that she had no control. "You are right. I do accept your offer of employment. I have only one question: why are you doing this? I must confess that I do not think that you really care who is housekeeper here."

She was right, of course. He knew he could choose not to answer, or make a joke of the whole thing. "Perhaps it is because I promised a friend not too long ago that I would make every effort to become kinder." This was more plain speaking than he had ever indulged in, and in front of a woman of inferior circumstances.

"This was the lady you lost?" she asked.

"If I must be honest, I do not think I ever really

had Libby to lose her! And that, *dama,* is enough from me. I will take dinner next door. Have a report tonight."

"Pues bien, señor," she said.

"One moment." He took her arm suddenly, and the gesture startled her. She pulled away quickly. "Beg pardon, Miss Valencia. Just tell me: what were you doing in there when I came in?"

She regained her composure quickly. "Something I learned from Sergeant Carr, *señor.* When matters were in confusion, he would call his men together and let them talk. They always suggested solutions to problems . . ."

". . . which my sister surely is," he interrupted.

"I am thinking your servants need to talk."

"I talk to them when I pay them!" he declared. "I ask them how they are doing."

"What do they always tell you?"

"That they are doing fine, Miss Valencia!" Benedict, you are a dimwit, he thought as his words sank in. He sighed at his own stupidity. "Let them talk, Miss Valencia."

"Claro, señor," she said, and went back into the hall, pausing long enough to tell him that she had already sent a servant with soup and toast to Sophie and to Luster. "Bravo, Miss Valencia," he declared. "You would probably not credit this, considering that I am a confirmed care for nobody, but that is precisely the errand I came on."

"I knew it was," she replied agreeably, and he thought she meant it.

When they came into the hall again, the chef had added his considerable presence to the congregation of servants. Without waiting for an introduction, he poured out a mouthful of rapid-fire French. By listening carefully, Nez could discern something about Lady Wogan. He sighed. Gussie, you can drive people into the boughs in two languages. That is surely an achievement, he thought. I suppose I must translate, even if my French is rusty beyond belief.

To his astonishment, Liria Valencia listened to his tirade calmly, and made more notations on her tablet. When the chef exhausted his argument finally, and paused to gather his breath for another assault, she replied in French as impeccable as his own. Well, what have we here? Nez thought as the chef sat down with a thump, surprised by Liria's fluent response.

"Miss Valencia, will you never cease to amaze me?" he asked.

"It is unlikely, sir," she replied calmly, with no hint that she was quizzing him.

She gave him a Libby answer, and he loved it. "Bravo, Miss Valencia," he said. "Do carry on, my dear housekeeper, in whatever language you choose! Shall I send the Bavarian stable boy 'round?"

"Jawohl, Herr Oberst," she said, and turned back to the openmouthed servants.

So it was that he went to dinner in perfect charity with himself. Audrey would know better than to place him next to his sister. And if it happened to be the deaf Miss Adams, with her infernal ear trumpet, on one side and the pontificating Mr. Potter on the other, he could tolerate it.

Audrey met him at the door. "Benedict, I have placated Augusta into a mood three or four shades from choler. Do try to act like the good brother, for the sake of my diplomacy, and Father's digestion."

He took her hand and kissed it with a loud smack. "Audrey, my concern for Sir Michael's large and small guts will overrule any low conversation on my part. And you know how devoted I am to his liver."

She laughed and snatched her hand away. "Benedict, the only liver you care about is pâté from ducks!"

"Geese, my dear," he murmured. "Are you still avoiding the kitchen?"

"Devoutly, Benedict," she replied. "Come, now, and face the lions."

Dinner went far better than he could have dreamed, and he gave Audrey the credit. He sat next to Sir Michael, who was never happier than when listening to stories from Spain. His only competition was Mr. Potter, who was compelled to shout down Miss Adams's ear trumpet.

"I think he concocts his scriptures from whole cloth," Sir Michael whispered to him while the fish was removed.

"I agree," Nez said. "What a good thing that Christ rose, else He would be spinning in his grave. It's the very, ah, devil, to be misquoted." Sir Michael turned purple and laughed so hard behind his napkin that Nez was forced to administer a hard thump between his shoulder blades. He scrupulously avoided looking at Audrey.

But he did look at her when Sir Michael was dutifully conversing with Miss Adams's only slightly younger sister, seated on his other side. Audrey will certainly never be a beauty, he thought. Her figure is not as tidy as it should be, and she needs a hairdresser younger than Methuselah's aunt. Her eyes are too prominent, and her forehead too high. All in all, though, he had to conclude that there was nothing disgusting about her. She was probably smarter than he was, and certainly a better conversationalist. She suffered no pangs when she had to order people about, and seemed unconcerned at being a year shy of thirty and unmarried. I see before me a woman who would never give me a moment's trouble.

He considered the matter during the next course, and did not object when the younger Miss Adams continued to monopolize Sir Michael. He concluded that if he could not have Libby—and he surely could not—then just about anyone else would do. I need an heir. Audrey knows how to set a good table, and she would probably prove proficient with children. I doubt any woman yearns to be an antique virgin.

He had settled the matter in his own mind by the time the sweets arrived, and Miss Adams directed her attention to a pudding and liberated Sir Michael. "Lad, are you still there?" his host asked in a whisper.

"Indeed I am," Nez replied. He looked down at the

pudding, suddenly less sure of himself. But on I go, he thought. "Sir Michael, I have been thinking that it is high time I courted your daughter."

He knew his host was a hard man to startle, but he had to smile at the way Sir Michael took a sudden jab at the dessert before him.

"Well, sir?" Nez asked.

"Last year, I would have said no." Sir Michael gave his dessert his entire attention, finishing it before continuing, as though he feared the eccentric Miss Adams would snatch it away. "But this year? Benedict, you are a year farther away from the bottle, and Audrey is a year closer to thirty. You may court her. I cannot guess at the outcome, however." He looked at Nez's pudding. "If you're not going to eat that, do slide it my way. If it is returned belowstairs uneaten, my cook will tear his clothes and sit among the ashes. Benedict, have you any idea how hard it is to find a good cook?"

I suppose it's almost as hard to find a good housekeeper, Nez thought as he crossed the park between the two great houses later that night. To his relief, Augusta had chosen to continue her pique at him and elected to spend the night at Ash Grove. "I do apologize, m'dear," he told Audrey when he found a private moment with her before leaving. "But you know how ramshackle we can be at Knare, sometimes."

"I know nothing of the sort, Benedict," she replied. "While you have always been our district's most, ah, colorful resident, you have never mistreated your estate. I cannot imagine that you hired someone unqualified to run your house."

"Never, Audrey," he said. "Do come reassure her that I am an excellent fellow."

She twinkled her eyes at him, and he had to smile, if only because Audrey was beyond the age of coquetry, and the effect bordered on caricature. " 'Excellent fellow?' I know nothing of the sort! You have been a rascal for ages." She laughed and then her eyes became solemn in her lively face. "But didn't you give away your wine cellar to your best friend, and engage a competent fellow to run your armory? What other surprises await me?"

Oh, Audrey, he thought. Oh, my dear.

He nearly didn't go belowstairs when he returned to Knare. A footman greeted him, blinking awake from his seat by the front door. "You know you needn't wait up for me, Haverly."

The young man turned shocked eyes upon him. "Your Grace, I could never abandon my post! What would Luster do?"

"My butler puts more fear into you than I do?" he asked mildly, pleased down to his toes that Luster was feeling more argumentative now.

Haverly was young. He gulped. "He does, Your Grace," he replied simply.

"Go to bed, Haverly! I am going belowstairs to see if I still have a housekeeper."

"She is there, Your Grace."

"What do you think of her?" he asked suddenly.

Haverly did not search around for what would be the correct answer, one for a duke. "Your Grace, she listens to us." He leaned closer. "Rather like you do."

The footman straightened up quickly, and Nez could tell that the disclosure embarrassed him. Do I listen? he asked himself. Well, damn me, perhaps I do, and didn't realize it. "Thank you, Haverly. That will be all."

Liria Valencia was sitting at the table in the servants' hall, her head propped against her palm. He could not tell if she was asleep, so he hesitated at the door, unwilling to disturb her. The soft light from the overhead lamp made her seem absurdly young. For a moment, he wondered if she was even beyond her teen years yet. Now, who is being absurd, Benedict, he told himself. She has a son who must be five.

He cleared his throat, and Liria opened her eyes, then rose to her feet.

"Sit down, my dear," he said, taking a seat. "Did you find a bed for Juan?"

"He can share mine tonight. Haverly says he will

find a cot tomorrow." She indicated the sheaf of papers before her. "I have been getting to know your servants."

"Then, you will stay?"

She answered his question with her own. "Do you always take a chance on people?"

He mulled over the question, and thought of Libby and Tony Cook, who had taken such a chance on a London merchant when he crashed his curricle in front of the Ames estate. "I don't know that I do, Miss Valencia," he replied, "but perhaps it is high time I did, since others have taken a chance on me. Does fifty pounds a year seem fair to you? That includes room and board, of course. I will provide your uniforms, and it will be a small matter to enroll Juan in the vicar's school this fall. Will you shake on that?"

She did not hesitate to extend her hand to him, and he was touched by her willingness. "One thing more, Miss Valencia," he said before he released her hand. "Do your best to make me look good here at Knare. I have decided to court my neighbor's daughter. I should be married." Almost before the words were out of his mouth, he wondered why he said that.

Liria did not seem surprised, which relieved him of any embarrassment. "Excellent, sir! My suggestion to you now is to find a way to encourage your sister to return to London, so you can court in peace."

He rose to go as Liria turned down the lamp. "We are obviously of one mind on that, Miss Valencia. A man hardly needs his older sister breathing down his neck when he attempts to convince a lady that he is a virtuous bargain. I welcome suggestions."

"Just tell her to leave. You're the duke," she said.

He laughed and went to the door. "Such plain speaking, Liria," he teased. "One would think you had practiced the matter yourself!"

She only smiled, dropped a graceful curtsy, and went into Mrs. Burlew's room, leaving him to wonder, and then shake his head.

Chapter Six

Liria didn't sleep well that night, lying in a dead woman's bed and wondering why she had ever allowed herself to take a position of such responsibility in a duke's household. She could not toss and turn because Juan lay beside her in peaceful repose.

It wasn't an uncomfortable bed, just a strange one. And maybe not so strange. Juan edged against her until his back pressed against her stomach, a familiar pose that made her smile and put her arm around him. She had held him close all the nights of his life from the first one—a raw January midnight—when a company laundress delivered him, wrapped him in one of Sergeant Carr's old shirts, then gentled him down to root around for her nipple, latch on, and make satisfying little mews that bound him to her forever.

She knew that Juan was the only reason she had agreed to stay at Knare. The realization came after the duke had left the mansion to walk across his park to Ash Grove. She had listened to the servants' worries until her head was aching, then excused herself to find Juan, who had disappeared from her side. His trail had been easy to follow. After two days of rain, the late afternoon was warm. She smiled to see his ragged jacket—one she had cut down from one of the sergeant's uniforms after his death—and then his broken-down shoes, as he discarded them.

The grounds sloped away from the house, and she knew she would find him at the spot with the best view. He was lying on his back with his hands behind his head, wriggling his bare toes in the spring grass, and staring across the slope to the avenue of elms, the ornate gate, and the river beyond. She slipped off her own shoes. I think we have walked enough on dusty roads, my son, she thought as she sat down beside him. She remembered the clouds of dust that she had walked through with the Nineteen, a cloth over her mouth and nose, and Juan pressed into her breasts to shield him from the choking dust. "Do you like it here, Juan?" she asked.

"I could stay here," he said after a long silence. He said it hesitantly, as though afraid that the saying would somehow uproot them again. "Mama, have we stayed with all of the sergeant's relatives?"

"I believe we have, son."

"You don't think the senor would mind that I have my shoes off on his grass?"

She thought to herself that even as little as she knew about the senor, he might be inclined to do the same thing himself. "I think he would not mind."

"We should stay here," he told her, and resumed his contemplation of the river and low hills beyond. "I could work, too."

"You are only five," she reminded him, touched by his willingness to help.

"The senor likes my drawings," he told her seriously. "I could sell him one."

Liria kissed the top of his head. "You probably could! I will ask the senor if there is something you can do to help around his estate."

Juan nodded, still serious. With a sigh, he moved closer. "I carried water for the surgeons," he reminded her suddenly. "I didn't like doing that."

"I know you didn't, *hijo,* but we needed your help."

"Do you miss him, Mama?"

"Oh, yes."

"I do, too."

She sat up in her bed now, careful not to disturb Juan, who only cuddled in closer to her hip for warmth. The senor promised me a school for you in the fall, she thought. I have merely to manage his household. That she could do it, she had no doubt. After her sister's marriage and her mother's death, she put aside her own pleasure in riding with her brothers, picked up Mama's keys, and stepped into the role she had been raised for. Then her brothers went to war, and Papa retreated into his study to dream, and nothing was the same again. She contrived food where there was none, and kept order in a household until the servants gradually slipped away, some to the army, and some to safer havens than that of a Spaniard who loved the hated French.

But I will not think about it now, she told herself. She got up quietly, stood still for a long moment until Juan returned to sleep, and then dressed herself. She had learned in the course of those hurried interviews yesterday that the senor employed a seamstress at Knare. With a tape around her neck and paper in hand, the woman had measured her for two dresses last night. "One will be gray and one will be black, miss," the seamstress had told her. "I imagine that Mrs. Burlew, God rest her, has caps in one of these drawers, and surely a petticoat or two that you can take in and hem."

She had made an outline of Liria's foot, and promised shoes in a week from the cobbler in Knare that the estate employed on occasion. "It's all sensible and plain, miss, but maybe better than what you've seen lately," the seamstress said, in her rough, blunt way. Liria held her breath and waited for the judgment or censure that usually fell her way, but there was none this time. Maybe this is because I have been listening to the servants, she told herself in surprise. Perhaps it is even because the senor is better thought of among his servants than he realizes, and they trust this sudden decision of his. I wonder, is he always so impulsive?

She found her rosary then, and fingered it as she sat in the chair by the window and watched her son. The Ave Maria meant nothing. God had ceased to have any particular interest in her after the storming of Badajoz, but she knew that the act of smoothing each ebony bead would calm her, and focus her mind on the task ahead. If the servants' regard for the senor is great enough, they will overlook my strangeness and my son, she thought. To make it last, I must show them that I can do my job.

She had no squeamish notions about looking in a dead woman's bureau drawer, she who had searched dead soldiers' haversacks for food. She found a lace cap and settled it on her neat coil of hair, then left the room, closing the door quietly. I will only remember what I already know of household management, and add to it what I learned from Sergeant Carr about managing people. She leaned against the door for a moment, almost overwhelmed by the great debt she owed Richard Carr. She knew that the time for sorrow was past. If she would honor him in future, it would be by using what he taught her, every day of her life.

The house was so still. The sun streamed in the fascinating many-paned little windows, but the halls and corridors were cool as she glided through them. She paused for a long moment in the grand gallery, thinking of the El Greco over the altar in the estate chapel near Bailen, and the Velasquez that hung in her family's gallery. She wondered if they were still there.

Great houses are great houses, she thought as she walked the next floor with its bedchambers. True, there was no pleasant courtyard with a soothing fountain in an interior square to look down upon, and no tile anywhere, but the row of doors was familiar. She watched as the small 'tween stairs maid—was her name Eliza or Emma?—walked with deliberate, slow steps toward one of the doors, her hands occupied with a copper can. She nodded to the child, who nodded back, her face serious.

Liria noticed that she was smiling when she came out. Liria waited for her by the stairs, and touched her cheek when she came close enough. "Good morning, Emma."

"It's Eliza, miss," the maid said. "Emma is the scullery maid."

"Eliza. Eliza. I will do better next time. Is the duke awake?"

The maid smiled. "As quiet as I am, he is always awake when I come into his room! He tells me good morning, and he asks about my mother."

"Your mother?" Liria asked, mystified.

"She used to work here, but she is sick now." Eliza leaned closer. "He didn't take away our cottage, even though she cannot work, and he found me this job." Her face darkened. "Mrs. Burlew said he was wasting money, but he didn't listen to her." She sighed. "He told me just to make sure that he had hot water every morning and that the hearth was swept, and not to worry about anything else." She looked at Liria, unable to disguise her anxiety. "Is that all right still? I do my best."

Liria touched her cheek again. "It is exactly what I want, too. Luster says that you help in the scullery. Is that what you want to do?"

Eliza hesitated. "Yes, Eliza?" Liria asked. "Go ahead."

"Someday I want to be a pastry maker like Betty Gilbert." She looked at Liria quickly, as if expecting her to laugh.

"Perhaps you could work with Betty, instead."

"After I take hot water to His Grace and sweep the hearth?" Eliza asked.

"Most certainly. That will remain your principal duty. I will ask Betty if she can use some help," Liria promised. One task done, she told herself as Eliza dropped a delighted curtsy and hurried down the steps. She looked thoughtfully at the duke's door. Your servants are not afraid of you, and you have a kind heart, even if you would have left me in the rain. She laughed softly to herself and continued on her rounds. She was halfway down the grand staircase before she realized she had not laughed aloud since Quatre Bras.

Ordinarily, Nez would have gotten out of bed directly after Eliza left the room, but he was content this morning to lie there, perched on his elbow, and look out the window by his bed. Eliza's other task was to draw back the draperies, and she always did it with a flourish, as though pleased to present him with something as pleasant as Yorkshire. I wonder how her mother is doing, he thought, admiring the view. I wonder if Liria could invent some work for her. Eliza tells me that she is sitting up still, and chafing at her inactivity. I will ask.

He was halfway through shaving his face when he heard a familiar knock. "Luster, that had better not be you," he admonished, "but do come in."

Looking thin through his neck, but bearing with some dignity the scars of chicken pox, his butler came into the room. "Your Grace, is there anything you wish from me this morning, beyond my usual duties?"

Nez wiped the foam from his neck. "I wish that you would return to your bed Luster. Does Liria—Miss Valencia—know you are about?"

"She does, Your Grace. I do not know why it is that women, even Spanish women, get that pinched look when they are irritated. I am well enough."

"Which means that you are still three parts wasted, Luster, and hardly able to do me any good at all. I insist that you return to your bed."

To his total amazement, his butler agreed. "I will, Your Grace, since you insist." He coughed politely. "I did want to advise you that your sister has returned from Ash Grove and is waiting in the breakfast room."

Waiting to pounce, more like, Nez thought. "Very well, Luster. Haverly can perform your duties in the breakfast room, and you can return to your bed. On this I am firm."

"As you wish, Your Grace." Luster paused at the door. "Do you know that Miss Valencia has been up for hours, walking around and observing your staff?"

He winced. "I suppose they are not enjoying that sort of scrutiny, Luster."

"On the contrary, Your Grace! The upstairs maid

informs me that Miss Valencia helped her change Lady Sophia's sheets, the downstairs maid is already mixing up a furniture polish that our Spanish lady recommended—she adds vinegar to the linseed oil and muriatic antimony." He smiled. "When I passed the library, she was on a rather tall ladder, handing down books to be dusted." The smile left his face. "I will have to speak to Haverly. He left the library to inform me that Miss Valencia has neat ankles."

With a straight face, Nez nodded to his butler. He waited to laugh into his towel until Luster's steps receded down the corridor. "Miss Valencia, this is a curious style of management," he said as he gazed into his mirror and decided to take a little more time with his clothing than usual.

He dreaded the thought of breakfast with Augusta, and delayed it by a visit with Sophie, who informed him that Miss Valencia had already been there with the physician she had summoned. "He says we are—I am—to spend one more day in bed, Uncle," she told him. "I am ill-used."

He sat on her bed and tickled her toes. "No, what you are is spoiled and accustomed to having your own way, like your uncle and mother. You will do precisely what you are told, and then tomorrow we will release you to roam the park like a Barbary ape." Sophie grinned at him, and he left her looking slightly less mutinous.

There was no avoiding the breakfast room. The door loomed before him like a siege engine. He put a smile on his face and opened it. "Augusta, how well you look!"

He knew he had never told a bigger lie. What a sour woman, he thought as he regarded his sister stalking up and down the room, oblivious to early summer right outside the window. "Glorious morning, isn't it?"

She stopped. "It is impossible to get hot tea or a proper baked egg in your ramshackle household. I scold and scold, but things never improve!"

I could be rude in return, he thought, but it occurred to him that such a course of action would offend Libby, and Liria, too. "Well, my dear, let us send back what offends you and try again," he said calmly.

"Benedict, you are such a simpleton!" she snapped. "I have already done that! Reduced that lazy maid to tears, I might add."

It also occurred to him that Augusta had to go. He looked at his sister with what he hoped was serenity. "My dear, you know how it distresses me to see you so upset."

She stared at him, but sat down. "Benedict, I know nothing of the sort."

I am about to prevaricate, he thought, but any military man knows the value of diversion. It will be a whopper. "Augusta, you see before you a man in love." His sister's eyes opened wide. "Last night I told Sir Michael that it was high time I courted his daughter." He held up his hand. "Now, now, it is far too early to congratulate me, Gussie, but I have a hard time worrying about baked eggs when I am on fire with love." My, my, that was spectacular, he told himself. He studied the pattern on the cutlery before him, not daring to look at Augusta.

"With . . . with Audrey?" she managed at last. "You told me once that her father should enter her at Newmarket, with a long jaw like that!"

"I was so rude, wasn't I?" he replied. "I trust you will overlook it."

He was spared a reply when Liria came into the room carrying a tray. Her face inscrutable, she placed the tray on the sideboard, then turned around to curtsy in her magnificent way, and stand there, her hands folded gracefully in front of her. He held his breath, hoping that Augusta would not turn her attack on Liria.

"Have you brought me a proper baked egg and hot tea this time?" Augusta asked.

"Yes, Lady Wogan. May I serve you?"

Augusta ignored her and glared at Nez. "I see a

housekeeper who has no idea of her own duties! I sent the maid, and what do I get but a Spanish drab, dressed in rags, dignifying herself with a lace cap, who claims to be a housekeeper!"

God, he thought, I cannot allow this. He started to rise, but Liria Valencia drilled him to his chair with a look. "When the food is inadequate, I wish to know," she said, her voice low. "Marcel has prepared another baked egg. I brought it to you because my maid was in tears."

"*Your* maid?" Gussie said elaborately.

"She is a member of my staff and I have her best interest in my heart, Lady Wogan. I would never send her where I would not go myself."

"*Her* best interest?" Augusta shouted. "What about *my* best interest?"

With a graceful motion, Liria indicated the covered dish on the sideboard. "There is your baked egg, Lady Wogan, and the tea, as well. We here would never be remiss in our duties to His Grace's guests."

"I am his sister, you simpleton, not his guest!" Augusta declared, her voice rising to unpleasant heights. "I can do what I like here!"

She stopped. I wonder if Gussie realizes how childish she sounds, Nez thought. Liria, you're right. This *is* my estate. He looked at Haverly, standing uncomfortably against the wall. "Really, Gussie," Nez said. "Your egg is getting cold. Take it down a peg before you frighten away my help. I believe Liria is right. You are my sister, but it doesn't follow that you can do what you like here. I am the only one who can do that, and I have hired a housekeeper who has a strong notion of what she owes her staff."

Lady Wogan gasped. "You have hired a brazen, inappropriate housekeeper who will run this household into the ground. I hope that Audrey dismisses this baggage as her first duty as the Duchess of Knare!"

He looked at Liria, who did not even flinch, but continued to regard his sister with a gaze so steady that he felt his admiration growing. He got up and went to the sideboard, where he removed the egg from the dish and took it to his own plate. "It's a little cold now, Gussie, so I'll eat it for you. I like 'um this way, and besides that, I don't think the egg was the issue anyway. Sister, I'd like a little peace and quiet to court Lady Audrey. May I recommend your own place in the country? Thank you, Miss Valencia." He got up and held open the door for his housekeeper, who left the room. He leaned into the hall after her. "Tell Lady Wogan's dresser to start packing, will you?"

He ate the egg in a room filled with awful silence. It didn't want to go pass the lump in his throat, but he was damned if he would let Augusta know that she still had the power to chill him. If my housekeeper in a faded dress and old shoes can face her so bravely, surely I can, he told himself. "Haverly, you may remove these dishes now."

The footman couldn't leave fast enough. Nez watched him go, content. He knew that Haverly would tell the other servants how brave Liria was to face the dragon. Touché, Benedict. He turned to his sister. "Augusta, I mean what I said. You're welcome to leave Sophie here for the summer, but your presence is no longer required."

"You can't get rid of me that easily," she began.

"I can," he replied. "What would Fred say if I told him how consistently you apply to me each quarter to cover gambling debts you'd rather he didn't know about?"

She stared at him. "You promised you would never tell," she hissed. "On your word as a gentleman."

"I was drunk and puking when I made that promise. I am no gentleman, a fact that you have been drilling into me for years. What I am is sober now and destined to remain that way." He hauled out his watch. "One o'clock, Gussie, and then no more until I actually invite you here."

After Augusta left the room, he contemplated the Ming vase that shivered on the mantelpiece and wondered if he should call an architect to check the building for soundness. What an arm, Gussie, he thought. I did not know that anyone outside of a dockworker could slam a door so hard. He felt only the tiniest twinge, knowing that Tony Cook would probably say that he had taken several steps backward in his attempt to mend the family fences. "What of it, Tony?" he said at last. "I am a duke, and I can do what I like. Liria Valencia says so."

The thought satisfied him, and he left the room smiling. If I cannot be good in large measure, perhaps I can atone in a small one, he thought. As he strolled toward the door, he was pleased to notice Haverly engaged in intense, if subdued conversation in the library, where several maids had gathered. He heard another door slam overhead, and figured that Gussie had reached her own bedchamber. Pack swiftly, dear sis, he thought. Surely you can blight someone else's life. I mean, what's a husband for?

He left his house. He walked past drying laundry toward the stables, and found himself grinning up at Juan Valencia, who had seated himself in the crook of an apple tree. "You're a little early for picking," he teased. "Are you drawing the blossoms?"

Juan held up his tablet, the same one Nez had found for him in the village, where the invalids convalesced. He was drawing sideways now across the pages he had already filled. "It appears that you need some more paper," Nez said, and made a mental note.

"I can keep crossing these lines," Juan replied. "Mama told me to be thrifty."

"Well, perhaps, but it does turn drawings into jumbles. Hop down, now. I have a assignment for you."

The boy did as he said. "Mama said I was to be useful, too."

"Tell your mother she is to meet me at the side door in fifteen minutes with some of Mrs. Burlew's petticoats and shifts." Nez repeated his instructions in Spanish, then continued toward the stables while Juan ran in the other direction, stopping several times to replace his shoes when they flopped off. Nez made another mental note.

From the expression on the ostler's face when he asked him to hitch up the gig, Nez decided that this must be everyone's day for surprises from the duke. "Yes, the gig," he repeated. "My horse only seats me, and the barouche would make me appear more vulgar than I really am. We'll save it for Lady Wogan."

Clothing over her arm, Liria was waiting for him when he reached the side entrance. "You, too, Juan," he said, and pointed behind him. "I need you to open the gates for me." He helped Liria into the gig. "I see you found Mrs. Burlew's clothing," he said, after looking behind to see Juan sitting in the box. "You know my little water girl?"

She nodded. "Eliza. Senor, with your permission, I am going to have her work with Betty, your pastry cook. Did you know that Betty loves your armorer?"

He looked at her in surprise. "My dear Miss Valencia, for someone who has only been here a day, you have an amazing grasp on the complexities of life on my estate."

"I told you that I listen, senor," she replied, her eyes merry. "When I asked her, Eliza told me that she wants to be a cook like Betty, but only if she can continue to deliver your shaving water and sweep your hearth."

"*Claro.* I depend upon her. Did she tell you about her mother?"

"Is she quite ill?"

"I believe she is, but Eliza tells me that she chafes even more from knowing that she is the recipient of my charity. Miss Valencia, I mean to ask Mrs. Tucker to hem those petticoats and take in the shifts so you can wear them."

"Won't it tire her?"

"It will." He halted the gig and called over his shoulder. "First gate, Juan. Open it, then close it after us. Tell me, Miss Valencia, is it worse to feel useless or tired?"

She looked at him. "Senor, Libby would be proud of you."

He shrugged and spoke to the horse when Juan was seated. "That is just small stuff anyone would do. I didn't come off too well this morning with my sister. I am certain the Cooks mean that my good turns should be large, the kind that matter."

"If you say so, senor."

"Of course I do," he retorted. "I should know the monumental effort that goes into reformation of character, Miss Valencia! I intend to become an expert! These are little things that anyone would do. And speaking of little things, Luster tells me that you have been doing servants' work. Miss Valencia, this is an odd way, indeed, to command respect."

"That was what Sergeant Carr did," she replied quietly. "He let his men know that there was nothing he wouldn't do along with them. Did the Nineteen ever fail the army?"

"Quite the contrary," he said after a moment's thought. "So you are going to practice his army management on my servants?"

"I think I am," she replied.

Tell me more about the sergeant, he thought, then dismissed the idea as supremely silly. "I thought you were rather brave this morning with my sister," he said. "Most people I know are terrified of her. I'm one of them," he concluded, hoping to get a laugh from her. "Or perhaps you are not afraid of anything, Miss Valencia?"

"Not anymore, senor," she replied.

Mrs. Tucker was sitting up in bed when her neighbor let them in. It required the effort of only a few minutes to explain what he expected of her. "I'll pay you five shillings for the lot of them," he said. "I wouldn't trouble you with it, except that my seamstress is overburdened, and she suggested you." He came closer to the bed. "Mrs. Tucker, you should know that Eliza is doing a wonderful job. I don't know when I've had a better 'tween stairs maid."

The woman in the bed beamed at him, and beckoned Liria closer. "You're a long way from Mrs. Burlew's size, but I believe we can do this." She sat up straighter, her face showing the effort. When she could speak, she addressed him. "Your Grace, you and the little boy will have to leave so Miss Valencia can put on this petticoat for me to measure."

He bowed and she giggled. "Very well, madam. Come, Juan, and let us admire the view elsewhere." He strolled into the nearby field to watch his sowers; Juan trailed after him. He didn't quite know how it happened, but soon the boy was holding his hand. "Do you miss Sergeant Carr?" he asked, when they stopped at the edge of the field.

Juan nodded and leaned against his leg. "He made Mama laugh." He looked at Nez. "Could you make her laugh, senor?"

Nez felt his face go red. My God I am thirty years old, and I am blushing, he thought. He pointed to the sowers. "Soon it will be a field of barley. And that is rye in the other field." He thought about what Tony had said, and what Libby expected. I wish I would not always come up against such small events, he told himself, matters that anyone could deal with. How can I possibly become a better man if the larger challenges of life continue to elude me? I am ripe for a major effort, and what does the Lord Omnipotent deal me but a Spanish woman of a distinctly low class and her illegitimate son?

"Make her laugh? I can try, Juan," he said finally.

He dined that night with Audrey and Sir Michael, but what he remembered about the day was Liria doing the work of the maids, staring down his sister, and then riding beside him in the gig, so composed and calm. I can try, he thought.

Chapter Seven

Nez decided that there were worse things than courting Audrey St. John. The effort involved little exertion on his part, beyond strolling across his park to Ash Grove. He was pretty certain that Sir Michael had communicated his intentions to Audrey. It flattered him that even with such a daunting prospect before her, Audrey did not seem to mind.

Long acquaintance rendered the formality of calling her Miss St. John unnecessary. She had always been Audrey. It was an easy matter to pay his respects to Sir Michael, then walk to the sitting room and plop down on the sofa he already knew was comfortable. Audrey was there with some handwork, ready to ply him with—depending on the hour—tea or lemonade. She never offered sherry, or spoke about his former bad habit, as the vicar did occasionally, proving to him that the Church of England didn't entirely trust the doctrine of repentance. She listened to a report of his day, offered suitable commentary, and made the duty of courtship as unexceptionable as she was.

It was just as easy to sit and say nothing, or read through the newspaper, while she did her needlework or knotted a fringe. He could lean back in the sofa, half close his eyes to feign an afternoon nap, and she would not cough politely to waken him, or appear in any way disturbed at his inattention. It gave him ample opportunity to observe her.

Her figure was tidier than Liria's, to be sure, but the occasional creak as she leaned into her work suggested a corset on duty under her well-made frocks.

He couldn't decide if her ankles were any trimmer than those of his housekeeper, but he could admire the rose hue of her handsome English complexion; it looked like the kind of skin all the ladies of his acquaintance aspired to, so it did not strike him as remarkable. Her hair was light brown and cut short in fashionable curls, so he knew he would never have to wonder what it looked like spread out long across a pillow. His mind did not need to wander much with Audrey.

Now, that face. True, it was long, but Audrey was clever enough to hide the defect of a high forehead with a row of wonderful curls. Her eyes were blue, and quite easily her best feature, but they didn't have the depth of Liria's brown eyes. She had an honest English nose, straight and not too long. He considered the matter, and decided, as he observed Audrey, that Liria's deep-lidded eyes fit her face. Oh, the complexion, too, a creamy color with an olive cast that would have sent an English lady rushing to the apothecary in the hopes of remedy, but which had never been known to cause him any disgust in Spain.

He must have been staring too hard. Audrey put down her needle, cut another length of wool thread, and made a face at him. He laughed, and she picked up her needle to thread it. "Really, Benedict, you hardly need to memorize my face!" she said in her usual quizzing tone. "If you don't know it after all these years, then I will think your wits have quite dribbled out of your head."

To try to fool her with a compliment was folly, but he reminded himself that he was courting. "I was thinking how well you look, Audrey."

"Then, why the frown?"

Why, indeed, he asked himself as he walked back across the park that evening after dinner was long done, the dutiful cigar smoked, the vicar ignored, his host complimented. He had hung around to rejoin the ladies in the sitting.room and play a hand of whist at one of three tables set up. Their whole country society seemed to be assembled, the families and faces he had known since early childhood. No one had anything new to say, and he struggled to keep awake. He watched as Audrey circulated throughout the room, the perfect hostess. She moved quickly on her feet like Libby, but for some reason, her tireless activity wearied him.

He amused himself by thinking of his own servants then, and the amazing way that the females among them had already begun to imitate Liria's gliding walk. The effect served to render them a little foolish at first, but as they settled into the cadence of her graceful movement, the tone in his entire house seemed to change. While he could not attest that the days drew out any longer, there seemed to be more time, less anxiety, even. The pace was slower in his house now, and he found it restful.

He never played whist well, mainly because he hadn't the patience for cards. He would have been happy enough to transport himself home, where he would kick off his shoes, stretch out on his sofa in the library, and listen while Sophie read to him. Juan was usually nearby at the table. He looked down at his cards and smiled, thinking of the boy's wide eyes this afternoon when he brought home two tablets of drawing paper and French-made crayons. Juan was probably drawing now, he thought, then flinched when the vicar scolded him for a careless discard.

"Really, Your Grace, that was—pardon me—a graceless move," the man teased, hugely pleased with himself. "Everyone knows that whist is the accomplishment of gentlemen!"

"No wonder I do not excel," he murmured. "I am fast finding it a total bore."

The sitting room became so silent. My Lord, is everyone listening? he thought in panic. Whatever will Audrey think of me?

And then she was there, her hand light on his shoulder for the briefest moment. "I think, Mr. Potter, that the duke has spent enough years in heavier waters than we know, to call whist slow, if he chooses," she said, somehow making that simple sentence droll beyond belief. The vicar smiled, and the conversation resumed. Nez winked at her, and she blushed.

He kissed her that night when he left Ash Grove, pulling her aside into the shadows into the end of the rose arbor, where she usually walked with him. She leaned into his embrace far enough to let him know that she must have thought it was a good idea, but not enough to convince him to repeat the event. So far, so good, he thought as he released her, then kissed her again.

"The vicar is correct," she said. "You are no gentleman."

She said it with the right amount of teasing, which told him volumes about her careful upbringing, but precious little about her heart. He smiled, nodded to her, and started toward Knare.

The house was quiet when he let himself in by the side entrance. I should get a dog, he thought, someone to greet me with unalloyed affection. One can hardly expect that of a footman, or even a butler, no matter how well he is paid. He looked at his watch, grateful that it was not too late to go belowstairs. He knew the cobbler had delivered Juan's shoes that afternoon, and he wanted to know if they fit. Liria's had come last week, at the same time her dresses were finished. Mrs. Tucker had sent several petticoats, as well, so now Liria swished pleasantly when she walked.

Luster met him in the hall. "Your Grace, if you would, there is a situation belowstairs that perhaps you can ameliorate."

"A situation, Luster? I thought I paid you and Liria Valencia to handle situations belowstairs," he said, amused.

"This crisis seems to be beyond us, and knowing how Juan likes to please you . . ."

Without a word, Nez hurried belowstairs. Juan sat at the main table, the shoes in front of him. "Don't they fit, Juan?" he asked, sitting down beside the boy and putting a hand on his arm. To his alarm, Juan burst into tears.

He looked at Liria, who sat across the table from her son. "They fit," she assured him, "but he will not tell me why that is troubling him. I have asked every way I know how." She stretched out her hand impulsively, and touched his. "It is probably such a small thing, but can you help?"

"I can try." Oh, when did I say that before, he thought. Juan asked me to make his mama laugh, and now one is in tears, and the other nearly so. He thought a moment. "Juan, I think they are nice-looking shoes," he began, "the kind that will be good for long walks. Will you tell me what is the difficulty?"

Juan accepted the handkerchief that his mother handed him, blew his nose, and shook his head. "He told me not to make my mama sad," he whispered in Nez's ear.

"Let us go in the little sitting room, and you can tell me. In fact, I insist upon it," Nez said. "Juan, I am employing you this summer to open gates for me, and to keep Sophie safe when she climbs trees. As my gate opener, you owe me an explanation."

He went into the housekeeper's sitting room, closed the door, and gestured to a chair, but Juan looked so distressed that he sat down and pulled the child onto his lap. "Now, what is so terrible about shoes that fit?" he asked, his voice gentle.

"They won't last very long."

Nez tightened his grip on the boy. "Probably not. Boys your age do grow fast."

Juan burrowed in close to him. "Sergeant Carr always said it was better to grow into things." He looked down at the old shoes he wore. "He gave me these before that place where all the cannons roared and it rained."

Oh, God, he is talking of Quatre Bras, Nez thought, and held him closer. "And he probably told you to take good care of them, didn't he?"

Juan burst into tears again. And you have probably

not cried enough for him, have you? he thought. Well, cry away, little one. As he held Juan close and rocked him in his arms, he thought of his own little corner in hell at Mont Saint Jean. I was twenty-seven and not three, he considered, and it sucked me right into a bottle. How is it that you're so much braver? Could it be you had a better teacher?

"I wish I had known your Sergeant Carr," he said. "I really do." He held Juan tight, and was gratified when Juan put his arms around him. When Liria opened the door, he motioned her to come inside. Her eyes wide as he had never seen them, she sat on the edge of a chair by the table. "Don't worry," he told her softly.

In a few more minutes, he handed the boy his handkerchief and helped him wipe his eyes. When he was quiet, Nez kissed his head. "Juan, I'm glad that your shoes fit and that you live in a place where you can get new ones when you need them. Do you see any of my servants wearing shoes that do not fit?"

Juan shook his head.

"Do I?"

To his relief, the boy chuckled. Nez felt his own spirits rise. He spoke in careful Spanish. "Things are different now, and I am certain that Sergeant Carr would be pleased. What would you say if I take those shoes he gave you, and have them repaired by the man who made your new shoes? You can try them on every few months, and when they do fit, you can wear them all you want."

"When they are too small, may I still keep them?"

"I will insist upon it. You might even want to loan them to Amos Yore to put in the armory. I am thinking about adding a collection of uniforms. These would be Juan Valencia's army shoes from Boney's Spanish War. We could write on a small card that they were given to you by Sergeant Carr."

"We could do that?" the boy asked. "I could draw a picture of him."

"I was hoping you would suggest that very thing."

Juan sat still a moment more, then leaned forward to remove his shoes. "They're muddy," he said. "Sophie and I went to the pond behind the stable today."

"Did you enjoy it? I used to play there." Nez laughed at Juan's expression. "I was your age once! Cross my heart, I was!" He looked at Liria then, happy to see a smile on her face. "Juan, I think you should go to bed now. Did Sophie tell me before I went to Ash Grove that you two are to accompany the goose girl tomorrow? She will be up early." He took the shoes from Juan and set him on the floor.

He stayed where he was when Liria led Juan into the bedchamber beyond. He heard their low voices for a few minutes, then the cot creaked. In another moment Liria rejoined him in the sitting room. "Thank you, senor," she said. "I do not think he ever cried for Sergeant Carr." Her own eyes filled with tears.

"Did you?" he asked softly.

She nodded. "When I could. We were so busy, even though so few of them lived. Most of the surgeons had gone ahead to Mont Saint Jean, and there we were at Quatre Bras." She sighed, and looked toward the bedchamber. "Even Juan had to carry water. He saw things no child should see, but we needed his help." She glanced down at her hands. "I did not know that they would never come clean."

"How long did your sergeant live after the battle?" She doesn't have to answer this, he thought, and I should have never asked it.

"A week," she said, speaking Spanish to him, like Juan. "His intestines were full of canister shot—the French were that close with their guns!—and we knew he could not live. All he wanted was water, and I could find none that was not red."

"We closed our eyes and drank, too."

She nodded and hugged herself. "He wrote letters to his relatives the first day. The second day he wrote letters to the families of his men. The third day he was hot, the fourth day he was cold. I put Juan in the cot to warm him, and he died on the sixth day."

"You were there?"

"Could I have left?"

I have a kinship with you, *dama,* he thought. You know what war feels like. "Did you ever see anyone celebrate after a battle, *dama*?" he asked. "I never did."

"Then, you were not at Badajoz, senor," she said after a long pause. The words seemed to be wrung out of her, and he looked at her in surprise.

As soon as he looked, the moment passed. She visibly gathered herself together, something he had watched her do before, but just before she became again his dignified housekeeper, there was an expression in her eyes that made him wonder if she was as old as he thought. He could have sworn a very young girl looked at him, and he shivered again.

"I was at Badajoz, *dama.*"

He waited for her to speak, but she did not; in fact, she did not even seem to be breathing. Impulsively, he took a deep breath himself, and let it out, as if trying to cue her. I have hit such a nerve, he thought. Maybe it was the look in her eyes, far beyond the soldier's stare that he was so familiar with. This was something worse, and he could imagine nothing worse.

"You weren't very old at Badajoz, were you?" he asked, almost afraid for her answer.

"I was fourteen, senor."

"Gracious, are you even . . ."

"I will be twenty in November." She touched the muddy shoes on the table, her face a study in composure that he could only marvel at. "Does this mean I am too young to be your housekeeper?"

He knew exactly what she was thinking. She will do anything for her son, he thought. If I say yes, she will ask me if she can stay on as a maid. She knows that she does not want to throw herself on the mercy of a textile mill in Huddersfield because of what it might mean to Juan. "Was the sergeant a good father to Juan?" he asked.

"He was not his father."

He stared at her, amazed, because he could tell from the look on her face that she had not meant to say that, even though he knew that she told him the truth. It shamed him to know that he had startled the truth out of a woman who must know that the truth only made her appear less acceptable than ever. And now you think I am judging you and wondering, how many men has this woman known in her young life? Say the right thing for once, Benedict, he ordered himself.

"Was he good to Juan?"

He could almost feel her relief. *"Sin duda, señor,"* she said. "Without a doubt." She hesitated. "And he was good to me."

"But . . ." he stopped, knowing he would be rude to ask more of an employee. It would be impertinent.

"You are wondering why I did not return to Spain, after the sergeant . . . after he died?" she asked.

Nez shook his head. "I should not have pried as much as I did, Miss Valencia. I hope you will forgive me."

"*Claro.* I assure you that I will perform my tasks here with all propriety."

He knew she meant it, and he also knew that she was dismissing him. He nodded, and went to the door. He opened it, then turned around. "Humor me, *dama.* Why didn't you return to Spain?"

"I have no relatives there anymore."

"None whatever?" he asked, surprised. "All are dead?"

She managed the ghost of a smile, and again it made her look young, even more young than her nineteen years. "Let us say, I am dead to them. Good night, senor."

After chatting for a few minutes with Luster—what he said he had no memory of even as soon as it left his mouth—Nez went upstairs. Too restless for sleep, he went into the Grand Gallery and sat down to stare at his relatives, the saints and sinners on his family tree. "What are you trying to tell me, Liria Valencia?" he asked as he gazed at his mother's portrait.

He nearly went to sleep there on the sofa, except that no sofa in Knare was particularly comfortable, other than the one in the library. He got up finally to go to bed, and looked out the window. Lights were still on in the armory.

Remembering that Liria had told him that Amos Yore was in love with Betty, he thought it best to clamber up the stairs, whistling as he went, and then knock and pause before he entered. Amos looked up at him with a smile, and set down the polishing cloth. "Major, you needn't be so heavy-footed on the stairs. Betty went to her own bed hours ago," he teased. "After all, her father is your gamekeeper and a far better shot than me."

Nez laughed and sat down on the workshop bench. "When are you going to marry her?" he asked straight out, abandoning forever any disinterest in his servants.

The smile left Amos's face. "I haven't asked her, Major. Don't think I will."

"Miss Valencia assures me that Betty loves you."

Amos picked up the rag again. "Her folly, then."

"Sit down here beside me, Amos," Nez ordered. "Put away that rag, look me in the eye, and tell me why that's not the greatest idea."

Amos sat down. On the space between them, he plopped his half leg up on the bench. "That's why," he said softly. "Don't you think a girl as pretty as Betty can find a man with all his parts? I do." He rubbed the stump.

"Hurt?"

"Not much. Sometimes I think it's still there, that if I look down quick enough, I'll see two shoes on the floor instead of one." He shrugged. "Betty can do better."

"I'm no expert, but I've noticed something about women, Amos. Sometimes they see things we don't."

He took a deep breath. "The lady I loved threw me over for a stout, nearsighted bumbler with a medical degree! And I'm rich, handsome, *and* sober, possessing a Waterloo medal and an estate with at least three peacocks."

Amos laughed, and Nez joined in. Still chuckling to himself, the armorer got up and leaned against the workbench again. "I don't know," he said finally.

"As one soldier to another, Amos, you've got both arms, and no one shot your balls off! Luster tells me Betty always has little pies and tarts just for you. Close your mouth, Private, and that's an order! It's not because she pities you; she loves you."

Amos was silent then, rubbing the bridge of his nose.

"I know you have a nice quarters off the armory because I had it refurbished," Nez went on. "I also pay you well, because if I didn't, one of my brother soldiers would probably snatch you away to his own estate, and we can't have that." He got up and put his hand on Amos's shoulder. "I can't order you to do anything, Amos, because I don't command you anymore. You work for me, but your opinion is yours. I'm just suggesting"—he chuckled—"encouraging you to take a deep breath and just do it. Don't miss out on the best thing you'll ever do because you're afraid."

Sounds good, Benedict, he thought. Too bad no one ever took you in hand with such terrific advice. He patted the other man's shoulder, then released him. "Well, sir?"

"You're probably right, Major," Amos said softly. "She's a wonderful lass."

"Of course she is! She was raised on my estate!" Nez teased, knowing that Amos needed the light touch now. "I'm never wrong about these matters." He went to the door. "Don't you have a wooden leg, Amos?" he asked.

"It doesn't fit well."

"I'll have the surgeon here in the morning. Maybe the padding's insufficient."

"You're determined, aren't you, Major?"

"Yes." He paused. "Have you written to Allenby yet about Sergeant Carr?"

"A week ago, Major."

"Let me know if you hear anything."

"I will, Major. And, sir, when am I to wish you happy? Betty's brother at Ash Grove says that Sir Michael is telling the world that you're courting Miss St. John."

"What? Oh! Yes, I am. Well, no news yet, Private. You first."

He went down the stairs slowly. Well, Libby, maybe I've accomplished another small thing or two. Juan is happy, I think, and Amos might propose. But Liria—I don't know about Liria. I may have made things worse there. Why is it that I take two steps backward for every step forward?

He was a long time thinking about Liria before he finally allowed himself to sleep. Even then, he dreamed of Badajoz and woke up too early, breathing fast with his fingers tight around his pillow. He lay there and forced himself to think of that place, the city three times besieged and finally captured by hard men who had lost too many friends. Dear God, the troops did celebrate, he thought, and the warm shame of it washed over him. Surely not. She was barely fourteen then, hardly more than a child.

The thought of it brought him out of his bed and on his feet in practically one motion. He wrapped a blanket about himself and stared out the window. He was still standing there when Eliza came in with his hot water and told him good morning.

Chapter Eight

He had little appetite that morning but he ate anyway, not relishing a scene with his cook, who had been known to come upstairs, tragedy written all over him, to wring his hands when anything was returned belowstairs uneaten. Besides, his sister had created a crisis recently about a baked egg. He ate his accustomed meal, but it might as well have been cork from a Portuguese tree.

He knew he had no liberty to say anything to Liria about his realization; indeed, he knew he would not know what to say, because she had indicted so little. Perhaps I am wrong to read so much into a few words, he thought. He tried to tell himself that she may have just witnessed the soldiers. That would not exactly explain Juan, now, would it, Benedict you cloth head, he told himself sourly. He wiped his mouth with his napkin and pushed his plate far enough away to allow him to lean on the table with his elbows, his chin in his hands.

I turned my own men loose, he thought. I did what the other officers did, and winked at what I knew was going on in back alleys, and even some open doorways in the broken town. And there was Beau Wellington, winking, too! We all did, damn us, for two days. How long that must have seemed to Liria! He rested his elbows on his knees.

"Your Grace?"

He looked up in surprise, forgetting that Haverly was standing against the back wall, directly behind his chair. He waved him away. "I don't require any assistance, Haverly," he said, and wished that his voice did not sound so weary. And now I suppose you will go belowstairs and announce to all present that I am monstrously hung over, and that the master is up to his old ways again. "It's nothing, really."

"Very well, Your Grace," Haverly replied in a voice as uncertain as Nez had ever heard. "I could get you some fresh tea or . . ."

"I don't want anything!" Nez shouted. He swept his arm across the table and sent the crockery, food, and silverware crashing against the wall. "Havcrly, leave me alone!" He felt ashamed of himself even before the door closed quietly.

He knew that Haverly would speak to Luster, and he was not surprised when he heard the familiar two taps—one moderate, one louder—on the door only minutes later. "Come in, Luster," he said. "Come in."

His butler entered the room. He stood still in surprise, staring at the broken dishes and glassware, and the greasy spots on the wallpaper. Nez dared him to say anything, but Luster merely looked, frowned, and then committed the unpardonable sin among butlers by seating himself on the next chair. Nez stared in amazement. "I have never seen you sit in my presence, Luster," he said.

"I fear, Your Grace, that the chicken pox has sapped me more than I care to admit. I trust you will overlook my lapse of decorum."

"If you will be so kind as to overlook mine," Nez said.

"Done, Your Grace."

Nez blinked in further surprise as Luster gave him a lengthy, appraising look, something else he had never done before. "Your Grace, you must reassure me that you have not begun to drink again," he said. His voice was even and low, and Nez could not help but think of earlier, painful interviews with his own father. I should resent this, he thought. I should also say nothing, because I know so little. I also know that if I do not tell this to someone else, I will begin to drink again.

He leaned forward, took a deep breath, and told Luster every suspicion he had. It pained him to see his old butler go so shockingly pale that his chicken pox scars stood out like hives on his bloodless face, but he knew he could not keep silent. "For two days, that's what good King George's troops did to Badajoz, Luster. The troops called it Baddyhof. We turned our men loose on the women and children and went back outside the walls. I even went to sleep. God! How could I sleep? But I did, Luster, oh, I did."

Nez wished he would not, but Luster got up and began to pick up the china from the floor. He nearly stopped him, then realized that the man had to occupy himself. "Luster, you have led a sheltered life, indeed," he said, his voice soft, as he came over to help his butler. He plunked the sausage back on an unbroken plate. "I didn't mean to distress you, but I had to talk to someone."

"You're telling me that a soldier did a terrible thing to Liria?" Luster asked, as though he could not believe such a thing.

Nez sat back against the wall. "Luster, we turned loose whole troops of men, and they hunted in packs!" He knew his voice was rising, and he tried to contain himself. "I know you can't imagine such a thing, but . . ."

"No more, Your Grace," Luster said. "Oh, do forgive me for interrupting you."

"No, I've said enough. I don't know that's what happened to Liria, but I strongly suspect so." He sighed and got to his feet again, lifting the window sash to lean out and take several deep breaths. "If you only could have seen the look on her face last night! And have you noticed how she shies away from coming too close to men?" He leaned farther out the window and vomited in the bushes, retching and gagging until he thought he would bring up his stomach lining.

He stayed at the window in utter misery until there was nothing left to throw up except his toenails. Luster left his side, and he could hear a whispered conversation in the corridor. In another moment Luster was back with a warm cloth for his forehead. He let his butler lead him from the window and sit him in a chair.

"And I was going to leave her in the rain, Luster," he said at last.

"I daresay she has already forgiven you for that, Your Grace."

"And the other?" he said harshly. Tears started in his eyes.

Luster did an extraordinary thing then that Nez knew he would never forget, not even if he became the oldest man in England someday. The butler placed his hands—oh, they were so cool—on his face and looked deep into his eyes. "*You* did not do a terrible thing to Liria," he said, his words crisp and bracing.

"No! I didn't!" Nez agreed. He did not try to stop the tears.

"And you never would," Luster continued. "You have not the nature for such a thing. Not even in war, Your Grace. You're far too good a man for that."

"Am I, Luster?" he asked, feeling like a child seeking approval from his parent.

"You are."

It was enough, and he knew it. Without saying a word for several minutes, he allowed the tears to slide down his cheeks. Luster kept his hands cupped on his face, in so tender a gesture that Nez felt the heart come back into his body. They stayed that way a moment more, master and butler, and then Nez shifted himself and Luster released his grip. He wiped Nez's face one more time, then turned back to the dishes, stacking the broken pieces neatly onto a tray that he pulled from the sideboard. Exhausted, Nez watched him. "What do I do now, Luster?" he asked finally.

"First, Your Grace, I recommend that you return to your bed and sleep awhile. When you wake up, I think you might consider how you can find out something about Liria Valencia. Does it strike you that there may be far more to her than we think?"

He nodded, and got to his feet. He swayed slightly, dizzy with tears and emotion, and smiled at the alert way that Luster watched him until he was in command again. "I wish Richard Carr were alive," he said. "We could ask him." He shrugged. "She told me last night that all her relatives were dead, Luster."

Luster covered the broken china with a cloth. "That was what she said?"

Nez thought a moment. "Well, no, not precisely. She said, 'I am dead to them.' " He leaned against the wall, so tired. "I think we were conversing in Spanish. I may have misunderstood her. Or, if it was English, she sometimes makes mistakes. No," he said, suddenly decisive. "She said, 'I am dead to them.' "

"Your Grace, there is a great deal of difference in the two ways of putting it."

He did go back to bed, but not before meeting Sophie and Juan, coming down the stairs as he was going up. He smiled at them, hoping that he did not look too ravaged. To his delight, Juan grinned at him and stuck out his foot.

"Oh! You're wearing your new shoes."

"Claro, señor," the boy said. "I think I will take them off, though."

"Why would you do that, Juan?"

The boy looked at Sophie, who nodded. "Senor, we are going to help the goose girl today." He leaned closer until his words tickled Nez's ear. "She doesn't wear shoes, and we don't want to make her feel bad."

"You're right to think of the goose girl, Juan. Just leave your shoes by the front door. Haverly will see that they do not go anywhere."

Juan leaned against him for a long enough moment for tears to well in his eyes again, and then he hurried down the stairs after Sophie.

"Do you have some paper with you, Juan?" Nez

called. "I know that you should draw at least one goose today."

The boy patted his jacket, then pulled out Sergeant Carr's artillery record. "It fits in my pocket, senor," he said.

"Good. Good day, and don't drive my goose girl to any acts of desperation!"

He did sleep then, until long after noon. When he woke, he had no firm idea what to do. He dressed again, looking out his window at the formal gardens below. Their tranquil order and the brave blooms of June restored him to some semblance of his own order. The summer's traveling visitors have arrived, he thought as he stood at the window, tying his neck cloth. "The garden is a tribute to you, Mama," he said, remembering the rather formal arguments his parents had indulged in regarding the expense. Foolish, spendthrift Mama, who had a predilection for beautiful clothes, and primrose and box elders. She who could spot a well-made bonnet in a milliner's window at a hundred yards, could also talk soil and compost with her head gardener.

He saw the magnificent result before him, and it was as though he saw it with new eyes. He watched one couple strolling at leisure down the graveled path, pausing to admire the well-organized beds of pansies. To his delight, the lady put her arm around the waist of the man accompanying her. Nez smiled as the man tilted back the bonnet she wore, looked around briefly, then kissed her cheek. "Oh, good for you, sir," he said. "It's that kind of a garden."

He thought of Audrey then, and wondered if he should invite her to stroll there with him. Of course I should, he considered. He knew he wouldn't, at least not now, when he wanted no conversation. Audrey was so witty and quick that he knew she could not be silent. It can wait, he told himself. What I really need to do—and I should have thought of this sooner—is take Liria down there. She needs to know what her duties are, regarding our estate visitors. That's it, he thought as he left his room.

She answered his summons and appeared in the open doorway of the bookroom. "Good afternoon, senor," she said with a smile and a curtsy. "Would you care for some luncheon? I could have it brought here, if you wish."

"Thank you, no I . . . I was a trifle indisposed this morning, and do not wish to challenge my digestive system, as of yet. Please sit down, Miss Valencia."

He could not overlook the wary look in her eyes, even when all else about her was calm. She did not so much hesitate to do as he said, but paused, just one beat overlong. He knew he could overlook her hesitation, because it may have been his imagination. "I think I should acquaint you with the workings of the estate in summer. Yorkshire seems to be a favorite touring ground for my countrymen with leisure, and Knare is a principal delight to many."

She leaned forward. "People just wander about your grounds, senor?" she asked. "I cannot imagine such a thing."

"It must be an English eccentricity," he said, taking his cue from her serenity and relaxing a little. "You indicated in something you said once that you were raised on a great estate near Bailen. Do the Spanish have this custom?"

"No. On my . . . on that estate, the orange groves march right down to the *estancia.* Oh, sir, you must remember what it is like: the interior courtyard is the place of beauty, but only for the family living there." She held out her hands. "We are a pragmatic, practical people, senor, not given much to touring."

He stood up and reached for her hand. "Then, I have been sadly remiss! Come with me, Miss Valencia, and let us stroll in my gardens." He watched her face closely, and the hesitation he dreaded was there. To her credit, she allowed him to take her hand, if only until he came around the desk and then gestured toward the corridor. She said nothing as they walked together down the hall, and out the back entrance to the terrace that overlooked the gardens.

"I'll only take a little of your time, *dama,* I promise," he told her as they went down the shallow steps.

"Am I to escort your visitors around the gardens?" she asked, her voice dubious. "I confess I do not know these flowers, even with labels I see. I mean, there is no jasmine, or mimosa, and not even a small orange. Would I look in vain for avocados?"

It was a small joke on her part, but he seized upon it. "In vain, *dama*! Any road, you could never compete with an Englishman who knows his violets from his Johnny-jump-ups."

"There is no accounting for the English," she murmured. "I miss orange trees."

He saw the longing in her eyes, expressive for a moment. "What you are to do when visitors are shown into Knare's entranceway is merely to greet them. One of the footmen on duty in the hall will escort them outside, then hand them off to one of the gardeners. I keep a register by the front door that you may invite them to sign."

They strolled through his mother's beautiful garden. He wanted to offer her his arm, but he did not have the courage. He was content to match his stride to hers, stop when she wanted, enjoy the sun on his face, and breathe deep of the fragrance of the earliest flowers of June. It was the first time he had walked completely through the gardens since his return from war, and the peace of it all nearly overwhelmed him. "There were times in the Peninsula and then in Belgium that I did not think I would ever live to do this again, Miss Valencia," he said simply.

She stopped, and her skirt brushed against his leg. He hadn't realized they were standing so close. "Would it surprise you to know that I was thinking the same thing, senor?" she asked, her voice no louder than his.

"I suppose we are both veterans, aren't we, *dama*?" he asked, and started walking again when she did.

They passed several couples—traveling visitors, from the look of their clothing—and he could not help noticing the amused glances they gave him. He stopped. "Miss Valencia, is there a leaf plastered to my face, or a vine wrapped around my ear that I am unaware of?"

She laughed, and he felt his heart melt right down into his boots at the sound of it. Oh, Sergeant, he thought, there you are. "Come, now, Liria. What is my problem?"

She stopped and turned toward him. "Senor, your neck cloth is most amazingly twisted. Did you not look in a mirror before you left your room? Your traveling visitors are perhaps curious as to who is the eccentric allowed to roam this *estancia* without a leash."

He touched his neck, and felt a blush spreading upward. "I was looking out the window when I tied it. Do I need a keeper, *dama*?"

"You need a wife, senor, so it is perhaps a good thing that you are courting Miss St. John. Hold still; I can repair this. Bend down a little."

He did as she said, holding his breath as she tugged his neck cloth around to the center of his shirt, untied it, and began again. Her wonderful full lips were pursed as she concentrated on the task before her. So close to her, he could only marvel at the length of her eyelashes. Her olive skin was as clear as a baby's across the gentle rise of her cheekbones. Her ears. He looked closer, and he felt an icy hand squeeze his backbone. The lace cap that usually covered the one he could see had edged upward as she adjusted his neck cloth. He stared at the scar that ran the length of the earlobe and knew that someone in a terrible time and place had jerked an earring from her flesh. He remembered that one of the officers in his regiment had joked that the women of Badajoz could be identified by their bleeding ears. He took a deep breath, and another, and knew for certain that his imagination had not run away with him last night.

"I am not strangling you, am I senor?" she asked.

She did not know what he was looking at, and she was sharing another gentle joke with him. Don't ruin the moment, Benedict, he ordered himself. With a hand that he knew trembled, he grasped his own neck and gave out a gargling sound that had her chuckling when she gave his neck cloth a final pat.

"There, senor. You can go in any company now, and not cause us embarrassment."

She stepped away and the moment ended. She resumed her graceful walk, and he fell in with her again, his heart sore. How you must have suffered, and here you are, doing your best to live your life. God forgive me when I whine.

The garden path took them past the maze, and then back to the terrace. He didn't want to go inside, so he sat down on the top step. She had no choice but to sit there, too.

"You like to be outdoors, don't you, senor?" she asked.

"Yes," he agreed, "although I should feel guilty to waste your time, I suppose."

She shook her head, and returned her gaze to the gardens, which allowed him to admire her Spanish profile, and the handsome way her dark hair coiled at the back of her neck. "I never thought to be in a place like this," she said finally.

"I hope it's better than Huddersfield."

"Perhaps I'll never know, senor." She looked at him then, and he saw the old uncertainty in her eyes. "You will let me know if there is anything you need done that I am not doing. I . . . I want to stay here with Juan."

"So far, so good. My sister claims that my impulsive nature is my worst enemy, but you've proven to be competent. You seem to know great houses, and there is always Sergeant Carr's army management." The army reminded him. "Oh, I should tell you that we can probably expect traveling visitors to the armory, as well as the gardens."

"Do I do the same with them?" she asked. "Does Haverly or one of the footmen escort them upstairs to Amos Yore?"

"I think that is best."

She touched his arm then, which startled him. "I forgot to tell you! Or did you know . . . you reminded me. This morning, Amos Yore asked Betty to marry him. He just blurted it out at the servants table over porridge!"

He laughed and leaned back on his elbow. "Over porridge? It's hard to imagine a more romantic setting, no matter how I try! I do hope she said yes, or he might have to propose again over stew at dinner. Think what that would do to a finicky digestion."

"Are you never serious?" Liria scolded. "She did accept, and then what did he do but burst into tears."

"I would say there was plenty of drama at breakfast."

She nodded. "He told me then to tell you that it was your turn, Senor."

So it is my turn, he told himself. He got up and brushed off his trousers, then offered Liria a hand up, but she was already on her feet. "You are right, Miss Valencia, and so is Amos. I think I will visit Miss St. John right now."

"To propose?" she asked, her eyes merry.

The thought unnerved him, even though he knew that was the course he had chosen. "Well, I, ah, Miss Valencia . . ." he stammered.

"You can't be afraid she will turn you down!"

"Not at all," he replied, and realized with a jolt that he feared she would accept.

If he had thought to spend a peaceful afternoon drinking tea in Miss St. John's sitting room, he was sorely mistaken. In his effort to make conversation, he mentioned Amos Yore's proposal to Betty Gilbert over breakfast. Audrey stared at him, laughed, and asked, "Why on earth are you so interested in your servants, Benedict?"

He felt his face go hot with embarrassment. "I care about them, Audrey," he said, and it sounded monumentally lame to his own ears. "You should have seen Juan last night, so concerned about his shoes, and sad because he didn't want to put away the broken-down pair that Sergeant Carr had given him. He misses the sergeant." He stopped. Spoken out loud in the sitting room, the whole matter seemed stupid.

She shook her head and picked up her tatting shuttle again. "Why is it your concern? It's well and good to give deserving servants every suitable kindness, and an extra fine dinner at harvest, Christmas, and Easter, but beyond that, Benedict, I think you would be interfering." She looked at him over the spectacles she wore while doing close work. "Perhaps this might be a good time for you to acquaint yourself with the workings of your estate."

"Too bad it is so infernally well run," he told her.

He must have sounded petulant, because Audrey set down her tatting. "Have you ever considered a good hobby, like riding to the hounds?" she asked in such kindly tones that he wanted to growl at her and repeat some choice phrases best left in the army.

Lord, woman, how trivial all this is, he thought in irritation, even as he smiled and sipped his tea. "I'm not overly fond of dogs, Audrey. You know that."

"Ah, yes, and more's the pity. Perhaps you will be able to overlook your dislike when we . . ." She paused. "I like dogs, Benedict. Horses, too." She picked up her tatting again and returned her attention to her tatting. He looked up when Sir Michael entered the room unannounced, then rose to his feet to shake his neighbor's hand.

Sir Michael nudged his shoulder. "Benedict, I stayed out of here as long as I could. Have you proposed yet, lad?"

Nez winced, and Audrey laughed. "Really, Papa, I think you can leave the matter to Benedict. He will have my leave to do so, when I think he is fully reformed!"

"I beg your pardon?" he asked without thinking.

"You know I am quizzing you, Benedict," Audrey said.

He couldn't argue with that. It seemed most likely, considering her cheerful nature, but something about her words struck him hard. "How will you know, Audrey?" he asked, keeping his tone light.

She laughed, stood up in that quick way of hers, and sat next to him on the sofa. "You have already abandoned alcohol, which shows such strength of character. Yet, my dear friend, it *is* a bit extreme to give away your entire wine cellar. Why could you not just eliminate some of your drinking? People will think you are a Methodist. Well, never mind," she continued when he opened his mouth to reply. "We already know that your estate is well run, and that you have hired a competent housekeeper, no matter that she is foreign." She touched his arm. "When you acquire a useful hobby, I will consider you fully rehabilitated." She leaned closer. "I can't agree that your servants are a useful hobby, however. Do find another one, dear Benedict." She hesitated.

"Say on, Audrey," he said, feeling suddenly weary.

"I think you should abandon your impulsive nature. And that is all," she concluded generously.

He stayed a few minutes longer, engaging in the idle chat that had once seemed so unexceptionable to him, but which now struck him as trivial. He shook Sir Michael's hand, kissed Audrey's, and left with a feeling of relief. He spent the next hour in his own park, shoes off, and watched Juan draw a goose. He didn't know how it happened, but after Sophie wandered indoors, Juan still remained on his lap, comfortably tucked close to his chest. "Show me the goose you drew, Juan."

The little boy opened the artillery tablet and pointed to the small picture he had squeezed next to the cutaway illustrations of canister and chain shot. Nez chuckled. "All I see is an open mouth."

"That's all I saw," Juan said. "Maybe I was too

close." He was silent a moment more, then he turned his head to look at Nez. "Senor, did you take my other shoes to the cobbler?"

"I'll have it done tomorrow, first thing," he promised, "and tell the man to make them good as new." He looked down at the boy in his arms. "What were your favorite things about Sergeant Carr?" he asked in Spanish.

It must have been a complicated question, because Juan was silent a long time. "He took care of us. He let me ride the caisson, too."

Nez smiled and kissed the top of Juan's head. "Good enough reasons, I suppose."

After dinner, he hurried upstairs to the armory, surprised Amos and Betty kissing, asked if he had heard anything from Allenby, and hurried back downstairs when the answer was a blush and a no. In half an hour, his horse saddled and bridled, he swung up on his mount and left Knare, bound for Pytch. I'm not reformed yet Audrey, he thought. I'm still impulsive. I must know more about Richard Carr. And when I find out more, I will have to eventually ask myself why it matters.

Chapter Nine

"Audrey, I do believe you are correct," Nez said out loud as he sank with a groan onto a bed in an inn near Lincoln that morning. "I will never be rehabilitated until I have become less impulsive." He waited long minutes before bending over to remove his riding boots, vowing never to throw his leg over another horse without regarding the possible implication of most of the night in the saddle, courtesy of a full moon. He decided that a wiser man would have taken the family carriage, or at least gone post chaise, then reminded himself that a wiser man wouldn't be so nosy about his servants.

Audrey had said as much that afternoon—it seemed so long ago now—as he sat in her parlour, sipping tea. He knew that his servants' lives were none of his business. They were there to do his bidding and keep his estate running smoothly. He had been raised to regard them as little more than furniture, there to serve a purpose, but not to call attention to themselves.

Maybe it happened when he saw Amos Yore, late of his Waterloo brigade, begging on that London street corner, and took him home out of a guilty conscience. Maybe it was later, when Luster lay so ill in the inn, not a butler then, but a man who shared the planet with him and who was too sick to piss without assistance. And then there was kind Tony, who thought that everyone was as nice as he, treated them as though they were, and recommended that Nez do the same.

Bootless now, he stretched out on the bed and watched the sun come up through the open window.

Tony, you've ruined me, he thought. Thanks to your meddling in my life, I care about the people who serve me. I found a job for Eliza, whose mother was so ill, and who needed the work, even though she was but eight years old. What did I care about that old armory, until I thought it might be just the place for Amos Yore, who probably saved my life fifty times during that long afternoon at Mont Saint Jean. Amos, why did it matter to me that you knew that Betty loved you, one leg or two? Do I really need all those gardeners to tend Mama's flowers, except that I know times are hard and jobs scarce.

He knew that only an impulsive man would have offered a housekeeping job to a foreign woman with a bastard son. That the matter had been precisely right was equally obvious to him. I am a good judge of character, he decided, and the realization warmed him. I was right about Eliza, and right about Amos, right about my gardeners, right about Liria. I was right to send that money to Private Allenby in Pytch, disguised as a gift from a fictitious relative, even though my solicitor was so disapproving and snitched on me to Augusta. At least I think I am right about Allenby, he amended. We shall see.

He stared at the ceiling and wondered if he had gone beyond the bounds in poking about in Liria Valencia's difficult life. Audrey would probably say he had, but Tony? Nez was not sure. He smiled then to think of Juan sitting on his lap, and leaning back against him with confidence. It doesn't matter to Juan that I am a reconstructed drunkard just a year away from the bottle, he reflected. He doesn't know or even care that my sister and I do not get along. I doubt he has the slightest comprehension of how much land I own or money I have. He just likes me, and I know he would like me even if I did not supply him with drawing paper and crayons, because I know people. This is my gift. Your gift, Sergeant Carr, was to be Juan's great example.

"He learned from you, didn't he, Sergeant Carr?"

Nez asked out loud. You and Liria, he thought. In the middle of an awful war, you three were a family.

He woke up in early afternoon to the rolling sound of bells from Lincoln's cathedral, content to lie there and think of Liria. He decided that there must be many fine women in the lower classes who were competent and well mannered, but something about Liria went beyond the place in life to which he would have assigned her, on that first meeting. No servant treated him as an equal, but Liria did. She did not fawn or simper or waste his time, but conducted herself with dignity in such a way that those she supervised sought to adopt those external qualities that made her so pleasing. He smiled. I may end up with the most serene household in all of England, he thought. With a housekeeper like Liria, it may not matter if I ever become rehabilitated.

The thought cheered him up, and he ate a hearty meal. Reason also prevailed, considering that Allenby had the audacity to live in Devon, practically in sight of the English Channel. He knew a good stable in Lincoln and took himself there to arrange for his horse to be ridden back to Knare, and to hire a post chaise. "I'm traveling as fast and far as I can each day," he warned the stable master. "Do your best for me."

As anxious as he was to speak to Allenby, he minded the long ride less than he thought he would. He had grown to admire the harsh contrast of the Peninsula, in particular the dramatic scenery of the Rio Tajo around Toledo, but he knew there was no substitute for June in England. He was riding through country he did not know well, but it made no difference. It was England, and he was satisfied.

He was chortling over a quelling religious tract he had picked up in one inn or another when the postboy announced Pytch finally. He sniffed the misty air when he left the chaise. "Ah, lovely Devon," he murmured, remembering the nursery rhyme. The postboys certainly knew their inns, as well as their livestock. He was soon involved in a late supper that made him want to kiss the cook. When the landlord asked if he wanted anything else, Nez hated to tell the man no. He leaned back in the chair. "You can give me some information, though," he said.

"Anything, Major," the landlord said, and Nez was glad all over again that he had signed the register with his army title, rather than as duke, which tended to provoke a level of service and tension at odds with his informal nature.

"Do you know a man named Allenby? He was a private in my regiment. He came into my regiment after several years in the Peninsula, when we were in sore need of replacements. I confess I do not know his Christian name."

That mere trifle seemed to be of no concern to the landlord. "Michael Allenby, I'll be bound. He had another brother in the army—in a battery, I believe—but that one died, so you can only mean Michael."

"The very one," he said. *I wonder if that brother told Allenby much about the Nineteen. I suppose I can ask.* "Where may I find Michael Allenby?"

"An easy matter these days. Major, he had a rare good turn of fortune about a year ago, after he was invalided home."

"Oh?"

"It seems a relative he had forgotten left him a pile of yellow dogs." He indicated with his head. "Just three doors down he started the Allenby Candy Company. Doubt he's there now, but you'll find him in the morning early, I'm sure." He came closer. "His wife keeps his nose right to the grindstone, she does. She was taking in washing to support them, and I know she doesn't want Michael's business to fail!"

He ate breakfast early the next morning, hopeful to see Allenby, and also hopeful that last night's magnificent fish soup was not a fluke in the culinary output of the kitchen. To his pleasure, it was not. "If the cook ever decides to leave you, do send him to Knare," he told the keep. He took a last sip of excellent coffee. "I know a duke there who would move heaven and earth to hire him."

The innkeep laughed. " 'Tis me own ball and chain, Major! How could I part with a woman who cooks like that?"

Three doors from the inn he found the Allenby Candy Company, a modest building by anyone's standards, but built solid. The sign painted over the door proclaimed what lay within. "Michael Allenby, Owner and Proprietor," he read out loud.

He went inside and was greeted by the fragrance of peppermint, and something more mysterious. He sniffed. Almond. Just a hint of it, and coming from the corner where that man was lighting the fire under that copper boiler. "Private Allenby," he ordered in his best brigade voice. "Step away from that pot and give an account of yourself!"

The man gasped, and turned around quickly.

"You can't salute me, Allenby," Nez said, stepping forward. "Neither of us is in the army. If you bow, I will not be happy, either. Would you shake my hand? I never have thanked you properly for Mont Saint Jean."

"I think ye have, Major," the man said quietly. He wiped his hands on his apron. "I never shook with a duke before." He held out his hand. "Mind, sir, it's probably sticky."

It was. "Very good, Private. I wasn't a duke then, back in our Spanish days."

"No, sir. You've always just been major to me." He did salute then and accompanied it with a heel snap that made Nez smile.

"You never were that militarily precise before, Private," he reminded the man. "As I recall, you were always on report."

"Aye, sir." Allenby grinned.

"And you were always watching my back at Mont Saint Jean," Nez added quietly. "Even after you fell."

Allenby swallowed and looked away. "That was a desperate day, Major, and weren't you doing the same for me?" he asked when he turned back. "Mary Ann!" he called, his voice sure and loud. "Bring a chair that's not sticky!"

In a moment a pleasant-looking woman came from another room, carrying a chair, and with a question in her eyes. "Mary Ann, this is Major Benedict Nesbitt, Twentieth Foot. Drop him a curtsy, dear, 'cause he's also a duke, God love him."

"Delighted to meet you, Mrs. Allenby," he said. "I hear you took in washing to support this useless private when he was invalided home. Tell me if he doesn't treat you right, and I'll have him broken right down to recruit."

She stared another moment, then laughed. "He treats me right," she said in her strong Devon accent. "Your Grace, can I get you anything?"

Nez shook his head. "I just ate. You know, I would like to take with me a pound of whatever it is I smelled when I came in here. Was it almonds?"

"Aye, Major," Allenby said. "Yesterday we made almond sticks. Today it's peppermint, and tomorrow anise."

"Almond sticks? Oh, Lord, I haven't had those since I was a child. Better make it two pounds. No. Three, and I'll pay."

"You have children of your own, then, Major?" Allenby asked as his wife hurried to the counter to measure out the candy.

Nez thought of Juan, and felt the sharpest longing to see him. "No, alas, but I know a boy who would like to sample what you obviously do better than soldiering, Private."

"I was pretty awful, wasn't I?"

"Only until it mattered, lad, only until then." He looked at Mary Ann. "My dear, could I take some of your husband's time this morning? I can see that you are busy, but since he didn't answer Private Yore's letter, I had to ride here from York."

Mary Ann glowered at her husband. "I told him ta answer that letter straight off, but what did he do but hem and haw and nearly dig his toe in the ground. 'What do I say to a duke,' he asked me. Didn't ya, Michael?"

"I did, Mary Ann, me love."

"No matter, Mrs. Allenby," he said. "I didn't come here to get a husband in trouble. It's a grand week for a ride, and I also wanted to see your candy factory. Private Yore told me about your good fortune."

Mary Ann left the counter and hurried to his side. She thrust an almond stick in his hand. "I never knew I married a man with connections! What came ta him ten months ago but a bank draft and a letter about a cousin who died in Virginia, now, then."

"Amazing," Nez murmured.

"That's what I thought, too, Major," Allenby said. "But I wasn't to look a gift horse in his mouth, now, was I?" He motioned Mary Ann closer and clapped his arm around her shoulders. "She's been a candy maker since she was a little girl. We thought and thought, and this is what we decided ta do."

"Are you making a go of it?" Nez asked.

"Aye, sir," Allenby said proudly. Mary Ann beamed at him. "Orders come from all over Devon now. Do ye know who're my best customers?"

"I couldn't guess."

"Sea captains!" He nudged his wife, who colored up prettily. "The second thing they crave when they get on land seems ta be candy."

"That's enough, now, Michael," Mary Ann warned. "He's a duke! Take him inside."

In another moment he was seated in their sitting room behind the shop. "I won't waste your time, Private," he said. "Did Amos tell you in the letter what I was asking?"

Allenby nodded. "Something about a Spanish housekeeper, and Sergeant Carr of the Nineteen. Me brother Tom's battery."

"I know. I'm sorry he died, Private."

"Nearly all the Nineteen did, didn't they?"

"Yes, and bravely, too. I hired this woman—her name is Liria Valencia—on an impulsive whim, I'll admit. She's not one to talk about her past, but I am curious, especially since she has a position of real responsibility on my estate."

"Stands to reason you'd want to know more."

"Did your brother Tom ever mention her? I know you visited Tom several times when the Third Division was close by with the Nineteen," Nez said, and added, "And often sometimes when we weren't, if I can believe the morning reports."

Allenby blushed and looked down at the carpet. "Guilty as charged, Major!" He looked up again, and there was a strong gleam in his eyes. "If I'd have known he wouldn't live past Quatre Bras, I'd have gone more, begging your pardon, Major."

"And I'd have let you, had I known," Nez replied. "It doesn't matter now. I just want to know something about Sergeant Carr. Do you remember him?"

"I do," Allenby said. "He got on me once about being away from me brigade."

"Reamed you up and down, did he?"

"Nay, sir, not him! Sergeant Carr could make you feel tiny with a look and a word."

"Was he a good man? Did Tom like him?"

"He'd have done a jig into hell, had Sergeant Carr asked him," he said softly. "Like us in the Twentieth, Major."

It was a compliment that took Nez's breath away. "Thank you, Private. Now I expect you'll want me to overlook all your sins and misdemeanors," he teased.

Allenby understood completely. "I'll expect you to."

"Do you remember a Spanish woman with the sergeant? Did Tom ever speak of one?"

Allenby sat back in his chair and gazed at the ceiling for a long moment. Nez felt his heart sink. I've run dry, he thought. What did I expect? "I suppose I ask too much."

"Nay, nay, that's not it, Major," Allenby said. "I'm just trying to remember if it was before Baddyhof or after."

Nez let out his breath slowly, and sucked on the almond stick.

"It was after," Allenby said, his tone decisive. "I know it was, because Tom told me later how she got the Nineteen out of a jam."

"Really?"

"Yes. If I remember, the Nineteen had gone with Hill's Division, and Picton took us after Soult."

"He did. Do go on."

"Tom told me later, they were having the devil of a time finding a reliable interpreter. Oh, we had Spanish women aplenty with us, and so did the Nineteen." He looked at the open door. "Mary Ann don't know about those women."

"My lips are sealed, Private."

"Tom said none of 'um could speak English. His major was trying to get directions, and no one could help him. He said that a girl sitting by a spot where the road forked came forward and translated. He said her English was beautiful."

It is, he thought. "A girl?"

Allenby shrugged. "That's what Tom said. Said she was young, any road." He put his hand to his head. "And she had them torn-up ears like the women in Baddyhof." He looked away. "You know."

"I know."

"And he said her dress was bloody. God, Major, I hate to think about it again!"

"I hate to ask you, but I have to know," he said quietly.

"For some reason, Tom didn't know why, Sergeant Carr took her along. He plunked her on top of a caisson and took her along." He leaned forward. "I remember this because Tom was so surprised. Sergeant Carr was older and quiet-like, not the sort of man who would pick up a drab. Not at all."

"Older?"

"Yes, he was. I remember that. I guess he was forty at least. Maybe older." He shrugged. "Maybe she reminded him of his daughter somewhere, if he had one." He chuckled. "Of course, Tom said in a few months she was wearing her apron high, so I guess she didn't remind the Sergeant of his daughter!"

Nez put down the almond stick. Think how many women were wearing their aprons high after the troops got through at Badajoz, he thought, some of them my troops, damn me. "I don't suppose anyone in the Nineteen joked about her in front of the battery sergeant."

"Oh, no! As I remember it, Tom said she was a good 'un. Never complained, and really useful, because her French was as good as her English. He said she got them out of some serious scrapes." He looked at the ceiling again. "And that's all I remember Tom telling me."

"Do you remember her name?"

He shook his head. "Amor said in the letter it was Liria Valencia, but I don't remember Tom calling her that." He paused. "It was something else, maybe a nickname. Let me think a minute."

Take years if you want, Nez thought, only please remember. Unable to sit still any longer, he went to the window, and was rewarded with a view, two buildings over, of the inn's stable yard and necessaries.

"I remember. You'll laugh. Sergeant Carr called her *La Duquesa*."

"What?" Nez demanded, startled.

"Well, Tom thought it was funny, and that's how I remember at all. He told me, 'Sergeant Carr must think she's royalty.' We had a good laugh. I mean there she was, a camp follower with the Nineteen—a pretty, serene thing to be sure—but you know camp followers, Major."

"Serene?"

"Oh, it's odd, but Tom told me that's what he remembered. 'She's calm like the battery sergeant,' he told me." He shrugged. "And that's all I know." He stood up, too, and joined Nez at the window. "That's also why I didn't write you. You can tell I didn't know anything to tell you. Sorry, Major."

"You never heard what might have been her real name?" he persisted, wondering now why he was bothering a man who was obviously busy. "You know the Spanish have so many names."

Allenby grinned. "Almost as many as you dukes, begging your pardon, sir."

"Oh, well hit, Allenby! My housekeeper's boy is named Juan. Does that set off any bells? Did Tom ever mention the baby?"

Allenby was silent again, and Nez knew better than to interrupt.

"He did mention the baby, mainly because when I . . . well, when I slipped away once to see Tom, the baby had just been born. It was January. It struck him funny that La Duquesa had demanded—and she never demanded anything—that the boy be baptized." He grinned. "Apparently it was the only time she ever raised her voice to the battery sergeant, and he got permission from his major to stop long enough to have the baby christened."

"Why would that have interested your brother enough to tell you?" Nez asked, puzzled.

"Somebody in the Nineteen had started a wager that the baby was the sergeant's and out of curiosity they went to the christening, just to find out what they named him. He was christened Juan Mora y Valencia. I don't know how that name is spelled, but it sounded like Mora. Guess he wasn't the sergeant's, but Tom said you never could have guessed that, from the way Sergeant Carr carried the baby to the front." He shook his head. "No telling what some folks will do, Major."

"No, indeed." Nez held out his hand to Allenby, and the man didn't hesitate to take it this time. "Thank you for your information."

"Wasn't much."

"It was more than you think," Nez replied. "And now, if I can pay your wife for those almond sticks, I'll let you get back to your work, Private."

"You can try to pay her, but I doubt you'll succeed, Major."

Mrs. Allenby wouldn't hear of payment. He tried, then backed off when she got a mulish look in her eyes and rested her hands on her lips. "Do me this, then, Mrs. Allenby. Send me two pounds a month of whatever you make and invoice my estate. Your husband has the direction. I think I can find you some more business in York."

She smiled and handed him the package then. "He told me about you, Major, and how you all stood together in your square at Mont Saint Jean." Her eyes welled with tears, and she surprised him by standing on tiptoe and kissing his cheek. "That's from me."

"You're welcome, Mrs. Allenby," he said, and never meant anything more.

Allenby walked him out the door and shook his hand again. "This could become a habit," he confessed with a grin. "Pretty soon I'll feel all democratic, like an American!" He turned serious then. "By the way, Major, I know I don't have any long-lost relatives in Virginia."

Nez snapped himself to attention, and Allenby did the same. "Private Allenby," he said crisply, biting off each word. "You're just the kind of slacker who would lose a relative! As you were now." He laughed and turned on his heel. Well, Tony, he thought, I'm still doing small deeds. He returned to the inn, alerted the post driver, paid his bill, and was on his way back to Knare in less than fifteen minutes.

He stopped the chaise at the first mile marker on the highway, and directed the driver to take him to London first, instead of directly to Knare. Of course, I could possibly do a greater deed, he told himself as the chaise continued along the south channel road, something that might be more significant than a paltry bit of goodness here and there to my servants. Anyone can do that. "I believe I will call on the Spanish ambassador," he murmured. "I wonder, do I have a decent enough outfit to meet a diplomatist? What a meddler I am."

Chapter Ten

He couldn't find a good suit of clothes when he arrived at Half Moon Street, which didn't surprise him; he knew the deficiencies of his wardrobe. He thought briefly about dropping in on his friend Eustace Wiltmore, but discarded the notion almost immediately. While they were of similar height and build, a visit to Eustace would require endless explanation that he was not prepared to provide.

"Pomeroy, what should I do?" he asked the footman who ran his residence when Luster was elsewhere. Pomeroy, who seemed to have scarcely recovered from the shock of the sudden descent, gave the matter his attention. "Your Grace, I believe that when all else fails, the employment of a well-brushed and bemedaled uniform is considered unexceptionable."

"That's a good notion, Pomeroy," Nez said. "I have resigned my commission, but the ambassador of Spain probably will not be aware of that." He looked around the Yellow Saloon with real pleasure. Mama's faux Egyptian antiquities had been replaced by elegant tables, and sofas that looked almost comfortable enough to sit upon. The walls were now a soft blue. "We shall have to rename this room," he said, "and high time. Well-done, Pomeroy."

"Thank you, Your Grace, it was a pleasure."

He went upstairs with Pomeroy, admiring the lighter draperies, the clever use of cornice-like railings to display Mama's collection of ceramic roses. His room, however, was much as he had left it, which made him positively giddy. Thank goodness no one had fiddled with his combination of cast-offs from other eras, and the bed that sagged in all the right places.

But there were more important matters at hand, considering that he had ridden long and late to get to London. "Pomeroy, do you think I should send a note 'round to the Spanish embassy to let them know I will be dropping by, or should I just pop in?"

"The Spanish embassy?" Pomeroy repeated.

"Yes, indeed. I have a matter to discuss with the ambassador," he said patiently.

"The ambassador?"

"Pomeroy, you are repeating me," he said. "Luster would never do that."

His mild criticism caused Pomeroy to draw himself together. "You Grace, as pleased to see you as I trust the ambassador will be, I would not advise popping in. It may be that the Spanish are funny about that. I should recommend a note of some sort."

"So would I," Nez agreed. "Maybe I could use a secretary after all. Too bad I do not have one. Pomeroy, a pen and paper, if you please." The note took little time. "I believe 'Your Excellency, I wish to see you as soon as possible on a matter of some importance,' about covers the subject, " he read to Pomeroy when he had finished and blotted the sheet. He signed his name carefully, folded the note, and fixed on a seal with the family crest. "It's nice, at times like this, to be pretentious," he told his footman. "Please see that this is delivered to the Spanish embassy."

Pomeroy placed the document on a silver tray. "Your Grace, have you any idea where the Spanish embassy is located?"

"Of course not. That is your job, Pomeroy," Nez replied, seeking for more serenity than he felt. "I can't help but note that Luster would never have asked such a question. I recommend that you wait for a reply, once you locate the building. Look upon this as an opportunity to consider London in a whole new light."

"Indeed, Your Grace," Pomeroy murmured, and withdrew from the room, a portrait of studied irritation or contrition. Nez observed that it was hard to tell with Pomeroy. How I miss my butler, he thought, and the secretary I should have, and the valet I have not yet stirred myself to hire. He had a happy thought: If I propose to Audrey immediately when I return to Knare, I can have someone available at all times to manage me. *She* will get me a secretary and a valet. Why should I plague Luster forever?

He was asleep when Pomeroy returned, but woke quickly to his knock. "Come in." He eyed the tray with a note on it in Pomeroy's hand. "It appears to me that you located the embassy. Well done. Just out of idle curiosity, may I ask how?"

Pomeroy permitted himself a tiny smile. "Your Grace, I hailed a hack and told the driver—a scurvy-looking man—to take me to the Spanish embassy. Simple."

"Excellent! And now, what is the news?" He took the message and opened it. "Well, well! I can come at my leisure this very afternoon. So I shall, Pomeroy. You say you know where my uniform is?"

"Indeed, Your Grace, although I fear it will give off a strong odor of camphor."

"That is scarcely a difficulty," he replied, getting up. "As I remember, Spanish cologne is extremely powerful. I doubt anyone at the embassy will notice my puny contribution."

To his amazement, the uniform still fit. He couldn't help but admire the contrast of the handsome gold trim with the red and white. How kind of the Portuguese and Spanish to be so generous in awarding medals to us Englishmen, he thought as he looked at himself in the mirror. While Pomeroy and one or two of the maids who had gathered outside his open door watched, Nez took the Waterloo Medal from its case and held it up to the light by its ribbon. "I never thought to wear this, Pomeroy," he said, his voice soft. "At least not until in my coffin, hopefully years from now."

"Your Grace, do you plan to be buried in uniform?" Pomeroy asked.

"Oh, no." He ran his finger over the raised image on the medal. "But I want this medal in the coffin with me. Pomeroy, I earned it. Help me get it straight, now."

He went downstairs into the Yellow Saloon to wait for his carriage. Magnificent room, he thought. He looked at the mantelpiece and smiled. "I'm grateful that no one removed the cup," he said to his footman.

"Luster told us to leave it alone."

He went to the fireplace and picked up Amos Yore's battered tin cup that he had placed there nearly a year ago to remind him that he was a civilized man. Tony, I am thinking of others, he told himself. He handed the cup to Pomeroy. "Put this with my saddlebags. I do not anticipate that I will spend much time in future here, and I want that at Knare with me." He looked out the window. "And here I go, Pomeroy. Do send word to the stables to prepare my chaise for the return to Knare. I intend to leave early tomorrow, and sleep on the way back."

He slept on the way to the Spanish embassy, too, worn ragged from constant days of travel. It was only when the carriage slowed and then stopped outside the iron gate, that he woke. Well, the Spaniards understand the value of location, he thought as he noted Kensington Palace Gardens through the trees.

He announced himself in the entrance hall and didn't even have time to admire the beautiful portrait of the *Madonna and Child*—surely it was by Zurbarán—before the ambassador himself came into the hall. He took Nez's hand in his, a gesture of such equality that Nez felt himself relax.

"*Vuestra Merced,* I am Jaime Gonzales Almeida, the Duke of Montressor y Calatrava," he said in a voice obviously used to command. "I believe that my son served with you in the Burgos campaign. Diego Almeida, el Conde Lucar?"

"My God," Nez said simply. "I never met a braver man. I can only wish our encounter with Soult and Marmont had produced a better outcome. Please accept my sympathies, Duke, even so long after the event."

The duke bowed. "He was a noble son. *Que lástima* that the god of war has no children and feels no pity." He came closer. "You, sir. You are still in the army? I would hardly be surprised, but why are you yet a major? From what Diego wrote me from time to time, your talents were ample."

Nez smiled. "I resigned my commission after Waterloo, and only wore this uniform to impress the Spanish ambassador! Your son would have appreciated that. As I recall, his wardrobe was almost as careless as mine."

"Then, you were brothers under the skin, Duke."

"Please call me Benedict," Nez said. "Diego always did."

The ambassador indicated a door. "Let us go into the garden, Benedict. This is far too fine a day to be indoors. Since you are merely Major Nesbitt, who does not stand on ceremony, it will be suitable."

It was. He thought of Liria, and her comment about Spanish courtyards as the duke led him through the door and into a haven. He could hear a fountain nearby, but it was hidden among the flowers. He sat down. In another moment he was leaning forward, telling the Duke of Montressor y Calatrava what little he knew about Liria Valencia and Sergeant Carr, and the Nineteen.

"She is my housekeeper, and she has never told me anything outright about herself," he concluded. "All that I have told you is surmise and conjecture on my part. I could be completely wrong in all aspects, but, Duke, the way she carries herself!"

The ambassador made a graceful gesture with his hand. "Benedict, you know Spanish women—even the most common is a queen in her own eyes."

"I do not argue that."

The duke was silent a moment. "Do you know her name, beyond Valencia? You mention orange groves and horses, but, sir, I have those. Most of us from the south do."

Nez stood and stretched. He walked to the end of the tiled patio, following the sound of the water, until he saw the source, a small fountain that was curved like a baptismal font. "That's it," he said, turning back to his host. "I forgot to mention it. According to one of my former soldiers, Liria's son was baptized Juan Mora y Valencia. I do not know how to spell that but . . ."

". . . I do," exclaimed the duke, rising quickly. "M-O-U-R-A." He clapped his hands together, his eyes lively. Nez could hardly look at the father without remembering his son, his enthusiasm cut short by a shot from the walls of Burgos. "The Mouras of Las Invernadas. It is east of Bailen, maybe closer to Torreperogil, and that was just the main estate. He owned . . . Well, never mind that!"

"Moura?" Nez asked, puzzled at the ambassador's sudden energy.

"Lad, he was a *grande* of Spain," Almeida said. "The only man who outranks a *grande* is the king. I would say you have quite a housekeeper."

"I believe I'll sit down," Nez sat, and returned to his bench. "La Duquesa," he murmured.

"Your Sergeant Carr obviously took a few secrets to his grave, Benedict. Maybe she told him more than she told you, or maybe he guessed." The ambassador resumed his seat. "I will tell you more." He rubbed his hands together. "The old man was an *afrancesado.* Do you know the term?"

Benedict nodded, leaning forward again, this time not so much to talk, but to listen. "Didn't they want Spain to ally with Napoleon?"

"They did, damn them to perdition." Almeida leaned back and sighed heavily. "And yet I can see why. You have campaigned in Spain. You know better than most how backward my country is, how superstitious its people are. Don't be shy to admit it."

"I know." Nez rubbed his forehead. "I once saw a woman stoned for witchcraft."

"Only one? You are fortunate," the ambassador said dryly. "There were those among us—Moura most prominent—who wanted closer ties with Europe. They learned English and French, and drilled their children in these languages and customs." He shrugged. "In truth, we have had poor kings of late. Fernando may have been better than his miserable father, but he was ripe for destruction, and Napoleon was not a man to shirk an opportunity." He clapped his hands together again. "And who was the first to ally himself with José Buonaparte when he was placed on our throne but the *Grande* of Moura y Valencia?"

"Liria's father?"

"The very same, if your housekeeper is who you think she is. Tell me, Benedict, is she a small woman, with a creamy skin, deep eyes, and a beautiful mouth?"

He nodded.

"A family trait."

Nez shifted on the bench. "But, sir, she made a reference to her family and said she was dead to them. I don't understand."

"That is the pain of civil war, lad. The duke had two sons and three daughters. One of the daughters, now dead, was married to a most inflexible man, but a patriot nonetheless. One of the sons was an *afrancesado,* and the other was loyal to Fernando. Napoleon ripped that family in half. The only one alive that I know of is the present *grande.* You would probably call him a duke."

"And the other two daughters you mentioned?"

"Young, sir, very young, at the time Buonaparte seized the throne, and still in the care of their father, who practically raised them to be more French than the French. No one knows what happened to them.

We do know the old duke died during that final siege of Badajoz, but the girls vanished, poof! Like that!" He snapped his fingers. "From what you suspect, Liria became a victim when the town was sacked." He looked hard at Nez. "There was no need for you British to sack the town, sir."

"I know," Nez said quietly. "I am ashamed for my part in letting my men do what they wanted. It is something I must live with, I suppose."

The ambassador leaned forward and touched Nez on the knee. "There are some who believe war is glorious. I think they have not been to war, eh?"

The subject was too uncomfortable, so Nez changed it. "What could have happened to make Liria flee the country with the English? Where is her sister?"

"I think that is for you to find out." The ambassador rose, and Nez knew his interview was over. "It may be that she chooses not to tell you. I have heard much of Badajoz. Very bad things."

"They are all true, Your Excellency." He bowed and left the ambassador in the garden. In the main entrance, he spent a long moment contemplating the Zurbarán and wondering about the pull that Spain continued to exert on him.

The servant had opened the door for him that led out to Peel Street when he heard the ambassador's voice. "*Un momentito,* Benedict!" He waited for the ambassador.

"I was remiss, Benedict. Let me suggest this to you: it is the time of the month when I send dispatches to Spain. Do you wish to compose a letter to the present *Grande* of Moura? You could tell him all that you have told me."

"Do you think he will want to know about that side of his family?"

The ambassador shrugged. "Who can say? A letter from you will give him the opportunity to decide. If he chooses to ignore it, what have you lost?"

"You say the girls were so young. Surely he would want to know what happened to his little sisters?"

"It may be that there are too many hard feelings to overcome, even now, six years later. I cannot say. Civil war is merciless. But if you wish to send a letter, I will hold the dispatches here until nine o'clock tomorrow morning."

Nez bowed. "Very well, Your Excellency. I will think about it."

He thought about it on the ride home, and through the early evening hours, well aware that Liria Valencia, the daughter of a grandee, had given him no leave to meddle in her life. He shook his head when Pomeroy suggested dinner, and paced the floor of the Yellow Saloon instead. He reasoned that a woman who left Spain because her relatives had no wish to see her again knew what she was doing. He also knew how angry it made him when Gussie tried to make decisions for him. No one had given him leave to force Liria's hand.

He went to bed, only to toss and turn and think about his own sister. True, Gussie is a boil and a wart, he reasoned, but if she were to vanish from my life, I would wonder what had become of her. Liria is no pain to anyone. It could be that her brother has worn out the world searching for her. He counted off each hour as it gonged in the corridor clock outside his bedchamber. Exhausted finally from wrestling with his conscience, he went to his desk, lit the lamp, and hunted for paper and ink—began to write.

A thought struck him, and he nearly tipped over the ink pot. If she is reconciled to those relatives, she and Juan will leave me. The thought was so disquieting that he put down the pen and stared at what he had already written. He picked up the pen a half hour later, and wrote until dawn had come and gone. Bleary-eyed and exhausted, he summoned Pomeroy, handed him the sealed letter, and told him to hurry with it to the Spanish embassy. He dressed quickly and was gone in the chaise before his footman returned from Peel Street.

His ride back to Yorkshire did nothing to settle his

anxiety. The letter was irretrievably on its way to Spain, and he knew that diplomatic pouches traveled more swiftly than any other correspondence. Within weeks Liria's brother would receive his letter. What will he do? Those Spaniards are a proud lot. There may be more bad blood than anyone can overcome.

With that in mind, his misgivings about mentioning to Liria any of his meddling grew stronger. Disgusted with himself for all his presumptions, he decided that Audrey was right; he probably wouldn't be rehabilitated until he became less impulsive. He sighed and looked out the window, moodily watching the countryside in full bloom just outside the glass. He thought about Richard Carr then, an older man, and from some accounts, a quiet man who kept to himself, at least until that moment at the crossroads when he saw a ragged young woman and stopped. What was it about her, Sergeant, he asked himself. What singled her out to you, after a lifetime of war, and work, and solitude? I know she is no English beauty, but what is it that compelled you to take a second look and then another? You had obviously resisted such an impulse before; why then? What was it about her? What is it about any man and any woman?

He thought of Libby then, and her love for Tony Cook, the clumsiest man on the planet, a nearsighted, overweight surgeon who would always be too busy. "I don't pretend to understand it, Libby," he said. "You could have had me, and you chose him." The thought kept him quiet and distracted through the days of travel and the nights of restless sleep in inns frequented by people of quality, but with mattresses not his own and unfamiliar food. By the time Knare came into view, he decided that love was a miracle not given to everyone. He also knew that he would say nothing to Liria Valencia about his impulsive letter to her brother.

I think I will not leave Knare again, he decided as he saw his own mansion finally. He wanted to walk in Mama's gardens again, and breathe in the fragrance of the flowers. Perhaps Liria would come with him, if he asked. She was a quiet woman, who knew it was none of her business whether he was rehabilitated or not. Everyone wants me to change, he thought sourly: Gussie, Tony and Libby, Audrey for certain. I wonder if Liria wants me to change, or Juan.

The carriage stopped in the driveway, and he looked out to see the row of servants, everyone orderly, and expectant, with none of the confusion or distress after Mrs. Burlew's death. He saw the little goose girl by the pond with her charges, and he waved to her. There were traveling visitors, too, on the walkway that lead around to the gardens in the rear of the house. They stopped to gawk at him, and he wished he had thought to comb his hair better, or make some attempt to find a better suit of clothes before leaving Half Moon Street. Here I am in all my dirt, he thought. If you were expecting something grand, I hate to disappoint you.

He got out of the carriage when Haverly let the steps down, and was gratified to see Luster standing next to Liria and Juan. *"Qué pasa, Juan?"* he asked.

Before Liria could react and hold him back, Juan ran to him from the line of servants. Without a thought beyond his own pleasure, Nez picked him up, held him out to look at him, then pulled him close. "I missed you, Juan," he whispered.

The boy burrowed in close to him. "I thought you were not coming back," he said.

You don't care whether I am reformed, or not, do you? he thought as he rubbed Juan's back and enjoyed the moment. You just missed me. "Of course I was coming back. I live here, Juan," he said.

"I'm sorry, senor." It was Liria, close now, frowning. "Forgive him, please, if he seems to think you are his special property. I will talk to him about it."

"Please don't, Miss Valencia," he replied. "I like a greeting like this." He shifted the child to his hip and walked with her toward the entrance. "I didn't think I would be gone so long, but I went to London." He turned to Luster. "By the way, Luster, you will be pleased to know that Pomeroy has carried through all of the redecorating on Half Moon Street. You were wise to leave him in charge."

"Indeed, Your Grace. Thank you," Luster replied. "If you will excuse me, I think I will go lie down again." He gestured toward Liria. "Miss Valencia has been of vast help during my convalescence, but she gets remarkably imperious when I do not rest."

"Certainly Luster," he said, mystified. "Shall I come and see you later belowstairs?"

"If you wish, Your Grace."

A frown on his face, Nez watched as Luster actually permitted one of the under footmen to help him up the front steps. "What has happened to Luster?" he asked Liria.

"I fear he is not recovering so quickly from his illness," she said. "I make sure that he lies down, which vexes him."

"I fear that retirement looms," Nez said.

With one gesture, Liria indicated for the servants to return to the house. "The servants tell me how devoted he is to you."

"There's no accounting for some people, is there?" he joked. "I'm no paragon—far from it! But there is Luster, always at my side. I think he was crushed that I would not take him to Spain seven years ago, when Father bought my commission."

Liria leaned toward him, and he held his breath, deeply aware that it was the first time she had ever moved closer in his direction. "I do spend a great deal of time with him, and he has told me so much about how to run Knare."

He smiled at her evident enthusiasm, something he had not really noticed before in her quiet, dignified competence. I could almost suspect that you are beginning to enjoy life at Knare, he thought. "I trust that you have managed everything to my satisfaction, Miss Valencia," he told her. He purposefully kept his voice low, so she would not move away. "Hopefully none of the traveling visitors have walked off with my silverware, and Juan and Sophie still have all their fingers and toes after helping with the geese." He looked around. "By the way, where is the Empress?"

Somehow that question broke the spell. Liria sighed and moved away from him slightly. They climbed the front steps, and he nodded to the under footman, who held open the door. Nez set Juan down, but the boy stayed next to him. "I do not know if I have done the right thing with *la Infanta,* senor," Liria said, and he enjoyed her quiet Spanish double play on words. "I let La Senorita St. John take charge of Sophie, and she has been spending time there, learning to embroider."

"That sounds perfectly unexceptionable, particularly since Audrey will probably be spending quite a lot of time here, herself." Did I just say that? Nez asked himself, wondering that the words seemed to be coming out of someone else's mouth.

"That was what I thought, too, senor, but Sophie is not pleased with it," Liria said. "I do not understand it, but she tells me she would rather count sheets with me in the linen closet than learn something more suited to her station."

"Maybe she sees embroidery as boring beyond belief, Liria," he said.

"And sheets are interesting?"

He knew she was teasing him then, and he relished the moment beyond anything he had experienced in recent days. When she joked with him, her eyes lighted up and she looked less like a housekeeper and more like the young woman he knew she was.

"My dear housekeeper, sheets are fascinating!" he said. "You can make tents in the breakfast room on rainy days, or knot them together and escape from your bedroom."

"You never did that as a child!"

"No, I never did, Liria, and more's the pity. When I have children of my own, I believe I will. Why, we could even hoist a sail on the terrace and search for the New World."

She looked him in the eye as he spoke such idiocy, and he knew how pleasant it was for a woman to do that. You are indeed my equal, Liria Valencia, he thought. Even more; if what the ambassador says is true, you are my superior.

"Senor, I hope you and your children do these things someday," she said. "Although . . ." She stopped and looked away.

"Although what?"

"I do not think that La Senorita St. John would entirely approve. She has already been over here, and expressed her views on estate management." Liria frowned. "I am not so certain they include the wearing of sheets."

"We shall see, Liria," he said. "Juan, help me carry my saddlebags upstairs, will you? I believe they are in the carriage."

Accompanied by Juan an hour later, he crossed the park to Ash Grove, and made himself known to the butler, while Juan remained outside. Sophie leaped up from the sofa where she was embroidering, and in a moment he was swinging her around as she shrieked. "I hear that Miss St. John is turning you into an accomplished young lady," he said with a wink to Audrey, as he set down his niece on the sofa again.

"And not a moment too soon," Audrey said. "Benedict, I tell you that she only has ten years until her come-out, but it doesn't seem to make much of an impression."

"I doubt it does," he agreed, flopping down beside her on the sofa. "What did you think about when you were eight, Audrey?"

"My come-out!" she declared.

Too bad it never took, he told himself, and then dismissed the unruly thought as highly unworthy of him. "Well, let me free Sophia from the constraints of tutelage now, my dear Miss St. John. I promise to return her tomorrow . . ."

"Uncle!" Sophia pleaded. "All I do is make knots in thread!"

"It must be good for you," he told her. "Only think how accomplished Miss St. John is. Why, she probably has drawers and drawers of doilies and things." My God, and they will probably come to haunt my house in a few months, unless I can restrict them, he thought. "Miss St. John, would you like to go strolling with me in my mother's garden this afternoon?"

Audrey shook her head emphatically. "Under no circumstances, Benedict! I only sneeze around all those flowers." To soften her words, she took him by the arm. "That is also something I wish to discuss with you in the near future, Benedict. Since the flowers make my eyes water, perhaps you might consent to turning at least some of that area into an arena to show horses. To begin with, you could save a lot of money by letting go some of the estate's gardeners. Think how practical that would be."

Surely she is quizzing me, he thought. "Audrey, where would they find work?"

She shrugged. "Many of the people around here are going to the textile mills."

Stunned, he engaged in a few more minutes of conversation, then led his niece home with him. Juan had been waiting by the front entrance, and he skipped along beside Sophie. Nez was grateful that the children did not require his attention because he was still reeling from his conversation with Audrey. True, Sir Michael always sang his daughter's praises. "She is prudent and knows how to manage a household," he had told Nez on more than one occasion.

"She will manage me into a house pet," he said, then looked around quickly to make sure that the children had not overheard him. I will be reformed, and docile, and everyone will declare what a good job Audrey has done with me, he thought, feeling more miserable with every step. The Duke of Knaresborough? Oh, he's a wonderful fellow, potters around his estate and never does any harm.

He watched as Juan ran ahead to visit with the goose girl. Sophie hung back, and soon she was walking hand in hand with him. "Uncle, I really don't want to embroider," she told him.

He sat down with her on a bench by the pond. "Miss Valencia tells me that you would rather count sheets with her in the linen closet."

Sophie made a face. "Oh, we do not particularly like to count sheets, Uncle, and we are so glad that someday we can employ someone to do it in our own household." She laughed when he tickled her. "Oh, very well! Sheets make my hands rough."

"Then, what is the attraction?"

Sophie leaned against him, and he was content to sit there with her as the afternoon's shadows deepened. "It is Miss Valencia, I think," she said finally, and he could tell that she had given the matter some thought. "She always wants to know about me, and my life, and what I think and care about." She sat up and turned around slightly to look at him. "And most of all—oh, do not laugh—she touches me."

"I'm not laughing."

"She puts her hand on my arm, or sometimes around my shoulder." She sighed and leaned against him again. "Once she even put both of her hands on my face! Oh, it felt so good, and she looked right in my eyes when she spoke to me." Sophie tipped her head up a little to look at him. "Has anyone ever done that to you? I mean you are tall, and I suppose it is hard to look in your eyes."

He thought a moment, and the answer surprised him. "Two people I suppose, Sophie: One is Luster, and the other is Miss Valencia, too."

"It makes me feel lucky," she said after another long silence.

"Me, too."

"I don't understand why, though."

I do, he thought.

Chapter Eleven

He asked for dinner on the terrace, ate with Sophie, and admired Mama's gardens. Oh, Mama, you were so wrong about some things, and so right about others, he thought as he ate and listened to his niece's chatter. Is that the way we are? Does it all balance out in the end somehow?

He couldn't answer his own questions, so he listened to Sophie, and then sent her off to play, when Juan came onto the terrace and requested her presence in the stables. "The groom says there are kittens," he announced, and that was enough for Sophie. He watched her go with some amusement, and resisted the urge to join them. He liked kittens, which only served to remind him of Audrey's preference for dogs, and her suggestion that he might take up the hunt. He put down his fork.

Once Sophie was gone, there didn't seem to be much point to eating. After telling himself that he only went belowstairs to find Luster, he went beyond the green baize doors and soon found himself sitting beside Luster, who had taken to his bed. His butler tried to rise, but Nez shook his head. "You're tired," he said.

"Alas, Your Grace, I also fear that I am old," Luster said.

For a long moment Nez contemplated the man lying in the bed. "Perhaps it is time for me to pension you off," he suggested. "You could name a place you'd like to live, and I would happily provide you with the means to do so comfortably."

"This is my home, Your Grace," Luster said, and Nez could sense his agitation, even though it did not show through his perfect butler's demeanor. "I was born here at Knare. As you were," he added.

"So we were," Nez said, startled to see tears in Luster's eyes. "I didn't mean to upset you." He thought a moment. "That can keep. Liria . . . Miss Valencia . . . tells me that you have been teaching her all about this estate. Thank you."

"Truth to tell, Your Grace, there isn't much I need to tell her about running a place such as Knare. I don't understand it; perhaps she has an intuition about the matter."

"It's . . . it's rather more than that, I think, although I am not at liberty to say," Nez told him. "Indeed, I do not know any more." He stood up. "I do know that I have no cause to regret my impulse in declaring to my sister that I had already hired a housekeeper." He laughed. "We just didn't know how true that was, did we?" He hesitated, then remembered his conversation with Sophie that afternoon. He reached down and gently squeezed his butler's arm. "Luster, I will think of something. I do not like the idea of you ever leaving Knare, either, even though I think you must be kinder to yourself."

He went into the servant's hall again, but Liria was not there. Disappointed, he went upstairs and back to the terrace. His heart lifted to see her there, supervising the removal of his partly eaten dinner. "Aha! I trust you will not tell the chef that Sophie thought his trout less than tasty, and I lost my appetite," he said from the French doors. "I didn't mind facing *chasseurs* in Spain and the Imperial Guard at Mont Saint Jean, but I confess to some terror around my chef."

To his relief, she did not seem startled by his sudden appearance. "What I will do is suggest that he leave the head off next time," she assured him. "There is perhaps not a child alive who would look a fish in the eyes." She turned to him, her hands folded at her waist in that pose he had come to like. "Would you wish me to leave the table right here? Dinner on the terrace in summer is a good idea."

"Yes, do," he said. "If the traveling visitors gawk, I can throw a bun at them."

"Or invite them to join you, Senor," she said, amused.

"Only if they are sparkling conversationalists, so I do not have to say anything beyond an occasional 'H'mm,' or 'Really.' " He came closer when the maids left. "Stroll with me through the garden, Liria. Mind, if you say no, I will have to wonder how I am offending the fairer side of the population. Miss St. John already turned me down flat."

"Then, I would not dream of disappointing you, Senor."

"Audrey says the flowers make her sneeze," he said as they walked down the steps. "She would like me to plow under the blooms and put a show horse arena in my backyard."

She looked at him with wide eyes, but said nothing. When they reached the bottom of the shallow steps and he offered his arm she hesitated, then took it. He had no difficulty adjusting his stride to her gliding walk. There was no need to say anything, and he was content to see what else had bloomed since his last walk in the garden. He had strolled with Liria then, too, although they had not stood so close.

"She means to manage me," he blurted out, and then was ashamed of himself for dumping his concern on her. "Oh, never mind that," he said hastily. "It's not your worry." He stopped. "Liria, does everyone on this place bring their troubles to you? Is this all part of Sergeant Carr's method of managing Battery Nineteen?"

"He did listen to anyone who had a complaint," she agreed. "Invariably they would talk, and solve their own problems."

He could tell the memory pleased her, and he was grateful. "Liria, everyone is telling me what to do, except you, I think! 'Think of others, Nez.' 'Find a wife right away!' 'Stay out of the wine cellar.' 'Do good deeds.' 'Change yourself.' "

He stopped by the roses, letting their peppery fragrance fill his head. "Liria, when the war ended after Waterloo, I was a drunkard. It's true. I neglected my surviving men in hospital, and some may have died because of that neglect; I do not know for sure. I fell in love with a wonderful lady who had no rank, and generously offered to make her my mistress. Oh, yes! My . . . my mother died last winter, and I didn't even mourn her until a month or two ago. I have been instructed to make amends with my sister, and I cannot seem to get it right. I . . ." He stopped and looked at her then, and realized that he had struck a deep chord. She bowed, her forehead nearly touching his arm where her hand rested. "Oh, Liria! I have said something else that is wrong, haven't I? I can't get it right!"

As he watched in horror, she gathered herself together with that strength that awed him, and then looked him in the eye. "Your sister? I have a sister . . ." Her voice trailed off. Carefully she extracted herself from his arm, curtsied, and turned away to walk swiftly back up the garden path. He watched her go, his heart heavier than he could remember since his horrible mistake with Libby Ames.

Stay out, Benedict, he told himself. You know she had sisters. This is not something you can meddle in and fix, more like. But he could not stay out. "Wait, Liria," he called, "please wait!"

She slowed down only slightly, and he ran to her, surprising the gardener weeding the alyssum by the path, who stared at him. He walked beside her, said not a word, but took a deep breath and clapped his arm around her shoulders, matching her longer stride now as she hurried toward the house. She flinched and tried to draw away, but he would not let her go. "I will never hurt you," he said in a low voice, "but it stands to reason that you do not have to hurt alone."

She stopped then, not looking at him, but shivering

in the warmth of the late June evening. She said nothing, only let him clasp his arm around her shoulders there in the middle of Mama's herb garden. "The war is a long way from here, Liria," he said at last. "I have to realize that, and I think, so do you. Go on now. I hope I did not frighten you. That is never my intention."

He let go of her then, and for a moment she remained where she was. For the smallest fraction of a second, he thought that she might talk to him, but then she turned to him, curtsied again, and hurried into the house without another glance behind her.

He stood a long while watching her, then turned around to see the gardener still staring at him. He shrugged, then knelt beside the gardener. "Which ones are the weeds?"

"These, Your Grace," he said when he collected himself. "And those."

"I'll finish this bed, then." He looked at the gardener, who seemed to be holding his breath. "Carstairs, isn't it?" The man nodded. "And when I'm done here, I think I will go to the stables. I hear there are kittens."

The gardener grinned, at ease now. "A little hot to go inside now, Your Grace?"

Nez laughed. "Yep. I'll wait until I am certain she is belowstairs. I really can't afford to lose a good housekeeper." He pulled a weed. "Like this?"

"Almost. Grasp it a little closer to the roots. That's it, Your Grace."

He weeded the bed, happy to concentrate on nothing more important than making sure he did not tug up alyssum. When it was too dark to tell the difference, he brushed off his trousers, wiped his hands on them, and walked slowly to the stables. Sophie and Juan were already gone, and he hoped, in bed by now. He admired the new kittens, blind little lumps of fur, and watched them root around for their mother's teats. She did allow him to scratch her under the chin, and he stayed there in the hayloft, resting his chin on his hand and listening to the cat purr. I won't meddle again, Liria, he thought.

He spent the early part of July in the saddle on most days, riding from field to field, and listening to his bailiff, who made remarkable good sense. It gave him real satisfaction to know that his land had a good heart in it, and that his father had employed only the finest agriculturists. He thought long and hard about the querulous father he remembered, the one who railed at him for drinking so much even before he went to Spain, who wrote chastising, moralizing letters which occasionally reached him on Spanish battlefields, but which always piled up at Torres Vedras, almost daring him to read them when Wellington withdrew behind his Portuguese lines. He wished now that he had known this side of his father better.

More often than not, Juan would accompany him to the field. It had started simply enough. Juan, who didn't feel Sophie's attraction to Liria's domestic duties, followed him to the stables. The boy was small and light, so it was a simple matter to swing Juan up in front of him on his horse and take him into the fields, or to the pastures where he liked to sit and draw sheep while Nez talked to his shepherds.

Nez spent nearly every afternoon at Ash Grove. He already had a high regard for Audrey St. John's excellent qualities, and could see all around him the results of her firm management. He could argue with none of it, except that he had a nagging suspicion that the St. Johns's staff toed the line because of a certain fear, rather than a wholehearted desire to please. He chided himself for his own suspicion, and wondered why, each day, he felt less and less like proposing. He knew that Audrey was beginning to regard him with amusement, even as her father fumed in the book room, where he regularly retired, to give Nez full opportunity to express his feelings to his daughter.

"Sir Michael is going to demand an account of me soon," he told Liria one night after the household was shut down, Juan asleep, and only him, Luster, and her in the butler's small sitting room. He never tried again to pry or intimate any knowledge of her family, and she gradually relaxed again in his presence.

"You can hardly blame him," Liria said. "Didn't you tell me that you had already secured Sir Michael's permission to court Miss St. John?"

"I did, and I don't blame him," he replied. Liria—or was it Luster?—had set him to work polishing silver. He rubbed a fork to a fine finish and dumped it in the warm water. "Miss Valencia, we all tell you our troubles. What am I to do?"

She handed him another fork. "And how many times have I told you that Sergeant Carr always let the battery talk and figure out their own solutions! You have to come up with your own answers."

And there it sat. Beyond the rides with Juan, his pleasure at the crops, and the evening's relaxation belowstairs, his greatest enjoyment came in hearing traveling visitors exclaim over his mother's gardens, and increasingly, visit his armory. Walking with his visitors, mainly veterans, he could forget his own difficulties in their enjoyment of the Nesbitt-Knare family's collection of weapons through the ages. Rarely a day began or ended without unfamiliar carriages in the driveway, the ladies to admire his mother's gardens, and the gentlemen to walk among the swords, arquebuses, longbows, and modern weapons that Amos Yore had lovingly restored and now handsomely displayed.

I have done something right, he thought one afternoon as he stood on the front lawn and watched a barouche come up the long lane and circle into the driveway. "What do you think, Juan?" he asked the boy, who seemed to follow him everywhere now. "Are they here for the flowers or the guns?" They watched as four men got out of the carriage.

"They are here for guns."

Nez turned around at her voice. Liria stood at the top of the steps, the open door behind her, ready to greet the newest traveling visitors. He knew this was not her favorite occupation at Knare because he had watched her greet visitors, her hands clasped in front of her waist as usual, but bound tight together, and the knuckles often white, especially when the visitors were men bent on visiting the armory.

I can at least relieve her of this concern today, he thought. "Liria, I will be happy to greet these gentlemen." He took a longer look at his latest guests and laughed out loud. "Indeed, I insist! These are officers from my own division. Do this for me, Liria, if you will," he said over his shoulder. "Set four more places for dinner."

"As you wish."

"Welcome!" he said to the four men. "We meet in much more pleasant surroundings, eh? Gentlemen, are any of you still in the trade?"

Captain Dowling, Twenty-third Foot, came forward first, his hand extended. "I suppose I should show a little more deference to a duke, Nez, but would you ever be appreciative?"

"Of course not," Nez said, and shook hands.

"I am yet in the trade, sir," he said, and indicated the next man to leave the barouche. "So is Harcourt here, of your own brigade, if you will claim him. We don't," he joked.

He barely remembered Harcourt, a replacement after Cuidad Rodrigo. He shook his hand, then turned to quiet Captain James Geddes behind him, and Major John Leakey, eager to clasp his hands on their shoulders. "I cannot imagine that either of you are still in the trade. Doesn't the army have higher standards in peacetime?"

"Indeed it does, and the army was eager to see my back, I vow!" the major agreed. "I am now involved in foul commerce in London, and fair bidding to be richer than you are, in one or two thousand years!"

They all laughed, and Nez remembered Morton Harcourt after all, whose high-pitched giggle had caused no end of ribald amusement among the men of the Twentieth. "What an odd collection we were, gentlemen," he murmured, and indicated that they come with him. "In thirty or forty years, we can sit around on our thin shanks—you will be the obvious exception, Geddes—gum our porridge, and bore our grandchildren with Busaco, Salamanca, and Toulouse!"

It gave him great pleasure to escort his friends through the armory, and even more pleasure to watch Amos Yore, fitted now with a better wooden leg, answer their questions with the authoritative power that came from mastering the collection. If I cannot get everything right, I am a good judge of character, he thought. Amos was a wise decision. He smiled at Jim Geddes, who grinned at him over the row of longbows.

Jim came to his side and they stood a little apart from the others. "Nez, I heard a rumor that you married Captain Ames's pretty daughter."

"Just a rumor," he replied. "I had a chance there and muffed it."

"It happens. I also heard that you gave away your entire wine cellar." He smiled. "That *has* to be a rumor."

"No, actually, I did just that. You see before you a man on the verge of rehabilitation."

"That's dismal," Geddes teased. "Well, I shouldn't talk out of school. Anne has made me swear off backgammon and limit my cheroots."

"I wish you had brought her with you."

Geddes made a face. "She's increasing again so I have ample leisure to roam the countryside with low company." He looked at his comrades. "It hasn't been so long since we all soldiered together, but already we have less and less to talk about. John Leakey there will tell you more than you want to know about the canal business. Adam Dowling has a new bride, and we could hardly pry him away. Morton Harcourt?" He shrugged. "He happened to be at the whist table."

"And you, Jim?"

Geddes patted his ample waist. "It appears that I

am increasing, too!" He touched Nez's arm. "I am content. Shall I bring Anne and the children to see you next spring?"

"Come in June, when the flowers begin to bloom. Anne will like that."

"So will I, Nez." He looked around the armory, and shook his head. "I'm through with war. Maybe your gardeners can give me some advice on growing roses."

"They can, and will."

Leaving the others, who were asking questions of Amos, Nez strolled down the stairs with his friend, then out into the gardens, where Geddes admired the roses up close. He glanced at the terrace to see Liria and Juan standing there. "You said you weren't married, Nez, didn't you?" his friend inquired. "And she has a little boy."

"She is my housekeeper, and that is her son," Nez replied, suddenly shy to say more.

"Well, you may have to let her go when you get a wife, my friend! What a beautiful woman," Geddes said.

"I suppose she is," he replied. "She's the best housekeeper Knare ever had."

"I'll take your word," Geddes said with a laugh. "I thought all housekeepers were born fifty years old with a permanent sneer!"

"Not mine," Nez said quietly. Geddes seemed to sense that the discussion was over. In a few minutes he was deep in conversation with the head gardener. Nez left them arguing the merits of mulch.

They all met again for dinner, which began with a magnificent soup a la jardiniere, followed by trout in butter, lamb and goslings (he could only be grateful that Sophie and Juan ate belowstairs and did not have to see the crispy little birds). The dinner concluded with meringues and cherry tartlets, brought in with a flourish by Betty and Eliza. Liria supervised the removes and serving, and he could tell that she enjoyed the exclamations of delight from Jim Geddes, who knew good food when he ate it. He winked at her when the maids and footmen removed the dinner plates, and smiled to himself when she pinked up like a come-out miss.

"Wonderful!" Jim exclaimed with a look around the table to his fellow travelers. "We could always get a good one in Nez's tent, couldn't we, gentlemen?"

"Hear, hear!" said Captain Dowling.

"Un más," Liria said, and left the room.

Geddes leaned closer to Nez. "I was wondering if she was Spanish," he said in a low voice that had a distinct question in it.

"Long story, Jim. I'll tell you later," Nez replied.

In a moment Liria returned with a covered tray. She set it in front of him and whisked off the lid. Steam poured out, and he looked down with a grin.

" 'Pon my word, Nez, I believe it's plum duff!" Geddes exclaimed. "Your housekeeper is a right one! M'dear, you know old soldiers, don't you?"

Liria smiled at him. *"Claro, señor,"* she said. His other friends at the table stopped their conversation and looked at the dessert. Dowling nudged Leakey, who cleared his throat, and began a particularly ribald version of "The British Grenadier." Morton Harcourt, his eyes bright, looked from one to the other and burst into laughter, which set Nez off, hearing that odd girl's giggle again after all these years.

He heard Liria gasp from her position against the wall behind his chair. Before he could turn around, Jim Geddes had leaped to his feet, knocking his chair over backward. He reached Liria just as Haverly, his eyes wide, grabbed her when she dropped to the floor in a dead faint. Nez squeezed out of his chair, careful not to bump the men behind him, who had all crowded around his housekeeper. "I say, give her a little room," he exclaimed as he fanned her with his napkin.

When she did not come around immediately, he dipped his napkin in the finger bowl and dabbed at her pale face. "I never saw anyone go so white so fast," Geddes declared. "Should I undo her buttons?"

"Let me," Nez said, and came closer. He watched as her eyes flickered open. She stared at the circle of men crowded close around her, and her eyes rolled back in her head again. "No. No. I won't, and neither will any of you," he said as it dawned on him what had just happened. "Haverly, carry her downstairs. I don't think she needs to see a doctor, but keep her down there, please. Gentlemen, I am certain she just fainted from the heat," he said, keeping his voice as calm as he could. "It is a rather warm July this year, wouldn't you say? Jim and I were remarking this afternoon that the roses seem to be drooping."

It was the smallest of small talk, but doggedly he kept it up for the rest of the evening, sitting with his friends around the table. Geddes smoked the one cheroot his wife would allow, Morton laughed over one of Leakey's stories about requisitioning pigs on the hungry march from Burgos back to Salamanca, and Dowling swirled his brandy around and around in the snifter and stared at it. Now and then he looked at Nez and frowned.

Geddes suggested whist in the sitting room, so Nez watched as they played their usual hard game, the one he remembered from campfire after campfire. The staccato slap of cards and the laugher did nothing to lift the stone from his chest. He wanted to order them to go away, but he gritted his teeth instead and as the perfect host, even took Leakey's place when the major declared he had lost enough for one evening. If I play enough rubbers poorly, surely they will quit the table, he thought, but he was partnered with Jim, his whist companion of old, and Jim seldom lost, even in a bad pair.

They didn't break up the table until midnight. Haverly showed them all to their rooms, and they went upstairs laughing and Dowling stumbling a bit, because he had finally gotten around to the brandy he couldn't drink at the dinner table. Nez immediately went belowstairs, where Luster waited for him. He didn't have to say anything, but he sank heavily into a chair at the servant's table and stared at Liria's closed door.

"She does not wish to be disturbed," Luster told him, his voice low. "Your Grace, the look in her eyes!"

"I know. I know," he replied. "Oh, Luster, I have vowed not to meddle in La Duquesa's life, but . . ."

"La Duquesa?" his butler interrupted, puzzled. "Is Miss Valencia truly royalty?"

"She is, indeed, Luster. That's what I learned at the Spanish embassy in London." He got up from the table. I have not felt this old since Waterloo, he thought. Sergeant Carr, how on earth can I help her? He climbed the stairs much slower than he went down them. By the time he reached the top, he knew just how much he loved Liria Valencia.

Chapter Twelve

He spent a beastly night, walking the floor as the clock chimed in the hall and wondering when he had last enjoyed a good night's sleep. So many times he wanted to go belowstairs and plead with Liria to speak to him, but some odd sixth sense told him that he would only find her gone. She has no money, he thought, and that will keep her here. His next thought told him how foolish the first one was. Face it, Nez—Liria is a veteran at fleeing the British. Liria had probably fled Badajoz with nothing, so leaving his house would hardly faze her. Was it Harcourt Morton's odd laugh that set her off in the dining room? Where does all this figure? He paced the floor, and willed the dawn to come.

It came and brought with it Eliza, with her can of hot water and eyes red-rimmed from weeping. "She's gone, isn't she?" Nez asked. His question brought another tempest of tears from his 'tween stairs maid. Wearily, he gave her one of his handkerchiefs, which brought on more tears. By the time he sent her on her way, the hot water was only tepid; he hadn't the heart to shave anyway.

He went directly belowstairs. It was still early, and the servants sat quietly at their table. No one could look at him except Luster, who rose and gestured toward the butler's parlor. He closed the door quietly behind him.

"She's gone, isn't she?" Nez asked.

"Your Grace, none of us heard her go," Luster said. "What happened upstairs? She would not say a thing."

"I'm not entirely sure, Luster, but I have a good idea," he replied. He leaned closer, even though no one else was in the little room. "I think one of my dinner guests raped her at Badajoz."

He hated to say that to his butler. He took in the pale face and shocked eyes of his old retainer, and realized all over again how naive Luster was, in many ways.

"She would have been safe with us, Your Grace," Luster said finally when he could speak. "You do not think she feared him."

"I don't know. I don't know anything," he said, and his voice rose in spite of himself. "I fear that her experiences may have put her to flight out of blind panic men can't understand." He managed a chuckle, and hated the sound of it. "I crawled into a bottle and pulled the cork after me when the war was over, Luster. Who knows what other people do when they are broken right down to little bleeding nubs? I can't explain it any better."

He went to Liria's room next, knowing it would be empty, but unable to go up the stairs again without a look around. It pained him to see two dresses hanging neatly on their hooks and know that she had fled with just the clothes on her back. His heart turned over when he saw under Juan's cot the shoes from Sergeant Carr he had had repaired. He pulled them out, clutched him to his chest, kicked the door shut with a bang that he knew could probably be heard all over the servant's hall, and just stood there in shock. Liria, you couldn't have meant to leave them. What will Juan do? He could see it all. She must have waited until the servants' hall was quiet, then snatched up her son and fled.

"You foolish woman, you have no money," he said. "It's not even the first quarter of your employment, and I have paid you nothing. Why are women so irrational?" Still holding the shoes, he lay down on her bed and tried to think. He breathed deep of the fragrance from her pillow, but it did not steady him.

Luster knocked at the door and Nez got up quickly. "What, Luster?"

"Your Grace, look here."

He followed his butler into the servants' hall. Haverly held out the little strongbox where the household funds were kept. It was open and empty, and there was a note addressed to him. He took it, embarrassed that his hand shook. He glanced down the row of careful lines denoting each household purchase that week to the bottom, where she had written: "I took the ten shillings remaining. I will repay you with interest when I earn it. Thank you for all that you have done for me. Please do not follow me. Your obedient servant, Liria Valencia." He looked closer. She had lightly crossed out "your obedient servant," and penciled in "your friend."

He held out the note to Luster. "What have I ever done for her that was good? I took her in, picked her up, and threw her down. Goddamn me, Luster."

He stepped back in surprise as his butler snatched the note, crumpled it before his eyes, and threw it on the table, his eyes blazing. "You did nothing wrong in all this! Nothing! Don't be so ready to blame yourself! I won't have it!"

Nez blinked. The servants were absolutely still, the under footman frozen with his hand in the silver polish, the scullery maid stopped in mid-scrape on a carrot.

Luster looked him in the eyes, his face full of compassion so extraordinary that Nez could feel his knees go numb. "Your Grace, there was always something greater here than we knew. We are only beginning to find it out." Luster looked at the box. "I only wish there had been more money in there."

"So do I."

"We know where she is," Luster said.

"We do, but we are going to leave her alone now."

"For good?"

"For now, Luster."

He nodded to the other servants, who started to

move again, as though he had kissed a princess and broken a spell. I have to face my guests now, he thought. I don't want to, but I have to. He took a last glance into Liria's room, and stopped to see something farther back under Juan's cot. Quickly he went back into the room, got onto his knees, and retrieved Carr's ledger. He carried the shoes and ledger book upstairs and left them on his desk in the book room. He stood a moment, glanced at the clock, then went to the breakfast room, hoping that he remembered his friends' habits.

He did. Only Jim Geddes sat at the table, tucking away ham and eggs. He looked up with a smile, and then a frown. "Bad night?" he asked.

"The worst." Nez poured a cup of coffee for himself, then shook his head at the underfootman, who left the room and closed the door without a sound. "What do you think happened last night?" he asked.

Geddes looked him in the eye. "I saw her ears. She was at Badajoz wasn't she? And there we were, all crowded around her like a wolf pack. You have to give her credit. I think my Anne would have died of fright on the spot." He paused, and Nez knew he was taking in his unshaven face and bloodshot eyes. "She's gone, isn't she? And by damn, you really care."

"She is and I do." He pushed aside his coffee, and it slopped on his hand. "Jim, were you the only one in that room last night with clean hands?"

Geddes was silent a moment. "No, I don't think so. If I remember, the good major was on quartermaster forage detail when we finally took Badajoz. No, you, Dowling, and Morton turned your men loose, but not Leakey, and by God, not me."

"Damn you, Geddes, why didn't you?"

It came from his heart, and he knew that Jim understood him. Geddes put his hand on Nez's arm and kept it there while he looked deep into his eyes. "God knows I wanted to. I led my men past those *glacís* with all those impaled soldiers, the same as you! I pulled dead men off the piles who were still warm because they were packed so tight together! I was so angry at that cursed town and those stubborn people, and the French, damn them still!" He was silent a moment, gathering his thoughts. "Blame Anne, Nez. I thought about her, and what would happen to her if twenty or thirty soldiers suddenly burst into our house." He turned pale from the thought, got to his feet, and went to the window. "I couldn't do that, not even to the enemy."

"Then, you're a better man than I'll ever be."

Geddes shook his head. "That's your biggest problem, Nez; you have to borrow everyone's badness. Stop it, will you? Stop it now. You're a good man, maybe not a great one yet, but you have some years to go. Quit flogging yourself." He walked back to the table and took a sip of Nez's coffee. "It was Harcourt Morton, wasn't it? She was standing behind your chair when he laughed, so you couldn't see her face." His confidence gave way then, and he set down the cup with a splash. "If ever I saw a wounded soul, it was last night. You'd better find her."

"Should I call him out?"

"And prove what? She's gone, and he'll deny anything you say. It was war, Nez, and we can't change that." He pulled out his timepiece. "What I can do is get up the others and get on the way. I'll make your excuses for you. Too much to drink last night."

"I don't drink anymore, Jim," he reminded his friend.

"Leakey and Dowling won't remember, and I'll wager that Morton wants to get out of here, too." He went around the table and did a surprising thing. He kissed Nez's cheek. "Let me know how it comes out. We'll come back to see your gardens next year, unless I hear otherwise." He let himself out of the room as quietly as the under footman.

Nez stayed in the breakfast room until he knew the barouche must be gone, and then went out on the terrace, sitting there all day, watching Mama's gardens and shaking his head when anyone offered him food.

He went to bed that night and stayed awake again. Then it was back to the terrace and no food and no sleep, until Lester must have called the surgeon. His stomach was too jumpy to keep down the powders the doctor forced him to drink. He ordered the man out of the house, and reeled back to the terrace, where he sat and stared at the flowers for another day until he finally fell out of his chair. The only thing he remembered before he hit the terrace was that Luster was there.

When he woke, his head pounded and his stomach gnawed on his backbone. The light was so bright that he put his hand across his eyes. The light dimmed then, and he felt a soft hand on his arm. "Liria," he whispered, but he was too tired to look. He slept again, and when he woke this time he was so hungry he had to stay awake. "I could use some water, if anyone is there," he said into the gloom of his bedroom.

" 'Pon my word, of course someone is here, you idiot. Now, let me sit you up, and you drink this before I astound everyone by getting testy. Don't think I won't, Benedict."

He knew the voice, but it puzzled him. Without a protest he allowed a strong arm to lift him up as he gratefully drank water that had been liberally laced with sugar. He opened his eyes and gazed at Lord Wogan, his brother-in-law. "Well, Fred" was all he could think to say. Then, "You must be a good nurse, old boy, because I'm still alive."

His bother-in-law sat back, his face wreathed in a smile. "Not me, you ungrateful whelp! I just got here. Your sister has been here ever since Luster summoned her."

"My God, Gussie?" he asked.

"Yes, my God Gussie, her very self," Fred told him. "I'm not much at this," he apologized as he fluffed the pillow up behind Nez's head. "There, now. Gussie is better at it, but the surgeon insisted that she get some sleep."

"H'mm," he said. It seemed remarkably intelligent to him, but Lord Wogan only snorted and told him to go back to sleep. "I promise to have some nourishing gruel here when you awaken."

Oh, no, Nez thought, and remembered a time when he had thrown a bowl of gruel at the door in Libby Ames's house. If that is all I am ever offered when I am ill, then I had better rise up and walk.

He was too tired to walk, but he was sitting up and finishing a baked egg on toast when his sister came into his room. "Lo, Gussie," he said. "I'm sorry I was trouble to you." He sighed. "I suppose you want to scold me about something, but please don't."

Gussie amazed him by pulling the chair up closer to his bed and taking his hand in hers. He flinched against the ferocious scold he knew must be coming, then gradually relaxed when she merely sat there holding his hand, her face so serious, and looking remarkably like Mama's. You do resemble her, he thought. Too bad that all I have heard from you for the last ten years is one long scold.

"Would you open the draperies, Gussie?" he asked at last. "And is the window up? A person ought to be able to smell Mama's roses from here."

He hadn't noticed Luster standing there, but his butler crossed to the window and pulled back the drapery. A breeze ruffled the fabric, and in another moment the scent of roses reached his nostrils. "Could I have some more food?" he asked.

"Immediately, Your Grace."

He came back soon enough with soup, a lamb chop, little potatoes cooked in butter with chives, and a pear. The tray on his lap, Nez ate slowly, savoring every mouthful, while Gussie and Fred watched him and said nothing. When he finished, he nodded to Luster. "Just put it on the table there," he said, "then I want the three of you to pull up your chairs and listen to what I have to tell you."

While they listened he told them about the terrible third siege of Badajoz, and the sacking of the town, the victories and retreats in the Peninsula, Waterloo, his drinking, Libby Ames, Tony Cook, his fierce regrets, his resolutions to do better, Liria and Juan Valencia, Mama's flowers, Audrey's expectations, the Allenby Candy Company, his visit to the Spanish embassy. His recitation went on all afternoon, with no interruptions except an occasional low-voiced question from Lord Wogan. Luster got up once to light the lamp, but they were undisturbed through the early evening hours. Gussie held his hand through most of his narration. When he described his desperate afternoon's work at Waterloo, she held it tighter.

Then he could think of nothing more to say. "You want me to change, and I have tried to oblige you all. Audrey can't wait to rehabilitate me." He twined his fingers through his sister's. "My dear, I know how much you want me to marry her and become someone you can be proud of, but I just can't do it. I'm so sorry to disappoint you all."

He leaned back then, exhausted from his efforts. Lord Wogan got up from his chair and came closer to sit on the bed. He took Nez's other hand in his. "My dear boy, perhaps I speak for all of us when I say that we are proud of you. Don't look at me that way! Do you have any idea how pleasant it is to drop by White's and always be certain that someone is going to ask after my brother-in-law, the Duke of Knare? Someone will say, 'I was with him at Busaco, or Vimiero.' Someone else will say, 'Did you see him and the Twentieth at Waterloo?' Someone else will mention an eagle—Good Lord, Benedict, did you capture an eagle in Spain? You never told us! Two or three men have told me about a remarkable hospital in Kent that you have named in your mother's honor."

Nez sighed. "You don't understand. These are things people wanted me to do!"

Lord Wogan only chuckled and patted his cheek. "Benedict, really! I think I know about the streak of real stubbornness you possess. Augusta, my love, you share it, too. I personally believe that the two of you, spoiled and willful as you both may be, have been doing good as long as I have known you." He shook his head. "The misfortune is that you are quick to see it in others, but unable to see it in yourselves." He leaned across the bed and kissed Gussie. "But I see it. Luster, you see it."

"Certainly, my lord."

Lord Wogan waved his arm to include the whole estate. "I have never known a more content and better run estate than Knare, since you came into its management."

"No, you don't understand!" Nez declared. "I have—had an excellent housekeeper! A fine butler! The best gardeners! The finest soldiers!"

"And who do they take their cue from, brother?" Lord Wogan said quietly.

They sat with him awhile longer, no one saying much of anything, because it had all been said. Finally Lord Wogan got up and held out his hand to his wife. "Come, my dear, and let us retrieve Sophie." He reached down to touch Nez. "I must take them to Wogan now." He sauntered to the window. When he spoke, his voice was casual. "You're a lucky dog, Benedict, to have so excellent a bailiff. You can probably take off in a week to go look for Liria, and your harvest won't suffer in the least."

Gussie nodded, and kissed Nez. "We could have been reared better, I suppose, brother, but Mama and Papa did get in the fundamentals. I'd think you rather rude if you didn't fetch Liria back here to run things." She shook her finger at him. "Mind you, I'm not totally pleased with you!"

"I wouldn't think so, Gussie," Nez murmured. "We mustn't abandon all our differences. How boring."

By the next morning, he was ready for a bath, a good shave, and then breakfast on the terrace. He spent the afternoon walking up and down in Mama's formal gardens, then composed a letter of apology that evening to Miss Audrey St. John, who deserved better. As he sat in the book room, he noticed the shoes and artillery ledger than he had placed there nearly a week ago. I must return those to their owner, he thought. If I knew for certain where she was, I would post them to her. It may be that she never wants to see my face again. And certainly not my armory, or those guests that must have been troubling her all summer, far more than she ever let on.

He picked up the artillery ledger from the edge of the desk, where he had left it during his agitation last week, and opened it again. He knew it would cause him a real pang to see Juan's little drawings here and there on the pages, but he had no idea, until he ruffled through the ledger, how heavy his heart could feel. He doubted he would ever meet other children quite like Juan, quiet, adaptable children who went about their daily business with a certain steely calm: children with no expectations of good fortune, who could be so surprisingly cheerful when something good did happen.

"Liria, you were hardly more than a child six years ago," he whispered, his lips against the ledger. Is that the secret of your serenity? he asked himself, and then found himself facing a more chilling thought. Are you really and truly serene, or do you just have no expectations?

He took another look at the ledger, not knowing if he was seeking answers, or just raking more hot coals upon himself, something Gussie had practically made him swear not to do when she and her husband and Sophie left that morning. He looked again at the pages of the dead, and Sergeant Carr's careful notation of letters sent, and their date. He turned the page with Quatre Bras written on the top. "You were determined to do them yourself, weren't you, Carr, a dead man writing to dead men's families? Were you that conscientious? You must have known you were dying. Did you want to spare Liria from this task?"

He turned the page and sighed to see the new handwriting that had seemed unfamiliar to him when he first looked at the book, but which he recognized as

Liria's lovely script, found now in entries in the household ledgers belowstairs. Carr wrote until June 22, four days after the battle, and then on June 23, it was Liria's writing. He leaned back in his chair, his finger in the ledger. And then, my dear, you could not bear to look at your sergeant's butcher bill, could you? he thought. You gave it to your son for his little drawings, because you were too frugal to waste the blank pages.

He turned to another page with a drawing of men on cots, and a small boy carrying water, and the tears welled in his eyes. *"Eres tu, Juan?"* he asked softly. He turned another page, and saw piles of dead horses and a man approaching them with a torch. True, they were a child's drawings, but he could almost smell the burning horseflesh; he had detailed his own men to do exactly what was done there at Quatre Bras. It hit him with the force of a blow that he was holding a priceless document of Waterloo, from a perspective so rare and personal that he felt only awe.

He turned one more page and looked closer, squinting to see both a drawing and words underneath. Under the drawing of a surgeon surrounded by a pile of what looked like sticks with boots on them, but could only be amputated legs, he identified the sergeant's writing again, ragged-looking, and slanted now across the page, as though written with great effort. He could barely see the words for the horrific drawing, but his heart stopped when he read *"Querida, La Duquesa."*

Barely breathing, he held the ledger closer. The other words were in English, as far as he could tell, and they were unevenly written. "My God," he whispered when he realized that he was gawking at Richard Carr's last writing on this planet. He dropped the ledger on the desk as though it burned, then opened the top drawer and looked for an eraser. He found one, and took a deep breath until his hand was steadier. As much as he disliked doing it, he carefully erased Juan's breathtaking drawing, done in pencil, to expose the ink below.

When he finished he looked hard at the words, not allowing his eyes to focus on them at first because he felt like a voyeur witnessing another man's most private acts. He began to read. When he finished, he set down the ledger gently, as though it were made of porcelain. "Liria, you have to read this," he whispered, knowing that if she had been aware of the note, she would have torn apart her room to find the ledger and take it with her.

He looked at it again and read:

> My Darling Duchess,
>
> When you read this I will be dead. Thank you for your many kindnesses to me and my men. I never told you, but I tell you now, how much I loved you. Everyone talked to me, and I listened. You could have talked to me. Was the wound too deep? I pray God you will talk to someone. God bless and keep you and your dear son. Love, Richard Carr, Battery Master Sergeant, the Nineteen.

Nez quietly closed the book and swiveled his chair around to look out at his mother's gardens. It was August and everything was a riot of color, as far as he could see. On the land sloping farther away, the harvest had begun. He thought briefly of the hops harvest in Kent last year, when he had lost Libby Ames, but the image dissolved almost before it completely formed, to be replaced by Liria and Juan, walking in his mother's garden, Liria and Juan walking in the rain by the highway, Liria with Juan on her hip walking through dusty Spain with the Nineteen.

He was still staring out the open window, his feet propped on the sill, when Luster came in to light the lamp.

"Your Grace, you did not eat the lunch that Betty brought to you."

He smiled faintly at the disapproval in his butler's voice. "Will you believe me if I tell you I wasn't even aware that she had brought it in? No?" He swiveled around in his chair. "Ask Haverly to fetch my traveling case. I mean to visit a textile manufacturer in Huddersfield tomorrow." He picked up the ledger. "Rumor has it that he is a benevolent employer, so he should be as easy to find as a solid-gold dinner plate in a midden."

He was pleased to see his butler smile. "Luster, it's time I delivered some possessions that don't belong to me," he said. He opened the ledger again. "And do you know, I have a duty to discharge for a soldier who has been unavoidably detained."

Chapter Thirteen

"Scipio Butterworth? You are quizzing me. That sounds like a name from an amazingly vulgar novel."

"Nay, your excellent worship!" The innkeep of The Hart took another brisk rub of the glass he held, spit on the cloth in his hand, and rubbed some more. " 'Course, I don't read those," he added virtuously.

"Neither do I. Next you'll tell me that his middle initial is *A,*" Nez continued, "which I will never believe."

The keep shook his head sorrowfully. "Pardon me, your solemnity. I have to wonder if all Yorkshire folk are so skeptical! The *A* is for Hafricanus."

"It's 'Your Grace,' my good fellow, and I would like a chamber and a parlor. Scipio Butterworth? Amazing. Will you tell me where his mill is located here in town? I must see the redoubtable Mr. Butterworth at once."

The keep nodded to the boy standing alert by the door. "Take His Graceful's luggage upstairs to the Blue Room." He turned back to Nez. "If it's after six o'clock, you'll find the mill locked up."

"My word, when there is still so much daylight left?"

"He won't open again until seven o'clock tomorrow morning!" The inn keep leaned across the counter. "Amazing what enlightened notions and domesticity do to a man!"

"Well, then, can you direct me to Mr. Butterworth's house?"

"He lives in Rumsey. Big brick house just on t'other side of the river." The keep rubbed his chin with the cloth, then applied the cloth to the next glass. "My boy there could send a message for you."

"Excellent. Can you tell me a place where I might get a good dinner?"

"Why, right here!" said the keep, astonished.

"I prefer to eat somewhere a short distance away so I can get some exercise," Nez replied hastily. He rubbed his knee. "Waterloo. You understand."

Waterloo, my arse, Nez thought. I'll have to tell Tony Cook that I am still pulling out gravel from my encounter with his blasted Kent road. He wrote a brief note, gave it to the boy, and limped, for the landlord's benefit, to the rival inn he had so grudgingly recommended for dinner.

When he returned, there was a reply waiting for him in his room. At first glance, with the sunlight behind him, he thought it was Tony Cook. Then the man stood up and bowed elegantly. "Your Grace, I am Scipio Butterworth."

Nez shook the mill owner's hand. "Mr. Butterworth, I did not mean to take you from your own hearth on this errand. I could have seen you tomorrow."

Butterworth shook his head. "When my dear wife Jane heard that you were staying at the Hart, she sent me over here to warn you about the food." He held out both hands. "And what does the keep in high ill humor tell me when I arrive, but that you had fled to another inn for dinner? Wise of you, Your Grace."

"I also confess to no enthusiasm about being waited on by a man who seems to speak in exclamation points," Nez said.

"And inspiring you to do the same, eventually, eh?"

They laughed together. What an overwhelming man, Nez thought. Too bad he does not live closer to Knare; think what fun he would be at an otherwise boring dinner party. "Do sit down, Mr. Butterworth. Is it safe to suggest tea from the Hart?"

"Only if the pot comes with water boiling," Mr.

Butterworth said, but his eyes were bright. He made himself comfortable again after Nez seated himself. "Jane insists it must be a full, rolling boil, but even she will admit that she is particular."

"Then, we shall insist upon such a thing," Nez said.

When the keep's wife had left the tea tray, Nez abandoned small talk. "Mr. Butterworth, I am wondering if you have hired a Spanish woman to work in your mill."

To his huge dismay, Butterworth shook his head. "She would never do in my mills," he said, then added, "What a waste of intelligence that would have been to stick her by a cotton spindle. No, Your Grace, I couldn't."

Nez leaned back in his chair and closed his eyes, unable to hide his disappointment from this man he had just met. Damn, now what?

"That is not to say I did not hire her."

Nez opened his eyes and sat up again. "What?" he asked, not in the least bothered that the word came out like an explosion.

"I feel a certain responsibility to my employees" was the mill owner's quiet reply. "But something tells me that you can be trusted." He smiled then. "When my wife claims I have excellent intuition, I remind her that a certain perspicacity is half the requirement to be a business owner."

"And the other?" Nez asked, amused despite his impatience to know more.

"Damn good luck," Butterworth said frankly. "Yes, I hired your Spanish housekeeper. Who would not? She is managing my dormitory for single females."

"Juan?"

"You like him, too," Butterworth commented, and took a sip of tea.

"You *are* perspicacious. Imagine what you would interpret from a long, involved sentence from me. Sir, my congratulations," Nez said, not even disguising his relief. "Tell me. Are they well?"

"Right as rain. Juan is attending the mill school."

"Liria?"

"Ah, these one-word sentences. Who knows? I never met a more contained lady."

"Nor I, and that may be the dilemma." Nez settled back in his chair. "Sir, I must acquaint you with La Duquesa. Do you have an hour?"

The mill owner did. Nez took a deep breath and told him all that he knew about Liria Valencia. In the telling, it chafed him to realize that so much was still surmise. "I want her back, sir, and that is the long and short of it."

Mr. Butterworth read the entry in the artillery ledger one more time, then returned it. He took a handkerchief from his pocket and blew his nose with considerable feeling. "I cannot compel her to act against her own will," he said finally. "Too many have made her do things against her will. Perhaps she will find some peace working for me. Should we just leave it alone?"

"I can't, and neither would Sergeant Carr," Nez replied. "I have an opportunity here to do a good turn for a man I never met. Somewhere under that serene, rather bloodless shell is a very young girl still trapped by . . . something. There is one more puzzle to this story. I am sure of it, and I need to know it."

Butterworth was silent for a long time. "If that is the case, it seems that your intuition rivals mine, Your Grace." He stood up and went to the mantelpiece, giving the little clock there a shake. "How the time passes! Jane will wonder if I have been set upon by road agents in the ordinarily tame two miles between Huddersfield and Rumsey. Yes, you may talk to Miss Valencia."

"She may not want to talk to me."

The mill owner thought a moment. "I believe she must," he said at last. "I hate to, but we can compel her. Didn't you just tell me that she embezzled funds from you? As her current employer, I will insist that she owes you the courtesy of an explanation." He perused his cuff. "Either that, or it is a trip to the ah . . . slammer."

"What? What?" Nez thought a moment then burst into laughter. "Ten shillings from the household money? Mr. Butterworth, you are a complete hand."

"We shall see, Your Grace. I can guarantee her presence, but you must give her reason to talk to you." He rose to go, then stopped. "You're in love with her."

"I know. It seems to be my lot in life to love women who are unattainable."

"I wish you all success tomorrow," Butterworth said. "Just remember, lad, who you're doing this for. It's not you, and it's not even the sergeant, God rest his soul."

Next morning, he looked long and hard in the mirror while he shaved, reminding himself that Liria could just as easily choose to remain where she was, and as she was. He knew that only a woman with extreme strength of will could have survived the ordeal. Face it, Nez, he told himself. She could ignore you and continue as she is.

He dressed and pocketed the artillery ledger, after another glance at what he thought of now as Sergeant Carr's last will and testament. At eight o'clock he presented himself at the Butterworth Cotton Works and was ushered into the mill owner's office. They walked three blocks in silence to a two-story brick building whose uniformity of windows, however softened with white curtains, proclaimed its purpose. My home is certainly handsomer, Nez thought. I wonder if she misses Mama's flowers.

They entered the hallway. The building was quiet, all of the workers engaged in Butterworth's two mills. In the distance he heard the faint sound of children reciting. "The teacher tells me that Juan is already picking up more English," Butterworth said.

"Good," Nez said, but he did not know if he was

altogether in favor of the boy losing his charming combination of English and Spanish in the same sentence. Come to think of it, I've been speaking that way, too, he reminded himself. Goodness knows *I'm* charming.

Butterworth stopped before the door marked Office, Inquire Within. He looked at Nez, a question in his eyes, and opened the door when Nez nodded.

She sat at the desk, dressed in a blue stuff gown that he already recognized as the factory uniform, from his brief stop at the cotton works. He was in the room before she noticed him, and then she rose quickly, her face draining of all color.

"Miss Valencia, I believe we have a matter to discuss!"

Nez widened his eyes in surprise at the sound of authority that boomed forth from the genial mill owner. Well, well, Mr. Butterworth, he thought, I would certainly pay attention if you aimed that much righteous indignation in my direction. "Good morning, Miss Valencia," he said. "I believe you and I also have something to discuss."

It nearly worked. For a second, he saw the frightened young girl behind the calm woman. Then with the steely character that he had to admire, even though it frustrated him, she performed that marvelous act of pulling herself up far taller than she really was. You are not a grandee's child for nothing, he thought; only please give it up now.

"Senor, whatever differences we have, surely they can be settled calmly."

He knew she addressed him, but Mr. Butterworth banged on her desk, and she jumped a little. "You are certainly a calm one, Miss Valencia, but we are talking about embezzlement," he told her, his voice rising until it seemed to fill the little room.

Her eyes grew wide then, and she took a deep breath and another. "Mr. Butterworth, isn't that where someone steals money? I would never do that!"

Nez saw that she had tightened her grip on her hands until the knuckles were white and almost straining through her skin. "What do you call the matter of ten shillings stolen from my household accounts?" he demanded. It sounded so petty that he couldn't believe he was saying it, but he marshaled all his memory and experience from his brigade major days, and bit off the words until they nearly crackled in the air.

He hadn't believed she could go any whiter, but she did. Her lips seemed drained of color. As she began to blink her eyes rapidly, he thought she was about to faint. Mr. Butterworth, made of sterner stuff than he, apparently, reached for her and took her by the elbow, even though she instinctively drew back. "Oh, wait," Nez said in a low voice, which neither Liria nor the mill owner seemed to hear, because Butterworth was rumbling something at her about trust, and the service one owed to one's employer.

When Butterworth finished his diatribe, Liria trembled and resisted as he pulled her closer. He handed her off to Nez. "Here! You take her outside and talk to her. Young lady, I don't keep people in my employment who mishandle funds!"

He didn't know how she could walk, but she did. He marched her out the door, down the block, and across the lawn toward the river. When they were far from anyone, he swung her around to face him. "Ten shillings, Liria! How could you do that?"

It was so absurd that he waited for her to laugh at him, turn on her heel, and go back to the office. I am not a bluffer, and I am a terrible card player, he told himself as he stared her down. Sergeant Carr, you had really better be right about this. "Explain yourself," he ordered in the voice he had used with raw recruits on the Spanish frontier, when death could be a hill away. "Do it now."

He didn't know he could be so heartless. He was on the verge of going down on one knee to beg her forgiveness when he noticed her lips start to quiver. Tears welled in her eyes as she drew herself up again, but with a difference this time. It took all his courage not to leap away from her as he watched her go from terror to the greatest anger he had ever seen in anyone in his life. He stared in amazement as her eyes turned from melting pools to the hardest, coldest granite he could imagine. He was grateful she did not have a knife in her hand. He reached for her. "Liria."

"You would blight my life for ten shillings?" she asked in a brittle voice as she pulled away from him in a frenzy. "Ten shillings?" she repeated, her voice loud now, with no manners or civility or serenity. "My God!" she exclaimed. "*Dios mio,* I am angry at you! You are a meddler! I am so angry!"

She struck him hard on the face then, once and then again, and he stood there and let her. "I could kill you!" she screamed at him. "I could! I could!"

Over her shoulder he saw people running from the mill, but there was Butterworth, talking to them. In a moment they had returned indoors. Liria continued to pound at him, and he was amazed at her fury and saddened to his very soul by what it told him about her suffering.

Her hair had come loose from its perfect coils at the base of her neck and swirled around her face, but still she battered him until her knuckles were raw and bleeding, and she was panting with exhaustion from the effort. He leaned over then to touch her shoulder, and she connected a fist with his eye that made him stagger back, feeling that his brain had exploded.

Over his own pain, he heard her gasp. When he could open the eye that still worked, she was slumped on the ground, dissolved in tears, the woman of calm possession completely gone. A child sobbed before him. He felt his heart turn over. Slowly he knelt in front of her. "Liria, *querida mia,* how on earth did you survive?" he said softly, as though he spoke to someone Juan's age.

He knew that if he lived into the twentieth century, he would never forget the look on her face as she raised her head. The depth of her misery appalled him. He thought he had seen it all in Spain and Portugal, all the death and destruction, all the homeless, all the ruined. He knew then, as he held out his arms and she collapsed in them, that he had only seen the smallest part of war. The woman sobbing in his arms now had felt its stripes on her back infinitely worse than he had ever experienced.

He held her close, his ears full of the sounds of the most terrible lamentation he could imagine, and he knew he had a vivid imagination. As he drew her into the tightest embrace he could manage without hurting her ribs, she wept as though she cried for everyone who had ever lived in the world. He crooned her name over and over, and in his mind damned Napoleon to the farthest, deepest rung of hell for the misery he had caused all across the face of Europe. Damn you, Bonaparte, for taking my youth, he thought, but damn you more for snatching this girl's soul. He knew then without a doubt how much he hated war, and how much he loved Liria Valencia.

When she had graduated to deep, dry sobs that wracked her whole body, he took out his handkerchief and wiped her face. She let him, raising her face to his as obediently as a child. "Liria," he murmured, "*menina pobrecita.*"

Her sobs subsided, and she relaxed in his arms. In a moment she took the handkerchief from him, and in a delicate gesture that made him wonder at the mystery of human strength, she wiped his face of the blood she had drawn. She leaned her forehead against his chest in what he knew was a gesture of contrition.

He picked her up. To his relief she did not struggle against him, but let him carry her closer to the river, where they could sit among the trees. He leaned against an oak tree, exhausted by her anger. She slumped against him. He put his hand on her head. "Tell me what happened, Liria. Tell me everything you can remember."

He dreaded to hear her story, but he knew that Sergeant Carr expected it of him. He knew that the patient man who had listened to others had been denied the opportunity to listen to the one person who could not talk, until this moment.

She was silent a long time, and he began to despair. When she did start to talk, he had to remind himself to breathe, so deep was his gratitude. She spoke in Spanish, and she was not the self-possessed lady so easy to call *dama*, but a much younger woman hardly more than a child herself.

"Papa was an *afrancesado*. You have heard of them? He wanted Spain to look outward, to join the rest of Europe. He made sure that we were educated in French and English. We went to a convent where there were French nuns." She shivered.

She was silent a while, as if picking out her sentences and arranging them in her mind. She sat up and leaned against the tree, too. "Where do I begin? When Fernando was forced from the throne of Spain, Papa welcomed Jose Buonaparte. He even went to Madrid for his coronation, and took Rosario and me with him."

"She was your sister?"

Liria nodded. "She was two years younger than I." She gave a little gasp, and began to breathe more quickly. Nez reached for her hand. "I have not said her name out loud in so many years!" She looked at him then, a quick glance as if to see if what she said was bothering him. "You need to know something about my family."

He almost told her what he had learned from the ambassador, but decided not to. "I take it that some of your brothers and sisters disagreed with your father?"

She nodded. "One of my older brothers was loyal to Spain, and so was my . . . oh *Dios* . . . my older sister Blanca. She was married to Don Alfonso Calderón y Victoria. Perhaps you have heard him called 'El Garrote.' "

"I have," Nez replied, remembering the guerrilla leader notorious throughout southern Spain. "I saw some of his handiwork. Made me almost pity the French."

"My other brother was an *afrancesado* who served on Marmont's staff. What a family we were!" she said bitterly. "I do not recall any pleasant family gatherings after 1809," she added with that touch of irony so Spanish. "And you complain about your sister, senor. Shame on you."

I think I will never complain again, he thought. All the more reason to reconcile with her. "How was it that you were in Badajoz in 1812?" he asked.

Liria drew up her knees and rested her chin on them. "Papa had been exiled from his land by Don Alfonso, his own son-in-law. We were on our way to rendezvous with Soult in Andalusia, who had promised Papa a voyage to France." She shivered again. "It was Papa and I and Rosario. We were in Badajoz when the siege began."

"Three weeks this time," Nez said, "but it was the third siege of that damned town. What was it like in there?"

She shrugged. "What do I remember? Boredom and hunger, and a great longing to go home, even though we had no home. Papa wouldn't let us leave his cousin's house during the bombardment." She rested her cheek on her knees so she could look him in the face. "I embroidered and counted the firing of the siege guns. Rosario read to me."

Her face changed then, and the tears welled in her eyes. "And then the bombardment was worse, and then finally one night the city fell." She closed her eyes. "At first I thought that was wonderful, because it would be quiet then."

He thought about what she said, calling to mind the great silence in Badajoz, followed by the cries of the British wounded and dying, calling for their mothers, or for water. He remembered his own huge anger, double quicking his men past the *glacís,* sharp swords with soldiers impaled there, and then the rush of entering the city itself, full of rubble. Fire crackled here and there, muskets popped, and rubble from the walls shook itself free, but after the bombardment, it seemed quiet. Until we turned our men loose, he thought. "Go on, Liria," he said, weary to the depth of his heart. He pressed his handkerchief, soaked with her tears, to a deep scratch beside his nose. "Go on," he repeated more softly, when she rested her forehead against her knees.

Her voice was muffled then. "I opened the window—oh, I don't know why I bothered, because the panes of glass were gone—and leaned out, and then I heard the most peculiar sound." She turned her face away. "It sounded like wolves."

He told her to continue.

She began to speak faster. "Papa told me to take Rosario and run for the British lines. He said that if we spoke English, he knew the soldiers would see us to safety."

In his mind's eye he could almost see the two sisters, hand in hand probably, skirting their way in the dark among the masonry from the walls and the bodies of the defenders, two young ladies gently reared in one of Spain's noblest families.

"I did as he said. I never disobeyed Papa," she said, and the anger returned to her voice. " 'Of course I will learn English, Papa,' " she said, mimicking herself. " 'Oh, French, too? *Por supuesto.* Napoleon is to be our liberator? *Naturallement.* The English will help us, Papa. They are such gentlemen.' " Her voice dropped to a whisper again. "He told us to put on our best white dresses, and make sure we had our biggest gold hoops in our ears. I wore Mama's gold crucifix."

You were living, breathing, moving easy targets for men enraged by too much bloodshed, too little food, and three weeks of taunts from the city walls of that horrible, arrogant town, he thought. "What happened then?" he asked.

She shivered and wrapped her arms around her drawn-up legs. "We were so close to a breach in the walls—I could see it up ahead—but then I got lost in that strange fog. Was it from the guns? I went down an alley, and there was no way out." She put her hands over her ears then, as though she heard the soldiers running toward them. "I turned around to leave the alley, but the way was blocked by so many men."

Liria stirred restlessly, and he thought for a moment she was going to leap up and run, like the girl in her memory. Instead, she crouched down, as close as she could get to him without actually touching him. "I stood there and called out to them in English, but they just . . . just roared! I grabbed Rosario and we ran, even though there was no place to run. They sounded like wolves. Did you hear them, too?"

"Yes, I did," he said, hardly breathing. I heard them getting fainter and fainter, because I had turned my regiment loose and was heading back toward the siege guns, he thought, hating himself. In a few minutes I was going to drop down by the guns and go to sleep. I was so tired, Liria. I had trained my men well, my dear. I knew they would return to the bivouac when they were through with Badajoz.

She was breathing too rapidly then, which made her press her shaking hand to her forehead. He didn't know whether he should pull her close to him, or not touch her at all. She solved his dilemma by burrowing tight against him like a small animal.

"You don't want to hear this," she told him, her voice barely recognizable.

"You must tell me anyway."

"I am not proud of what happened then," she said in a small voice. "Senor, someone grabbed me and threw me down. Rosario, too." She squeezed her eyes shut and tried to crawl inside his armpit. All Nez could do was hold her as tight as he could. "She was screaming and screaming! I could just reach her fingers with mine then someone stepped on our hands and made us let go. I think someone stuffed a rag in her mouth, because then all I could hear was her gagging."

Nez swallowed the hot acid that rose in his throat and closed his eyes.

"They held us there. Someone tried to pull my dress

over my head, but someone else was holding my arms so he could only work it up to my armpits." She stopped and was silent a long time. "I remember that the stones were sharp on my back, senor, but that was what I tried to think about. Have you ever really concentrated on something before? I mean, really? Really?"

He turned away from her then and retched in the grass by the tree, then pressed his stomach and willed himself to stop. He felt her hand on his shoulder then, and she rubbed his arm, as she would comfort a child. "Oh, I am so sorry, senor," she whispered, which only made him retch harder. His stomach continued to heave as he sagged back against the tree again.

"And then the worst thing happened," she said. She seemed almost eager to talk, to spill out the story she had tried to bury deep inside herself. "There we were, held down hand and foot, and one of the soldiers asked the man standing by my head—he was standing on my hair—if he wanted to go first with me." She shuddered then. "He laughed that awful laugh I heard at your dinner table. Oh, before God and the angels, he said no, that he liked them younger and went to Rosario. Senor, she was only twelve!" Her breath came in gasps. "He made one of the soldiers turn my head so I had to watch while he . . . he violated my little sister. O *Dios,* while he was jamming himself inside her and she was screaming behind that gag, he shouted to me, 'This is what we do to lovers of the French!' "

She burst into tears again, helpless tears. "It happened over and over, senor, until all the soldiers were through. Then it was my turn. I counted the soldiers at first, and then stopped because I knew I would go mad if I kept counting. All the time someone was pulling my hair and then yanking my earrings until they tore away, and that man was laughing. How dare he?"

It was a question for the ages. He could do nothing but gather her into his arms and hold her under the tree, his mind filled with the terrifying images of that alley in Badajoz. She stopped crying then and lay in his arms as limp as a doll, soaking wet from tears and perspiration even as he was.

She said nothing for a long time, and he heard a fish jump in the river. He breathed deep of the wildflowers in the field beside them, and listened as a bird perched in the next tree warbled its summer call. Somewhere farther off he heard a child laugh, and then people singing. It reminded him that he was in England and that it was high summer. He listened as Liria's breathing slowed. He told himself that they were both far away from a ruined city in a poor, tired country so remote that it might have existed only in his mind, except that he held in his arms someone who had lived a nightmare he couldn't even fathom.

"They left finally," she said. "I suppose everyone had his turn, and we had nothing more to give. Someone tried to take Mama's crucifix, but it was tangled in my hair." She heaved an enormous sigh. "I heard someone draw a sword, and I thought he was going to cut off my head for that necklace. What he did was hack off a hunk of my hair and carry off the hair and the crucifix. Then they left."

"What did you do?" he asked finally when she was silent a long time.

"I didn't think I could ever move again, but I did, after a while. I still had my dress, so I pulled it down and crawled over to Rosario." Liria covered her face with her hands. "Senor, she was just staring and staring! I pulled that gag from her mouth, and still her mouth stayed open. I think she must have thought she was screaming, but I didn't hear a sound."

"Was she dead, Liria?" He could hardly recognize his own voice.

"I . . . I don't know. I was afraid to touch her because she looked so . . . so broken. Her legs . . . I couldn't even cover her because they had ripped her dress to pieces. Jackals! May they rot!" She couldn't go on. He held her close.

"Did you go for help?"

"I wish you would not ask me," she replied. "I thought I would get some water for her. I just wanted to wash her legs. Benedict, why was I so concerned about washing her legs? What was the matter with me?"

He absorbed the fact that she had just called him by name for the first time. "I don't know, Liria. Maybe there's a part of our mind that wants to help keep us sane by doing something ordinary." He sat up straighter. "Do you know what I did when it was finally quiet at Waterloo?" He could feel her shake her head. "I took out my housewife kit—I'm sure Sergeant Carr had one—and I sewed a button on a dead man's shirt. Imagine that! I had glanced at him just before the Imperial Guard started marching toward us, and it really bothered me that he was so untidy."

She sat up, too. "I think you understand."

"I think I do."

She bowed her head suddenly, as if the break from terror was over, and she had to get back to the dirty work of telling a story that no woman of any age should ever be forced to think of, much less endure. "I did an awful thing then, senor, God forgive me."

"Tell me, *querida*."

She scrubbed at her eyes like a child. "When I could walk, I went to the entrance of the alley looking for water." She clutched his hand and held it to her cheek. "I found some in a rusty bucket and started to go back, but I couldn't find the alley again!" She sobbed against his hand. "She died all alone."

I must say the right thing now, he thought. Sergeant Carr, what would you say to this dear woman? Don't let me blunder here, Sergeant. Be like most sergeants, and keep this officer doing right. "Liria, I am certain she was already dead before you left the alley," he told her finally, his voice firm. "You didn't abandon Rosario."

"You don't know she was dead," Liria said bitterly. "You weren't there."

"Yes, I do know. Trust me now. She was a child and could not have survived those injuries, even if the gag hadn't choked her already. You didn't abandon her," he repeated. "It never was in you to abandon her. I know you that well."

Liria sighed then, and leaned against him. He kissed the top of her head. She tipped her head a little to look at him. "You're sure?"

"Positive," he said, his voice crisp.

"Then, why did my family abandon *me?*" she burst out suddenly. "You need to tell me that now." She grabbed his shirt. "Benedict, I am not done yet."

Chapter Fourteen

Liria was silent for a long time then. Finally, to his joy, she settled against him. "It's perfect here," she said, keeping her voice neutral. "I think you know who I am."

"I do, *dama,*" he said. "I confess to meddling. I took what little you told me, and added some from my own source . . ."

"Amos Yore," she interrupted, with just a hint of the regal indignation he knew now that she was capable of.

"Well, yes and no," he temporized. "He reminded me that Private Allenby in the regiment had a brother in the Nineteen."

"Tom Allenby," she said, her voice was soft. "I wrote a letter to his mother after . . . after Quatre Bras when the sergeant could no longer write."

His hand went involuntarily to the ledger in his coat pocket, but he left it there. "And then I went to your country's ambassador in London."

She sat up and looked at him intently. "I think you should tell me why you are going to all this trouble," she said quietly. "Why can you not just leave it alone? Why do you think you know what is best for me and my son?"

Because I love you, he thought, more than I thought I could ever love any woman. But would you believe me now? "Put it down to my curiosity, Liria," he told her. "Maybe I am more like my sister Augusta than I wish to admit."

She did not look as though she believed him. "Who is the ambassador?"

"Jaime Gonzales Almeida, Duke of Montressor y . . ."

". . . Calatrava," she finished. "He is my godfather. Did he tell you that, too?" she asked. "There was a time when Napoleon appealed to him. Don't look so shocked! We Spanish are remarkably adaptable." She leaned back again and pulled his arm closer.

He enveloped her in a protective gesture, and spoke into her ear. "We can discuss Spanish politics some evening this winter when we are bored and there is nothing to do, *dama.*" She nodded, and he wondered if she was even aware of the turn in their relationship that implied. "Liria, you were telling me . . . what happened after Badajoz?"

"You won't let me stop?" She sounded so forlorn that he almost hated himself.

"I can't," he said reasonably. "We've already agreed that I am a meddler. Besides, I have promised someone . . ." He stopped, but she did not question him. He could feel her tensing again, and he knew that she was thinking about Badajoz, and not what he said. "Tell me, Liria. You have told me so much, but you must give it all away now."

"I hid in a well all day and all night, and then stole a cloak from a dead woman," she said, her voice hushed, as though she could not believe that a grandee's daughter would do such a thing. "My mama would have been shocked."

"I would call you resourceful," he said.

"Then, why weren't you there when I needed you?" she burst out. "But you were there, weren't you?"

"I was. I told you that before," he said without flinching. "I was one of those officers who turned my men loose on the women and children of Badajoz."

"Please tell me that you did not do what that horrible man who laughed did?"

"Never. We can dissect my sins later. Go on, Liria."

"I waited for a long time before I left the town. I

went out the gate with a crowd of people. I suppose we all thought we had somewhere to go. I thought I did."

"Where were you going?"

"To Mérida, senor, where my sister Blanca lived."

"The one married to El Garrote?" he asked, and felt a distinct chill. Oh, God, please don't let this go where I think it is going, he pleaded silently. "That is thirty miles, isn't it?" he asked, striving to keep his voice as neutral as hers.

"I don't know. I just knew that was where she lived. There were two armies, neither I could trust now, between me and Blanca, but I had to get there. I couldn't walk too far that first day," she said. He could hear her humiliation. "I was in too much pain. I knew Blanca could help me." She sobbed then, a dry wracking sob that startled him with its unexpected despair. "Papa used to scold her for showing me favoritism." Her tears returned full force, and he marveled that she had any left at all. " 'But she is my little doll, my *menina*,' she would tell Papa. *Ay de mi*!"

He shuddered at the sound of her wail, remembering too many widows and orphans in Spain, lamenting at too many cemeteries.

"I hid out during the day and traveled a little at night. There were wild dogs, and I was afraid. I . . . I tried to tell myself that nothing was worse than what already had happened to Rosario and me, but I was still afraid when they growled and showed their teeth."

"I don't imagine anyone had ever been unkind to you before in your life."

"Never." She chuckled, which sounded worse than her tears. "There is something about being mounted and ridden by an entire troop of soldiers that wipes away any sense of privilege, senor! When they unbuttoned their trousers, they weren't too concerned that my father was a *grande*. Why should I worry about wild dogs? But I did."

He could say nothing to her artless admission, so weary in one so young. He stirred restlessly, and she quickly straightened herself and moved away from him. "Oh, no, Liria," he said, and tried to gather her back again. She shook her head; the humiliation in her eyes frightened him.

"I arrived at my brother-in-law's *estancia* at night. The porter let me in."

"Thank God for that," Nez murmured.

"Yes, let us thank God," she mocked. "How awful if He had ignored me! I was even allowed to sit down before my sister entered the room. Oh, I cannot!"

"After all you have been through? Of course you can. I insist," he ordered.

"You are a heartless man," she said calmly, "and a meddler and a drunkard still, for all I know. You probably even rewarded you soldiers when they came back with handfuls of earrings. How many Spanish women did *you* mount? You are scum that my servants skim off our ponds. I could spit on you, but that would be a waste of my spittle."

He was silent, letting her, in her sorrow, berate him with words this time. I can take that, too, Liria, he thought, as she called him every terrible name she could think of in three languages. She stopped for breath finally, and it was his turn. "You can call me anything you want, but I still insist that you give away your story to me, Liria."

"She never came any closer to me than the doorway," she continued promptly, as though she had been waiting for his cue. Her voice was again that of the young girl. "I told her what had happened in Badajoz, and that Papa was dead for all I knew, and that probably Rosario was, too." She knelt then, sobbed, and bowed her head to the ground. "She demanded to know why I had been so stubborn to live, when there was no place in her household for an *afrancesada*."

He reached for her then, but she moved away, holding up her hand to ward him off. He sat back, desperate to hold her, but equally aware of the emotion that compelled her to reject any comfort. Is this your Gethsemane, my love? he thought.

" 'You are dead to your family,' she told me, then took a stick and drove me from her house," Liria said simply. "My own sister! I was starving, and hurt, and bloody, and desperate, and she drove me away like a skinny-ribbed dog! And you think you have a troublesome sister? *Viva España, Señor.*"

Tentative, he reached out his hand to her, and held his breath until she took it. "When did you meet the Nineteen, my dear?"

He could see the gratitude in her eyes as his calm question bridged the awful chasm of her family's rejection and carried her to what he hoped and prayed was something better. Please, Sergeant Carr, he thought. Be the man I think you were.

"I met them in Mérida, at the crossroads. Perhaps you knew it?"

He nodded. "Yes. Daddy Hill took his troops south, and Picton's division went north with Wellington to Salamanca."

"Daddy Hill! I have not heard that in a while," she said, and her tone was lighter. "Yes. It was raining and I sat at the crossroads. I didn't know what to do. I was so hungry that I think I would have eaten sweepings from a pigsty."

"Private Allenby told me that the Nineteen needed an interpreter."

"Yes. There were Spanish camp followers with them, of course, but none who could speak enough English to exchange information."

"Why did you get involved?" he asked. "Weren't you afraid of them?"

"I was so hungry," she said simply. "I thought someone might toss me a scrap." She shrugged. "All they could do was throw me down on my back again, and what was that to me anymore? I wanted to eat," she said, emphasizing her words with a jab to his chest. She sat back and smiled then, and he watched the despair leave her eyes. "Sergeant Carr let me translate. He picked me up and set me on a caisson, and gave me a hunk of cheese. I would have followed him anywhere after that." Her voice was soft. "I suppose I did."

She relaxed then and leaned against the tree, her eyes on the river. "He took me in to his tent that night and found me another dress from a camp follower. He never asked me any questions about Badajoz, but I suppose he did not have to, did he? When . . . when I discovered that I was with child, I was terrified. That was the only night he ever held me on his cot. I had my heart back by morning, and we went on from there. I translated for the Nineteen, and helped in interrogation of French prisoners." She sighed.

"He called you 'La Duquesa'?" Nez said. "Did you tell him about your background?"

"No. The only person rude enough to ask or meddle is you, senor," she said with just a touch of asperity. "I don't know how he knew, or even if he did."

Nez smiled and took her hand again. "Oh, *dama,* you have an air about you. I can't imagine what the other camp followers thought!"

"They were my friends," she said simply. "We shared food with each other, they delivered Juan, and gave me a blanket for him."

"And Sergeant Carr?"

"He cared what happened to me and Juan." She looked at him shyly this time. "He told me once that his happiest time in the world was just watching me with my son."

"I don't doubt that," he told her. "Battery sergeants don't have many pleasant moments, I'll wager."

"Then he had three good years," she said, and got up finally. She swayed a little, and put her hand on the tree to steady herself. She looked at him then, and folded her hands in front of her waist, as was her habit. He looked more closely at her, and noticed the difference now. She still looked sad, but there was nothing hopeless or blank in her expression now. Thank God. Sergeant you were right, he thought. He stood up, too. His eye throbbed in good earnest.

"Oh, *Dios,* I can't believe I did that to you," she

said, reaching out to touch his face with delicate fingers. "Why was I so hard on you? Why did I call you those awful names? I don't understand this, except . . ." She sighed. "I did not know I was that angry. You should have stopped me."

"No. I couldn't. You needed to do what you did."

She clasped her hands in front of her waist again. "Do you know what else, senor? I was never an *afrancesada*. I love my country."

"I know you do." He offered her his arm, and she took it without hesitation. They started to walk back slowly. "*Dama,* there is a commission I have been asked to fulfill."

"I do not understand you."

When he pulled out the artillery ledger, she backed away, holding up her hand in that imperious way. Gently he took her hand and turned it palm-up and laid the little book across it. "Liria, you need to look at something in there."

Her eyes pleaded with him. "I cannot! After I finished those letters for Sergeant Carr, I gave the book to Juan for his drawings. Don't make me."

"My dear, I swear before God this is the last time I will make a decision for you. You missed a page from the book, something your sergeant added, I suppose, before he could no longer write. Please, Liria, I'll open it to the page. I insist that you read it."

She nodded, unable to speak, her eyes haunted again. While she held out the book to him, he turned to the page. "There. Just read it."

She did as he said, taking a deep breath as she began. The tears began to slide down her face before she finished the short entry. As he had known she would, she read it again then closed it gently. Her voice was low and unsteady, and he leaned closer to hear her. "Benedict, he was forty-three when he saved me. I teased him once about being the daughter he never had. I was more, wasn't I?"

"You were much more," he said simply. "When I read that, I couldn't turn down his request." He took her hand. "Liria, after Waterloo, I failed so many of my men in hospital. This was a chance to do a good turn for another sergeant." He raised her hand to his lips and kissed it. "Thank you for trusting me."

She laughed a little through her tears. "*Trusting* you? You were a bully, and you know it. Ten shillings!"

She stood on tiptoe, not to kiss him, but to rub her cheek against his in a gesture so intimate that he had to remind himself to breathe. Her tears wet his cheek. She did not let go of his hand, so he risked one more question. "Liria, this is truly none of my business—I know! I know! When did that consideration ever stop me? Don't give me that look!—I am curious about one thing: I know that there were other January babies after Badajoz. I also know that many January babies ended up in orphanages. A nun told me so once. Why did you keep Juan? There was no earthly reason for you to do that."

"There was." Her voice was kind, as though she spoke to a child. "I did not know who Juan's father was, but before God and all the saints, I knew who his mother was."

He let that sink in. He pocketed the artillery book that she had handed back to him. Sergeant Carr, you have helped me, too, he thought. He started to walk again, but she held him back.

"I hope you will not tell this to anyone, senor," she said softly, and he heard the plea in her voice. "As much as I love my son, what happened is shameful, and I bear the sin of it. You understand why I do not wish others to know."

"I understand. Your story goes no farther." He patted her hand, and tipped her head up a little, because she was staring at the ground when she spoke. "Look me in the eyes, Liria. I know I was paying close attention to the whole story, but I must have missed something. Where did you sin?"

She stared at him. "You don't think I will have to

answer for Badajoz before God's judgment someday?"

"No! Others will, Liria—maybe I am one—but not you." He gave her chin a little shake. "I have never been more sure of anything in my life."

Wordlessly, she gave him a fierce hug. He let her cry, but these were different tears. Well, Sergeant, he thought, I guess the good turn never ends, does it?

When they returned to the dormitory, Juan was there, perched on a corner of his mother's desk while Mr. Butterworth serenely catalogued invoices. As Juan jumped down and ran to his mother, the mill owner looked at her over the top of his spectacles. "I trust, Miss Valencia, that you were able to explain that ten shillings?"

"I fear that I am going to be rather high-handed about the whole matter, Mr. Butterworth," Nez said before she could speak. He held out the artillery ledger to Juan, who ran to him next. "Here, lad," he said, and picked up the boy. "I believe that Miss Valencia is obliged to continue in her employment with me until we settle the matter."

"H'mm." Butterworth peered closer to him. "Your Grace, it appears that you must have . . . ah, well, did you fall down? I should have warned you that the ground in Huddersfield is notoriously unstable."

"That accounts for it," Nez said.

"There is a remedy for your eye, sir," Butterworth continued smoothly. "When you return to the Hart, request a well-done beefsteak. It will come to your table quite raw. Just clap it on, Your Grace." He laughed, and turned his attention to Liria. "Miss Valencia, if you don't wish to return to Knare with this clumsy fellow, you may certainly stay here. I do not believe that His Grace will force you to accompany him, if you choose not to." He whispered confidentially. "I think you're good for the ten shillings."

"I choose to return now," she said quietly. She looked

at Nez, then back at Butterworth. "If by chance I choose not to continue as his housekeeper, could I find employment again with you, Mr. Butterworth?"

"You have my word. Would you like me to put that in writing?"

"It isn't necessary now. I trust you, Mr. Butterworth. Truly, I do."

Her voice was so calm and peaceful that Nez could only smile into Juan's neck. The mill owner clapped his hands. "Excellent, Miss Valencia! I propose that you and your son come to my home for dinner tonight. Your Grace, you are invited, too. I know you wish to keep an eye—oh, bad choice of words—on your housekeeper, in the event that she should wish to disappear again still owing you ten shillings."

"I accept with pleasure," he said. "I believe I will first return to the Hart to put a cold pack on my eye."

"Very well, Your Grace. We dine at six." Butterworth rubbed his hands together. "Now, Miss Valencia, if you will leave a detailed list of duties here, that will be sufficient for the day. What would you say if you pack your belongings now and bring them along to my home tonight? You can stay with us, and His Grace can retrieve you and Juan in the morning."

Despite the fact that his eye was purple and closed tight, Nez enjoyed his evening in Rumsey with the Butterworths and the Valencias. His cup ran over when Juan asked his mother if he could return to the inn with him. "Of course you may," she told her son, "if it is agreeable to the senor."

"It must be," Juan insisted with just that touch of Valencia in him that made Nez smile. "I have to show him my new drawings."

"Then, by all means," she said seriously, even though her eyes gleamed. "You can be the ransom to prevent me from fleeing in the night."

"Oh, Mama! I know you would not leave me."

"Never."

Juan fell asleep promptly on the drive back to the

inn. Nez carried him upstairs, and put him in bed, after taking off his shoes and shrugging him out of his jacket. After a moment's thought, he took from his traveling case the other shoes that the cobbler had repaired, and placed them next to the sleeping child, so he could see them first thing in the morning. I have a housekeeper again, he thought, as he drowsed next to Juan, warm against his back. Sergeant Carr, good night to you, or is it farewell? I intend to tell your Duquesa that I love her and want to marry her. This may not be an easy thing for her. I hope she will let me love her, but I can be patient.

He slept well that night, even with the compress on his eye. It still throbbed in the morning, but not with a force to make him grit his teeth. He didn't want to move. Juan was comfortable against him. He raised up on his elbow to look at the sleeping child. He touched his hair, a shade or two between Liria's dark hair and blond, with reddish glints. I wonder if you will be tall someday, or short, he thought. Your nose is straight, like Liria's. Your lips are much thinner, more British. He thought of Liria's full lips and wondered how pleasant it would be to kiss them. "We shall see," he murmured. "Your mother is a fine woman." And you, *mijo,* he thought, you are your own person.

He got up, holding still in a half crouch until his head quit pounding, and went to the window. A hay wain with two little boys perched on top rumbled through the street below, and he thought of his own land, and the harvest going on. There was a time when he couldn't wait to be away from his land, from his parents, but that time was over now. He looked at Juan, and the love that filled his heart made him swallow hard. It must be a mystery of the universe, how an incident more terrible than anything he could dream of could yield a harvest as beautiful as this child's life.

He leaned his head against the cool pane of glass at the window. When Libby Ames turned me down and married Tony Cook, I thought my life was over.

How did I know it was only beginning? My apologies, Mr. Cook, but I don't need to rush to you for advice. I only need to look within myself.

His deep feelings kept him silent for the early part of the ride back to Knare. Liria and Juan were seated opposite him in the chaise, and they conversed together quietly. Juan still clutched the shoes that had been his first sight when he woke up. A man could make himself jealous of the way Juan idolized the sergeant, but Nez knew the utter folly of that. I hope I have a lifetime with these two people, he thought. Sergeant Carr had no more than three years, and how well he used his time. Trust an artillerist.

He knew he wanted to talk to Liria, but not while Juan could hear. He closed his eye—one was already shut—and leaned back. He wasn't sure how much time had passed, but Liria must have wanted to talk, too.

"Senor, do you remember the first time we rode together?"

He opened his eye. Juan was asleep, his head in his mother's lap. "I was so rude and so eager to find a way to ditch you at the nearest opportunity." He grinned at her. "Praise the Almighty for chicken pox."

She laughed softly, and he doubted there would ever be a time in his life when he would take that delightful sound for granted.

"I want to talk to you about that man in the alley, that officer at your dinner table." She didn't look at him when she spoke.

"Liria, you never need to be ashamed to talk to me about anything. I think it's safe to say there is not a subject we can't discuss eye to eye."

She raised her eyes to his and held her head up. She nodded, but didn't say anything else.

"Liria, I've been thinking of him, too. There isn't really anything I can do about him. Whatever justice we seek would be in vain. It was war, there were no witnesses that lived. You could accused him, and he would deny."

"I know. Tell me this, senor. What is he doing today?"

He leaned back and closed his eye. "Oh, I did not know him well, even then. What did Jim Geddes tell me? I believe he has a majority now, and is returning to Belgium on occupation duty." He grunted. "I know he found soldiering not to his liking, Liria, if that is any comfort. Maybe he can't do anything else. I do remember that he transferred to the quartermaster department after Badajoz. He wasn't even at Waterloo."

"Those soldiers in the alley?"

He suddenly understood what she wanted to know. "Some probably died at Salamanca, or Burgos, or maybe of disease. I think we all had typhus once or twice. Maybe some survived Waterloo. They're in the army still, or back on their family's farms now. Just ordinary men, Liria, in more ordinary times."

"Then, why?"

The age-old question. He had nothing more than the age-old answer. "I don't know. Why did I turn my own men loose? I don't know. Why did Sergeant Carr have to die? I don't know." Why do I love you so much, he wanted to add. I don't know. What *is* it about people?

He knew she was bright, and somehow he knew she understood his feeble answer, because she nodded, even though there was the finest frown line between her eyes.

"Pues, claro," she said. She leaned across her son. "I have also been wondering why you were only a major in the Twentieth. Senor, you are a duke. I knew no Spanish dukes who were only majors."

It was a good question, one he had considered for years. He knew he had a partial answer after spending so many hours observing his mother's gardens. He also knew that the answer was more complete, after watching Juan sleep this morning.

"More properly speaking, I was a marquess then, because my father was still alive and held the title now mine." It was his turn to look at the floor, until Liria cleared her throat and made him look up. He smiled at her, and she smiled back. The moment was so intimate that he thought he could not breathe and live at the same time. When the moment passed, he continued. "I played a stupid prank at Brasenose, and he summoned me home. He told me he had purchased me a commission as a major in the regiment of a friend of his. I was furious to be just a major! He could have bought me at least a lieutenant colonelcy; I knew he could afford it. Oh, Liria, I even confronted him about it, and there we were shouting at each other. What must you think?"

"You'll remember I had brothers," she replied, and leaned back when Juan stirred.

"Ah, yes. You'll appreciate this: He sent me a letter that I opened on the crossing to La Coruña. He told me that he bought me a lower rank so I could learn something before I commanded a regiment. He wrote that he hoped a sergeant would teach me something before I died of stupidity. Luckily, several did."

"I do appreciate that, senor," she agreed. "But you stayed a brigade major."

"It's slightly different, my dear. It was a staff position, rather than line, and I worked with three regiments. I chose that, Liria, because the position involved skill in organizing."

"Something you're good at."

"Why, thank you! At Badajoz I was commanding a regiment after the colonel died." He sighed. "And you can tell I still had much to learn there, can't you?"

She shifted Juan slightly so she could move across and sit beside him. She hesitated for the smallest moment then took his hand and held it tight. "Did you learn?" she asked, her voice as firm as her grip.

"I did. Liria, I did."

"Claro," she said, and resumed her seat opposite him. "Your father was right."

The final realization came to him with such force that he had to look out the window until his vision cleared. "It's odd, Liria. My father was a remote man, given to sudden anger, unpredictable. He never treated my mother very well. She was a poor mother, with little regard for her offspring." It was his turn to take a seat beside her, much closer because Juan filled up the rest of the space. "For all his faults, he did the right thing and kept me alive in Spain. For all hers, she left a beautiful garden that overwhelms my heart every time I look at it." He moved back across the chaise. "I suppose we are all a collection of good and bad parts. I can forgive them for not being perfect parents."

The silence was long. He looked out the window and counted several mile posts.

"Are you saying I should forgive my father?" she asked. "And that officer? And the soldiers? And my sister Blanca?"

He shrugged. "Someday, maybe. If you can. I don't think there is a rush on the matter, though." He reached across and touched her hand, running his fingers lightly over it. "I'm ten years older than you, and I'm just getting a glimmer. I suspect—I can't prove it—that there is even time enough in the eternities to keep working on the problem."

It seemed to be enough. She relaxed visibly, then eventually leaned against the cushion and closed her eyes. He watched her hand that rested so lightly on her son, noticing that when the chaise hit a bump and the seat jostled, her hand tightened, even as she slept. Mothers and children, he thought, then remembered the sight of Libby Cook asleep in the chair, with her hands curved protectively around her belly. With an ache that he felt through his whole body, he yearned for his mother's flower gardens, which he knew now were her arms around him.

They lunched quickly at a nondescript inn and changed horses. "We'll be home at dark," he said, and she hurried Juan to finish his soup.

"I think I do not want to travel ever again," Juan told her.

"Nor I," she said. "I have done enough traveling for two lifetimes, *mijo*."

You don't have to leave Knare again, he thought,

and he smiled into his reflection in the window. Good. Now I have merely to gather the courage to ask you to be my wife. Juan, as much as I love you, go back to sleep.

He knew it would not take long. Juan curled up next to him this time.

"Liria, I . . . I . . ." He knew he could not continue, not now. How do I propose marriage to a woman who has every reason to want to stay far from men? Will she want the body that comes along with another title, a beautiful home, a sterling future for her son? Would I? He paused, disgusted with himself, and thought of his own rallying speech to Amos Yore about Betty Gilbert. Which reminds me, he thought.

"Liria, I am going to close the armory. It's too upsetting to you."

She stared at him, her eyes wide. "But what would Amos do?"

"That's not a worry. I have a myriad of assignments he can fulfill on my estate. In a few years, he might be an excellent bailiff."

"But he is so good in the armory!"

"Liria! It upsets you!"

She glared at him. He marveled how lively her expression was now, how open. And how short he was falling at the moment, in her estimation. From now on and ever after, I will always know what is going on in this woman's mind, he thought.

"You can't do that, senor," she said finally, and her voice was firm in that Valencia way he knew he would have to become accustomed to, or else they would have some lively fights. "Don't you see? If you close the armory out of fear that it frightens me, then that officer has won, and so have the soldiers in the alley. I don't want them to control me anymore. If you close the armory, then they are still pinning me to the ground, aren't they? I will learn to live with the armory."

No, I will not always know what is going on in this marvelous woman's mind, he thought with the deepest gratitude. "You're right," he said. "The armory stays open."

They arrived at Knare just after dark. The manor was well-lit, and he wondered for just a moment if another guest had arrived to see the armory. Most traveling visitors to the gardens were gone by dusk. When the chaise came to a stop, the door opened and Luster hurried down the steps, leaving the door open wide behind him.

"Your Grace, let me speak with you before any of you go inside," he said.

Juan leaped down. Still holding the shoes, he ran inside. Liria laughed and followed him. "No!" Luster called, but she was gone with a wave of her hand.

Nez clutched his butler's arm. "What is going on? Tell me quick."

"Your Grace, he came an hour ago!"

He ran up the steps and into his house, stopping to stand beside Liria and stare at the man in the hall. He was not tall, but he was broad, with a look of command about him, and great dignity. He was a stranger, but as Nez looked at him, he heard Liria's breath come in quick gasps. He looked closer at the man, and with a chill that seemed to squeeze his heart, he observed his mouth, as elegant in a man as it was beautiful in a woman. Oh, God, sometimes we get what we ask for, he thought. "Not now, not now," he pleaded.

As he watched in horror, the man slowly dropped to his knees and held out his arms. "Liria, *menina linda,*" he said, his voice hoarse with emotion. "Forgive us!"

"Brother," she whispered.

Nez wanted to hold her arm and shout no at the top of his lungs. Before he could grab her, she glided across the floor toward the kneeling man. When she reached him, she touched his head, then sank to her knees in front of him. In another moment his arms were around her, and he was sobbing.

Nez turned away and clapped his hands to his ears. I wanted this a month ago, he thought. I am still fortune's fool.

Chapter Fifteen

"Your Grace, he arrived an hour ago," Luster said, speaking low as Nez watched, with failing heart, the brother and sister embracing each other in his hallway.

"Did he? Well, no wonder. I sent a letter to him, courtesy of his country's ambassador in London. Luster, did you ever imagine that I would be so efficient? Tony Cook should be happy with me. I've thought of everyone now, so that must mean I am rehabilitated. Wish it felt better."

He reflected on the matter a moment as he watched them, then touched Juan on the arm. "Let's go belowstairs and bother the chef to find us some food."

Juan leaned against him. "Is he hurting my mother?" he asked, anxiously.

"No, lad, no!" Nez picked him up and held him close. He's killing me, but he's not hurting your dear mother, he thought. "That man is her brother, your own uncle."

Juan nodded, and Nez carried him down the hall. "Your Grace, I have put your correspondence on the desk in your book room," Luster murmured as he walked beside him, hurrying to keep up. "I think you will find some welcome news there."

"Oh?" he asked, not even trying to hide his bitterness. "Did Napoleon escape from St. Helena, and the Beau wants a foursome to find him? Did I lose my entire income on 'Change? Do you think it can wait?" He was shouting now, but he didn't care, except that Juan clung to him closer. "I'm sorry, lad. Let's eat."

Dinner was already over in the servants' hall. He knew how temperamental his chef was, but the despair that he suspected was on his face and he knew was in his heart must have told his servants not to give him grief. In a matter of minutes, the chef had prepared a simple meal. Nez chased the chicken and asparagus around on his plate while Juan ate as he always did, a child of the guns, never sure of another meal.

He found himself glancing at the door to his wine cellar, then staring at it, as if he could make the dusty bottles materialize again that used to nestle there in racks. I think I would start with Madeira, because my father liked it best, he considered. Sherry's too sweet after all that Madeira, but I would drink some next in honor of Spain, then move back to the British Isles and settle in for the next month or two with whiskey right from the bottle. Maybe some rye from America next, if I'm still alive, because I like the irony of that word. What could be more wry than my life?

He knew he was feeling sorry for himself, but he didn't care anymore. He had nothing to show for his life now except good turns, and they weren't enough. I have done what everyone wanted me to do, he told himself as he stacked the asparagus on top of the chicken. Now everyone can pat themselves on the back and feel proud that they had a hand in rehabilitating a rather shabby man. Now I am fit for polite company because I cared enough to bring a young woman back from the death of her soul, and let her brother know she was alive and well. Now they will return to Spain, and everyone will be happy.

He couldn't help himself. He sobbed out loud, and stared at his plate as though it had grown talons and scales. He pushed it away. Juan looked at him, startled.

"I'm sorry, Juan," he said, shame flooding his face with heat. "I think I am tired, more than hungry. Come sit on my lap."

He held Juan until the little boy grew heavy, relaxed in sleep. Betty was knitting at the end of the table, and watching him closely—too closely, he thought suspiciously. "Shall I make up his cot?" she asked him quietly.

He nodded. After a few minutes he carried Juan to bed. He sat on Liria's bed and watched him sleep, trying to memorize his face, and wishing he had skill in drawing, so he could capture the moment. Already he was forgetting the nuances of his own parents' faces, people he had only been peripherally interested in when they were alive, and whose lives only held meaning for him now. How long would it take him to forget what someone looked like that he loved right now? He rested his head in his hands, tired to his soul. How long would he be able to summon to mind Liria's beautiful face, and her slow way of looking at him, assessing him?

This is pathetic, he told himself. He watched Juan another moment, then went upstairs and down the hall to the book room. He didn't know where the Valencias—more properly the Mouras—had taken themselves. If they wanted him, they would find him. After opening the window to catch the evening breeze and maybe the scent of Mama's roses, he settled himself in his chair and glanced at the correspondence on his desk. He noticed that the breeze against his back was a little cooler now, more like fall than summer. Then would come winter, and spring again eventually, and on and on through his life.

He looked up at the familiar knock. "Come in, Luster," he called.

Luster opened his door, and he could see the Mouras standing behind him, arm in arm. "Your Grace, His Excellency the Duke of Moura y Valencia wishes to speak to you." He coughed behind his hand. "Your eye . . ."

"Bugger it, Luster," he said succinctly. Nez waved the Mouras in and indicated his sofa. "Please be seated. May I congratulate you on your good fortune."

"We have you to thank, Your Excellency," Moura said. He had removed his cloak and sat, impeccably clad, in a traveling suit of Spanish cut and flair.

"Your English is as fine as your sister's," he said, when no one else seemed to want to fill the air with silly words.

"We did have the same father."

"Of course." If you can't do better than that, Benedict, he thought sourly, you are losing your touch. Let him at least think you are intelligent. "I sent a letter to you in Spain six weeks ago through the Duke of Montressor y Calatrava," he said. "How is it that you have responded so promptly?" Too bad the ship carrying it didn't sink.

"He sent it to Paris, where I am Spain's ambassador to the court of Louis the Eighteenth." He smiled, but it was a self-deprecating smile. "My French is also excellent."

"He didn't tell me you were in Paris."

"He wouldn't," Moura countered. "In diplomacy one always plays cards close to the chest, Duke." He put his arm around Liria, whose expression was as inscrutable as it ever was. Nez looked away, dismayed. "I would have been here even sooner, but there were trade negotiations going on. Fishing rights in the Bay of Vizcaina."

And we all know how important they are, Nez thought, and felt the tiniest flicker of amusement. Good for you, Nez. One must find one's humor where one can.

His arm still around his sister, the duke leaned back and told Nez his story of exile and misery, and powerful longing to return to Spain and pick up the shards of his own life. "I was able to learn of my father's death in Badajoz, but no one knew what had become of Rosario and Liria," he said. He looked at Liria, and Nez could see deep affection for his sister in his face. "My dearest, Blanca would not say anything! I assumed she knew no more than I did. I thought you dead until the spring, when she lay dying."

Nez looked at Liria's face at this news. He could see only numbness there, and the blankness he had prayed never to see again. He felt only the bleakest kind of satisfaction when she slowly inched herself away from her brother. He may have imagined it.

"On her deathbed, she confessed that she had driven you from her house in Mérida. Oh, Liria! She told me how she had suffered in the years since, wondering where you were, or even *if* you were. Almost with her last breath, she asked me to find you, to beg your forgiveness and save her immortal soul."

"Here I am," she said, her first words since entering the room. "My son and I."

"Ah, yes, your son," the duke replied quickly. "Your son. Well. My dearest, I need a hostess at the embassy in Paris, or you may return to Las Invernadas, if you wish." He looked at Nez. "Dear senor, we will always be in your debt."

"I'm glad I could help," he said, wishing that the floor would open up and suck down the Duke of Moura y Valencia. "I'll miss your sister, Duke. She was a wonderful housekeeper." Stop there, Benedict, he warned himself. Make your exit in a dignified manner. He rose. "Please excuse me. It's late and this has been a long day. I am certain that you would rather talk about private matters."

The Spaniard stood up, too, and bowed. "Again, my deepest gratitude." He looked at his sister with uncertainty. "I have one question, something that I have been puzzling over since I found out where you were, Liria. Why did you go with the British, especially after what they did to you at Badajoz!"

Is he trying to insult me, Nez asked himself, surprised at the question. "Really, Duke," he murmured. "Weren't we allies?"

Liria stood up then, the lethargic look gone. "The British took me in when my family drove me away. Miguel, I was a camp follower because my sister chased me away like you would chase a dog! What would you have done?"

The duke flushed a deep red. "I hope you will forgive her."

Nez left the room, closing the door quietly behind

him, when he wanted to slam it off the hinges. He went out onto the terrace, grateful to stand there in the cool of the evening. Luster joined him in a few minutes. "Luster, I'm not going to do anything drastic!" he said, unable to disguise the irritation he felt, and his heart's soreness under it all. He sat down on the top step, wishing it were light enough to see Mama's flowers. "I had hoped that things would turn out better for me."

"I, too, Your Grace," Luster said. He cleared his throat. "Are we to wish the Cooks happy?" he asked.

"The Cooks? I didn't open that letter yet. Do you think it is about the baby?"

"It would seem so, Your Grace, considering that this is August."

"Even good news can wait. I think I'll be out here for a while. Don't wait up."

He went down the steps and into Mama's garden. He heard the fountain, and he went toward it, standing there watching the water, and contemplating the ritual of tossing a penny in for luck. I suppose my face is as blank as Liria's right now, he thought. I wonder why she looks that way again? I know why I do. I've lost the one person—the two people—who make me happy. I will go to my grave missing them. Did I ever think I would feel worse than I did after losing Libby?

He heard footsteps. "Luster, I promise not to drown myself in the fountain."

"I don't think there is enough water to drown you."

He smiled. "Always the practical one, eh, Liria?"

"Someone must be."

She stood beside him, and he wanted to grab her and never let her go. "I'm sorry, my dear. I suppose I was rude just then to your brother."

"No more rude than he was to make such a comment." She touched his arm with enough force to make him turn and look at her. "What should I do?"

"Do? Well, go home with him, of course. Isn't that what you want? Blanca is dead, he is contrite. Do you want me to tell you to stay? Liria, I refuse to tell you what to do. I promised you at Huddersfield that I would never be the man who would compel you to do anything! Hasn't enough been done to you? What do you want from me?"

He was aghast at his harsh words, but to her credit, Liria did not even flinch. "He said I could take Juan with me."

"Big of him! Liria, I'm tired. Let's just say good night. No, let's say good-bye. There's no law compelling me to see you off tomorrow. I can't do it, so don't expect it."

"Very well," she said, and she sounded agreeable, and more the woman he wanted her to be. "You realize that you're acting like a duke."

He smiled in spite of himself, amused at her ability to smooth him over, even as she broke his heart. "I suppose I am. I'll be all right, Liria." He held out his hand to her.

She startled him by taking his hand in both of hers, and kissing it. To his further amazement, she stood on tiptoe and pulled his head down closer. She kissed him, and her lips were as grand as he had hoped. He folded her in his arms, kissing her back with considerable vigor, and not worried about frightening her, or doing the wrong thing, because she had begun it. He kissed her with all the joy in him and all the sorrow.

When he finished, he cupped his hands around her face, and looked deep into her eyes. "I love you. The more fool me, eh? Go with God, Liria. I hope and pray that you and Juan have the wonderful life that you deserve and that is long overdue."

He turned and walked quickly out of his mother's garden. He wondered if he would ever have the courage to go into it again.

He didn't sleep all night, but the matter hardly bothered him, because he knew he wouldn't. He spent the early morning hours going over his farm ledgers. The bailiff had explained them to him before his trip to Huddersfield, and he wanted to make certain he understood the man's method of entries. It was straightforward enough. He considered his bailiff's suggestions about visiting an estate near Wales where the owner was experimenting with various strains of Belgian wheat. I can probably work a visit to the Waterloo Seed Farm into my busy schedule, he thought. Gussie's birthday is soon, and I will surprise her with a visit *and* a present. He laughed out loud. She'll be so startled she won't know what to do. He was sober then, thinking of Liria driven from her sister's home like an animal. "Gussie, we may be luckier than we know," he murmured.

First there would be a visit to Kent for a christening. Tony had told him not to return without a wife, but christening couldn't be put off forever. He lay down on his bed then because all the close entries from the ledger were making his eyes water. He thought about the little artillery ledger that was still in his coat pocket. He knew he should return it to Juan, but he knew he would keep it instead, even if he never looked at it again. He wasn't even sure he could. "Well," he said. "Well, on we go."

He pretended he was asleep when the 'tween stairs maid brought his water and swept his hearth. Each day would be the same, each night no different, not unless he made them different, and he knew he could. His father had kept him alive in Spain, and his mother had given him a garden. He had done a few favors for some friends, met a child he adored, and fell in love for the last time. All in all, it had been a busy summer.

He tried not to listen for it, but he heard the carriage leave promptly at eight. He was finally tired enough to roll over and go to sleep, but didn't. He would have his horse saddled and go into his fields, where the harvests continued. No, not today, he decided. I would miss Juan too much, and his usual perch in front of me. Maybe tomorrow.

He decided that he would read Tony Cook's letter and write back, to assure them he would be there for the christening. A letter to Gussie might be in order next. He could invite Sophie along to the christening. And since he would be in the book room, he could look over the household accounts. No, that could wait, too. He didn't want to look at Liria's neat penmanship just yet. Maybe tomorrow, or even the day after.

I do need a valet, he decided as he took his time lathering his face. Shaving is a dreadful bore, and I think I would not be inclined to bother anymore, if there is not someone to insist. By the time he had scraped the whiskers off his face and wiped it, he had thought up a creative solution for Luster's retirement. He frowned at his bleak image in the mirror. Heavens, Benedict, don't look so down pin! he chided himself. No reason for your misfortune to ruin everyone's day, even if they are just servants. Speaking of that, you need to hire a housekeeper. Tomorrow, maybe, he could look for another housekeeper. No, the day after.

He dressed carefully so Luster wouldn't scold him, and went downstairs quietly. If Luster heard him, he would likely try to bully him into breakfast he didn't want.

"Your Grace, may I suggest breakfast on the terrace? It's a lovely day."

Nez groaned inwardly. "I think not, Luster," he replied. "I'm really not hungry yet. Maybe something around noon."

"You didn't eat dinner last night."

"H'mm, that's right, I didn't. I'm still here, so I must have survived, Luster."

His butler bowed, but his back was stiff and Nez knew he was not pleased. He held out a tray, with Tony Cook's letter on it. "Your Grace, if you would read this."

With a sound somewhere between a growl and a groan, he picked up the letter. "You are even more determined than I am to know the news, are you not, Luster?"

His butler coughed politely. "If you please, Your Grace, we have a small wager going belowstairs as to the sex of the child."

"Very well, Luster!" he said and laughed. "Hand me a . . . oh, thank you." He slit open the seal and held out the letter. "Well, it appears that Libby and the good doctor are the parents of a baby girl." He read a few more lines. "Tony says that he is relieved to announce that Baby Cook looks very much like her mother." He read further. "The christening is a week from today, and will I please be there?" He looked up. "Luster, is that enough to satisfy the staff?"

"Almost, Your Grace. Does Mr. Cook chronicle the date of birth?"

Nez perused the letter again. "Ah, yes. It was August 18. A girl on August 18. I trust that is good news for someone belowstairs."

"I am certain it will be, Your Grace. I fear that some of your staff are inveterate gamblers. Don't laugh, Your Grace. It is true. Perhaps you should speak to them abut it."

"Oh, Luster! The houseke . . . Well, maybe I can later if you think it's a concern."

"Very well, Your Grace. Now I do wish that you would eat a little something on the terrace. How many more beautiful days do you think we will have?"

"Quite a few, Luster! It's only August 20. I'm not hungry, and I don't want to look at flowers. Don't give me that butler look, Luster! Very well. Tea. Only."

Smiling to himself, and a little touched at his butler's concern, he headed for the back of the house. He looked around. Curious, but all the servants seemed to be working in the rooms facing his mother's gardens. Perhaps there is a total eclipse going on right now that I am unaware of, he thought with amusement.

He opened the French doors and just stood there. Liria sat at the table on the terrace, chin in hand, gazing at his mother's gardens. He closed his eyes and opened them again, but she was still there, her dark hair perfectly coiled at her neck. She was properly clad in her black housekeeper's dress, but she wore no cap or apron. I'm losing my mind, he thought. A movement on the lawn caught his attention then, and he saw Juan walking with the goose girl, careful not to get too close to her charges. Two apparitions, he told himself. I am loonier than most madmen.

"I believe she is real, Your Grace," Luster whispered.

"But I heard them leave this morning," he whispered back.

"More accurately, I think you heard *him* leave, Your Grace," Luster corrected. "I hear he wasn't too happy, but you can ask Liria." He coughed quietly into his hand. "Provided that you decide to move, Your Grace. Please don't let me have to think of everything anymore. I am getting old."

Nez chuckled. "Luster, find yourself a quiet corner, and while you are at it, do reel in my staff and find them useful employment on the other side of the house."

Hardly knowing what he did, Nez walked onto the terrace. He sat down next to Liria, who smiled at him and nodded. "Lovely morning, isn't it?" he asked her.

"Claro señor," she replied, her eyes bright.

Without another word, he took her hand in his and kissed it, then rested it on his knee. "I don't think I have ever seen the flowers lovelier," he said finally, then he could play the game no longer. "Liria, what are you doing here?"

"Two things occurred to me early this morning, senor," she told him, her voice serene as usual. "One was that you really were not going to make any decisions for me."

"I told you I wouldn't, my love. The other?"

"I still owe you ten shillings." She reached over and put her fingers against his lips. "Don't laugh so loud! I am a woman of honor, and I always pay my debts. Of course, Miguel said he would be more than eager to leave ten shillings for you, but then I would owe him." She sighed and closed her eyes when he kissed her fingers. "I decided I would rather owe you."

"I love you, Liria," he said. "Plain and simple."

To his delight, she moved her chair closer to his.

"This is such a coincidence, because I love you, too, senor."

"Strange, indeed."

She was close enough to kiss him, and she did. He responded eagerly, relief mingling with pleasure. There was no hesitation on her part, no drawing back. "You are the only man I have ever kissed," she said when they finished. It told him volumes, and he understood something about the bravery of the woman he loved. He knew, deep in his heart, that he was her first love, and she was his last. What had happened to her was a terrible accident of war, but it had not blighted her. He loved a woman of great spirit and infinite courage. He knew he could never give his yet-unborn children a greater gift than their mother.

"I am a lucky man," he said. He moved his chair closer, too, and put his arm around her. "I have been wanting to say something to you, but the time never seemed right."

She leaned her head against his. "Before Huddersfield, it would never have been right. I owe you a debt far greater than ten shillings."

"I'm inclined to think we are even." He kissed her then, once or twice more, until she was rosy. "Liria Moura y Valencia, best woman I know, will you marry me?"

She considered the offer. "My dear, there may be some small element of protocol here. I am the daughter of a *grande,* and I may outrank you. You're not a royal duke?"

"Alas, no, just an ordinary duke," he joked, "the kind you see on every street corner. Does this mean I am ineligible? That would be such a disappointment. I seem to have the poorest luck proposing."

"You do," she agreed. "To avoid any continuing disappointment, I accept, even though I suppose I am marrying down, *casado abajo.*"

"Sergeant Carr would approve, though, wouldn't he?" Nez asked.

She nodded. "I wish he could know."

"He probably does, my love. Battery sergeants have a way of knowing what their charges are doing. Oh, excuse that dreadful pun!"

She touched his face, and her gaze did not falter. "I will marry you. I confess to some fear still, but you are a good man and I know you will be gentle with me."

"We'll take our time." He kissed her hand again. "Patience."

"Do you know something else? I fear I cannot forgive Blanca yet."

"Patience, my love."

She got up then. "I want to tell Juan by myself," she told him. "I know he will be pleased, but I know this is the last time he is only mine."

"Oh, God, how you honor me," Nez said. "He'll be mine, too, then?"

"Claro, señor." She kissed the top of his head, then looked at him, her eyes bright now with tears. "Do you know what else decided me?"

"I haven't a clue. I was so occupied with feeling sorry for myself that it couldn't have been anything I did."

"But it was! I went to the succession house to say good-bye to the gardeners last night, when I still thought I was leaving, and what did I see but that little orange tree! Benedict, you are a wonder! I said so to Luster, and he agreed. He said you had been searching and searching for one, so I would not be homesick."

While Liria was sitting on the lawn with her son, Nez looked for his butler. No one was in sight, so he strode to the front door, opened it, knocked on it, and then closed it again. Luster appeared from around the corner, polishing cloth in hand.

"That was deuced thoughtful of me to get Liria an orange tree," he said, looking his butler in the eye.

"Indeed, Your Grace."

"I only mentioned it once to you, Luster. How did you remember?"

His butler drew himself up. "Your Grace, I am a butler. Actually, I enlisted Pomeroy's help in London. I thought he would have an easier time finding one there."

Yes, Nez thought. He probably asked a hack to drive him to the nearest orange grove. "That reminds me, Luster. I have been thinking over the matter of your retirement. Consider this: I believe I will name you butler emeritus. You'll remain here at Knare, of course, in a cottage I will build you. Liria and I will consult with you on all matters up to and including . . . orange trees."

Luster permitted himself a smile. "Who will replace me as butler?"

"I was thinking that Haverly would do well, as long as you were nearby to supervise."

"Perhaps, Your Grace. May I suggest that you replace your housekeeper with a house steward instead? For an estate the size of Knare, it would be more appropriate, especially considering the influx of traveling visitors that I fear will only grow larger with each passing year."

"Excellent! I might suggest Pomeroy." Nez looked at the clock. "I think I will join Liria and Juan outside now. Luster, do you think you could find me some information about a special license? I did promise the Cooks that I would return with a wife, and the christening is in a week."

Luster bowed. "It would be my pleasure, Your Grace. Oh, there is another small matter. Could you tell me the precise hour and minute that you finally proposed to our dear Miss Valencia?"

"Another wager belowstairs, Luster?"

"Precisely, Your Grace."

Author's Note

The third siege of Badajoz (16 March–6 April 1812), is considered by many historians to be the turning point in the Peninsular War. Ciudad Rodrigo had fallen earlier, and with the total destruction of the fortress city of Badajoz on the Spanish/Portuguese border, all of central Spain was now open to Allied advance. Never again would the French mount an offensive in the Peninsula, although the war would continue more than a year.

The great tragedy of Badajoz was the forty-eight-hour nightmare of rioting, pillage, and rape by British and allied Portuguese troops that followed the successful breaching of the lines and the storming of the castle. Not a home in the town was left with furniture intact; a convent was fired; females of all ages were raped; children were bayoneted. Some of those officers who tried to stop the devastation were killed by their own troops. Other officers turned their backs on their men and by their tacit agreement, allowed the savagery to continue, until an exasperated Wellington finally set up gallows for his rampaging troops.

Military historians point out that such animal behavior was not unexpected, particularly after the three-week siege carried on in the mud and cold rain of early spring, the necessity to move faster than expected as Marmont began to threaten from the north, and the enormous bloodshed and suffering incident to taking a well-fortified position. At best, this is an academic argument.

Badajoz is a much larger city today, of course. The old walls remain in places, as well as the castle stormed at such a high cost on the evening of 6 April 1812. Many say that the town still seems to reflect sadness, even after nearly one hundred and ninety years.